PRAISE FOR
JEFFREY FLEISHMAN

"From the first page *My Detective* moves as smooth as a bullet train through the shadowy world of night. Its hypnotic prose and scintillating characters guarantee that once you're on board you'll be riding this one to the end."
—**MICHAEL CONNELLY**, #1 *NEW YORK TIMES* BESTSELLING AUTHOR, ON *MY DETECTIVE*

"The Sam Carver series is page-turning contemporary noir at its finest. Fleishman's novels take readers on an unforgettably atmospheric and riveting ride. It's a haunting fever dream you won't want to wake up from."
—**WILL STAPLES**, AUTHOR OF *ANIMALS*

"The writing is intermittently gorgeous: 'a city of ghosts, bright as paper lanterns.' The detective chats about Mozart, Bernini, and *The Great Gatsby*. The final confrontation between cop and killer isn't just written, it's orchestrated."
—***BOOKLIST*** ON *MY DETECTIVE*

"Fleishman's writing style is reminiscent of the 1940s style of the likes of Raymond Chandler, and yet Fleishman seems to take it one step further. The story is alive; it breathes; every paragraph brings the reader a sense of being there, of being Carver. Fleishman's writing in the first person ensures that the reader is always in Carver's mind."
—***NEW YORK JOURNAL OF BOOKS*** ON *LAST DANCE*

"Fleishman's writing is classic LA noir . . . He takes us on a tour of the big city's underbelly and those who populate it and profit from it . . . The ending is spectacular."
—*FLORIDA TIMES-UNION*

"[Fleishman's] style, his vocabulary, and his ability to engage the reader leave no page unturned. His fans will expect another winner soon."
—*NEW YORK JOURNAL OF BOOKS*

"Fleishman's Los Angeles is dark, brutal, and somehow still filled with moments of profound beauty . . . If something bad happens to me, I want Sam Carver on the case."
—TOD GOLDBERG, *NEW YORK TIMES* BESTSELLING AUTHOR, ON *LAST DANCE*

GOOD NIGHT, FOREVER

BOOKS BY
JEFFREY FLEISHMAN

The Sam Carver Series

My Detective

Last Dance

Good Night, Forever

Other Novels

Shadow Man

Promised Virgins: A Novel of Jihad

GOOD NIGHT, FOREVER

Jeffrey Fleishman

BLACK STONE PUBLISHING

Printed in the United States of America
Originally published in hardcover by Blackstone Publishing in 2022

First paperback edition: 2023
ISBN 979-8-212-18482-3
Fiction / Mystery & Detective / General

Version 1

Blackstone Publishing
31 Mistletoe Rd.
Ashland, OR 97520

www.BlackstonePublishing.com

For Lisa, my sister

CHAPTER 1

Rain falls. I roll down the window, feel the cool on my face. It makes Los Angeles another world—slick, clean, racing silver clouds. I cross the bridge into Boyle Heights. A kid on a bike flies off a curb over a puddle. Children splash and twirl past a mural of Our Lady of Guadalupe. The light over the taquería flashes like an erratic whisper, and on the corner two men step out from a bar and lean against a wall beneath the eaves, hands cupped, smoking a joint. The sweet sting of it mixes with the rain. The radio is midway through a trumpet tune. I don't know who's playing; the notes spin hushed and slow, a reverie against a sway of pepper trees and dripping awnings. I have a bottle of wine and a bag of takeout. Simple things at the end of a long week. I turn. The cross at Saint Mary's rises over Lily's house.

Blurs and blue lights.

Streams of yellow tape.

Something's not right.

I know the scene. I've been to this moment many times.

But why here? Why at Lily's? I stop the car. Rain rattles the roof, drenches the windshield. I get out and run to the house. The cop faces know me. Their eyes dart away. I see Ortiz on the porch. He steps toward me, wraps his arms around me. He speaks but his words fall silent. He holds me hard, then eases. I break from his grasp. Two uniforms block the open door. I see light behind them and the stairs that lead to Lily. I try to push through. They look at me, glance at Ortiz. He nods. The uniforms part. I run but there is no reason to run, not anymore. What's at the top of the stairs is the end of an act. Time frozen. I know this, but it tricks me. All is the same: the couch by the window, the painting I gave her from an artist in Lincoln Park, Lily's barbells and weights in rows and stacks, the stereo with the scratched Chavela Vargas record she has been playing for weeks. "I love vinyl," she told me. "The cracks between words." It is not the same, though. Men in white suits rummage and bag. They take pictures. They look at me and look away. They know. I am not on the clock; this is not my case. This is Lily Hernandez, my lover and almost partner, the woman I called two hours ago to ask if it would be Vietnamese noodles or Korean barbecue. I follow voices to the bedroom. She lies by the glass doors that open to the back porch. Bare feet, kimono robe, blood at the heart, eyes closed as if in prayer, short black hair wet from the rain spattering off the porch wood. I step closer. I know not to touch. I kneel beside her like a failed knight. I study the wound. A single shot. Close range.

"Find the casing?" I say.

"Not yet, Detective," says a voice behind me. "You really shouldn't . . ."

"She was a cop," I say.

"We know, Detective. Everyone knew Lily."

I look back to the wound, a bloom on silk. I lean closer to

her. Feel the rain. The first night we made love, it rained. We watched it from the bed, drinking scotch and listening to Chet Baker as a thunderstorm moved in from the west and wind blew through the porch doors and Lily laughed and said, "No, Carver, let it in." I want to say something to her, a last word she'll never hear. But what? She is still. Lily was never still. I want to lift her to the bed. Hold her and watch the rain.

I feel a hand on my back.

"C'mon, Carver, let these guys work," says Ortiz.

"I was coming over with takeout . . ."

"Neighbor called it in," says Ortiz. "Heard a pop. Place was dark when we got here."

"Robbery?"

"Don't know, but not looking that way. Get up, Carver."

"It's been raining for hours," I say. "It never rains for hours."

"It's winter. You never know in winter."

"She was training."

"I know."

"You got a smoke?"

"We quit."

"Yeah, but sometimes you can find one in a pocket. Check your pockets."

"No smokes," says Ortiz.

Two guys from the coroner's office walk in with a stretcher and a zipper bag. They unfold the bag next to Lily. The zipper sounds like a bee buzzing up a window. Crime scene. Hair. Fibers. Science. Fingerprints. All these faces looking at me, knowing that I know everything that's happening. A cop is down. Turn the badges black, polish the brims, march in unison. But not yet. Now she's just a vic in a bedroom, a number, a case file, a soon-to-be entry in the *LA Times* Homicide Report. I don't want to get up and leave her. If I turn away, she'll be gone. That's what happens. I know. All that was dies in increments. At least her still body is something, this quiet Lily in the rain.

"You need to see this, Carver," says Ortiz.

I stand.

"Weren't you in Costa Rica?" I say. "Weren't you fishing in Costa Rica?"

"Got back two nights ago."

"How . . ."

"That's not important, Carver. You're in shock. Just follow me, please."

We walk down the hall, past pencil sketches of LA through the decades that Lily picked up in a box at a yard sale in Hawthorne. She loved yard sales. "Never pay full price, Carver. There's so much good shit out there." Ortiz and I turn into the bathroom, which Lily hated; tiles loose, bad lighting, rust stain in the tub. I reach and feel her toothbrush slanted in a glass. Bristles still wet. She was waiting for me. We were going to watch something on Netflix and disappear from the world. I hear Ortiz breathing; footsteps in other rooms, voices soft as hymns. I look up over the sink to red words written on the mirror.

Hi, Sam. I'm back.

I cannot move. My eyes burn. They won't look away. The letters are written in lipstick. Perfect, precise, and clear. I knew before I read them. I knew as soon as I saw the blue lights out front, before I even walked through the parted cops and up the stairs. So did Ortiz.

"Is it her?" he says.

"Who else?"

"Shit. I thought she was gone. Thought she escaped to Europe or some other goddamn place."

"She did for a while. I told you about the picture."

"I know, but nothing happened after that. I didn't think, you know, it would start again. Lily did nothing to her."

"It's not about vengeance anymore," I say.

"What, then?"

"It's about me. She wants me."

"Why didn't she kill you, then?"

"She wants me to love her."

CHAPTER 2

I sit on the front porch with a scotch. A CSI guy hands me a cigarette. A radio bursts with crackle; a few uniforms peel away. Lily is carried down the stairs and out the door, sailing through the night and into the back of a van. Doors slam. The van heads up the street, turns left. Another part of her, gone. How many vic families have I watched when I handed them this moment? Narrowed eyes, tightened faces. A jagged wave running through their insides. Heads shaking, "No . . ." And then that empty air, that heavy, leaden air, pressing down, making them smaller than they've ever been. I blow smoke. The rain's still falling. A small river flows from the hill at Saint Mary's and runs down the street. Kid voices, splashing, playing tag. It's late, isn't it? Shouldn't they be in bed? Low, thin clouds mask the skyline, breaking every now and then to a half-moon. I sip. I'm cold. Ortiz sits beside me.

"It's not your case, Carver," he says.

"It's been my case for a long time."

"Not now."

"She wants me."

"Which is why it's not your case—that and the fact that you and Lily, you know, were together."

"Together?"

"Girlfriend, whatever. Some complicated thing like you always do. She's your partner, your lover. I don't know."

"She was my almost partner."

"She would have gotten her detective shield."

"Yes, but . . ."

"I know. You weren't sure if you wanted a partner. Mr. Solitary," says Ortiz, brushing back his thinning hair, tamping his mustache. He gets up and stands at the porch steps, looks into the rain. "The *Times* is already calling."

"Dead cop."

"The circus begins," he says.

"What are you going to say?"

"Under investigation."

"That never works with them."

"No."

"It'll leak."

"Yeah."

The CSI guys are done. Lights go off. They close the front door. They nod, walk into the rain, and drive away. Ortiz and I are alone on the porch. He sits beside me. Thunder rolls far off. Lightning flashes. It's too cold, I think, for lightning, but with the climate these days and the earth so spoiled and ruined, who knows? Fires in the Amazon. Fires in Siberia. Three billion birds vanished from the skies. The houses on the street are dark. The TV helicopter that had been circling has flown away. Ortiz sighs. "I'm sorry, Carver," he says. His big hand rubs across my back. "I liked the kid," he says. "Remember her on the Jimmy what's-his-name stakeout, that bar in Burbank?

The night she got grazed by the bullet when it went bad. She wanted to get back in, you know? She wasn't spooked. A lot get spooked after something like that." I remember but I stay quiet. Manuel Ortiz has been my captain and confessor for a long time. I didn't think he would come back from Costa Rica. I thought he was done with it all. He said as much when he boarded the plane. But here he is. The rain is not falling as hard as before. It is strangely soothing. But a new world—one I never invited—is settling around me. The empty house, Lily's bed, her badge in a kitchen drawer. "It'll be light in a couple of hours," says Ortiz. "It's worse in the light, don't you think?" He leaves the porch and walks to his car. He gets inside. I can see him on the phone. My car is parked crooked. I should get the noodles and the wine. But I can't move. Ortiz comes back after a while and sits beside me again. We look for the thin gray thread between night and day.

A woman comes out of the dark, stomping wet from her shoes, brushing the sleeves of her jacket.

"Detective Sam Carver," says Ortiz, "meet Detective Alicia Bryant."

"I work alone," I say.

"Maybe, but you're not working this case," says Ortiz, nodding toward the woman. "Bryant is."

"Sorry for your loss, Detective," says Bryant. "Sorry for the department, too."

"Did you know her?"

"Only that she was a good cop."

"Ortiz," I say. "This isn't going to work."

"It's the way it is," he says.

"Hey, Carver," says Bryant. "Why don't we take a ride and talk? You tell me what I need to know."

I stand and look at Ortiz. If I leave the porch, it's another increment, another way Lily is gone. Ortiz knows, but he nods for me to go. I follow Bryant to her car—not a cop issue, but a current-year silver Merc.

"Pulling a lot of overtime, Detective?" I say.

"My husband's rich."

"That's an option."

We drive. I look back at Lily's house—yellow tape, bedroom window black, Ortiz a ghost on the porch. Bryant skims through downtown and onto the 10. West through no traffic, palms blowing against clouds, rain pattering to drizzle, Solange playing low in the speakers, and Bryant, calm, not saying a word, having me in her car but giving me space. Smart cop. It'll be dawn soon. Lily's alone in the morgue, splendid and broken on a tray. I close my eyes and open them again. We pass the Lincoln Boulevard exit, curve and bend right onto the Pacific Coast Highway, the ocean on our left, the Palisades quiet above. Bryant pulls into an empty lot. We watch the waves; a sliver of light glimmers behind us.

"I'm always up before dawn," says Bryant.

"What precinct? We've never met."

"Hollywood."

"Ortiz?"

"Known him forever," she says.

"You're not that old."

"Cop years are like dog years."

"What's your husband do?"

"He's an artist. Trey Bryant."

"The guy who . . ."

"Yup."

"No shit."

"Hand to Jesus."

"You religious?"

"Situationally," she says, sliding her keys and gun on the dash. "Okay, Carver, you don't know me. But I'm on this case. And you're thinking, what the hell? Who is this? I get that. So, here's me. Condensed version. Black girl raised in Compton, teacher parents. Worked hard, kept me safe, sent me to boarding school with a lot of borrowed money. Then Duke. Neat. Tidy. Grand little success. The kind of story liberal white folks like."

"I thought Blacks were folks and whites were people."

"You know what I mean," she says. "Black woman with a fine education and a detective shield. How'd that happen? That's some mental math shit. Need a place to put that. I'm not bitter. It's part of me." She laughs, a bit nervously, and realizes maybe she shouldn't, but I don't mind. I'd rather think of Alicia Bryant skipping rope on the sidewalks of Compton than Lily with her unfixable wound and paling skin. It is too soon to know Bryant—tonight I'm too numb for first impressions— but she is self-assured, a little brash, yet there seems an inlaid disappointment brought by an unyielding truth that neither she nor her parents had anticipated.

"So why did it happen?" I say. "Why a cop?"

"Another conversation."

Incandescent curls of waves push through the dying night.

"Almost light," she says. "My dad called it the sacred time."

"My father used to get up and run before dawn."

"What'd he do?"

"He was a boxer."

"Any good?"

"More mean than good. He never went down. Except . . ."

Bryant cracks her window. Two seagulls circle and land. A kid hops on a Bird scooter and hums toward Malibu.

"Carver," she says, "tell me about Dylan Cross."

I look at her, rub my face.

"What do you know?"

"Ortiz gave me a brief on the phone," she says, turning in her seat, looking at me. "I remember some of it from the news. Not much. Bad scene."

"I caught the case two years ago. Vic with his throat slit outside an old hotel off Main. An architect. A few days, maybe a week later, another architect killed in an apartment on Grand. Place had a great view of the city and the mountains. Dylan was the doer for both. She was an architect, too. A good one."

"Don't think that kind of shit about architects."

"I think it about everybody," I say. "They had raped her years earlier. Got her drunk, slipped her something. She wakes up sure but not sure. In a haze for a long time. But it comes back to her in pieces over the years. The guys videoed it. She got hold of it. She's an expert hacker, but that's a long story. She takes her vengeance." I close my eyes, feel the cool air through the cracked window. "I'm getting ready to make an arrest when she breaks into my apartment, waits for me to come home, hits me on the head, ties me to a chair."

"I heard about that part."

"Everybody heard about that part," I say. "She talks to me for hours. Thinks I'm as damaged as she is and will understand what she did. She had hacked my laptop months earlier. Knew everything about me. She wanted absolution. Thought I was it. Her mother was schizophrenic or bipolar or something. A little rubbed off. The rape let all the demons out. That's what the shrinks said. But they didn't know. How could you really know? That night at my place, she walked around me, talking, wanting me to understand. I saw the rape video. I understood. She stood at my window looking out over Hill Street. She was tall, beautiful, and broken. That's not cliché. She was. She knew it. She didn't cut me loose. She was disappointed. It didn't work out like she thought. She left and disappeared—I thought to Europe."

"For a while," says Bryant. "Tell me this. If you were her absolution, why'd she leave?"

"I guess she wasn't convinced."

"It's tricky, Carver. Suspect getting that close. She get into your head?"

"You could say that."

"You said *beautiful*."

"Just being specific."

"*Beautiful* isn't specific, but I get what you mean."

I wish I had a smoke. I feel a tear, push it back.

"Ortiz tell you about Boston?" I say.

"A little."

"That your MO?"

"What?"

"Not knowing much."

She smiles, lets it pass.

"My mother has Alzheimer's and lives with my aunt Maggie," I say. "I visit when I can. Maggie had needed help with Mom—bathing and meals. Someone to lift a bit of the burden. One day a nurse shows up. Maggie thinks she's from the hospital. She had filled out forms. You know, an in-home care thing. The nurse comes a couple days a week. Gets close to Maggie and Mom. Maggie loves her. She tells me about her when I call." I take a breath, stretch toward the dash, lean back. "I'm visiting a year ago and Maggie hands me an envelope. She says it's from the nurse, Sara. I open it and a picture falls out of Maggie, my mom, and Sara. But it's not Sara. It's Dylan. She had dyed her hair red and was wearing a lot more makeup. A disguise, but one leaving just enough of herself revealed. She was looking right at the lens, right at me."

"Damn."

"Letting me know it wasn't over."

"Then what?"

"I kept waiting for the what. But nothing, went quiet."

"Until . . ."

"Last night."

"How do you know?"

"'Hi, Sam. I'm back,' written in lipstick on Lily's mirror, is how I know."

Bryant taps my arm, soothing but firm.

"You put a lot of guys away over the years, Carver," she says. "Could be someone else. Someone wanting to take something from you."

"I appreciate your open-minded approach. But this is Dylan Cross."

"Maybe. Got to look at all angles, though. No doubt the woman in the picture—Sara—was Dylan?"

"No doubt."

"You have the picture?"

"At home."

"I'm sorry, Carver, but you'd do the same."

"I know. But Lily's dead. Dylan did it."

"Let me handle it."

"It's about obsession. Don't you get it?"

"Obsession comes from a lot of places, Carver."

First light hits the ocean. A few surfers walk down to the shore. The waves are bright green and white beneath the clouds. I get out of the car and walk over the sand to a lifeguard stand, smell salt and kelp. Feel the damp. I strip to my boxers and run through the surf, diving through the break to deeper water. Cold, but not cleansing. I want to be someone else, christened anew—a man with the past few hours peeled away. I stay under for a long time, feeling weight above and below, suspended, remembering as a boy running with my father along the Rhode Island coast. He'd punch the air like a madman in the mist. *One, two, three, one, two, three.* Fists flashing. I see Lily, too, alone, in a current beyond me, slipping toward the horizon. I surface. Gasp. I am numb. My skin like ice. A lost man bobbing at the edge of a continent. Bryant is standing in the sand over my clothes. She's on the phone, waving for me to come in. Dawn widens and traffic gathers in the Palisades.

CHAPTER 3

Bryant drops me at Lily's.

"Get some rest, Carver," she says. "Hard days coming."

She drives away, over the hill, and past Saint Mary's. I get into my car. The bottle of wine and spiced noodles from last night sit on the front seat. It smells like another land. I open the noodles and eat them cold, staring out the windshield at Lily's house, white clapboard and pitched roof, trimmed windows, a garden out back. Yellow tape in the breeze. It's still early, the time Lily would go for her run. People are rising: the landscaper next door, the plumber down the way, girls in plaid dresses and necklace crosses. I didn't know where Lily and I were going. We were loners and lovers, changeable and constant, hard to pin down. But on those mornings, like this one, when the day was starting and she lay curled beside me, back-porch doors open to the sky, I would close my eyes one last time and pretend it was night. That is gone. I wonder about the new people who will move in and mow Lily's grass and live in her rooms, touch the places I have been. I start the car and drive over the First

Street bridge, past homeless tents and unfinished buildings, to my apartment on Hill. The pink-and-blue neon from the Hotel Clark across the street is glamourless against the day. I shower, put on coffee. I sit by the window and hold to the light the ring Lily's mother gave her when she was a girl. An heirloom from El Salvador that her mother found on a dirt road as a child when her family traveled north and crossed into the US in darkness. She would later marry Federico Hernandez, a Mexican American police cadet whose family had arrived a generation earlier. They had a baby, named her Lily, and moved to Boyle Heights. The ring is silver, the stone blue, but it is of no value except for its story. I picked it up last night from Lily's dresser and slid it into my pocket. I press it to my lips and put it in the small wood-and-pearl box where I keep possessions from vics, collected over the years. Things I've taken from crime scenes. I never want to forget that once, like my murdered father, those dead held a brief place among us. I don't know if the ring belongs in the box. Lily is not my vic—she's Bryant's—but I know that if it's there, I won't lose it. Her. I still have the lace from my father's boxing glove, dried blood, tips fraying—the single thing he left me. I close the box, slide it under the chair. Ortiz is calling. I don't answer. I close my eyes but can't sleep. I throw on clothes and head to the morgue.

"Shouldn't be here, Carver," says Lester, dressed in white in the gleam of a bright light while standing over a dead man with no cuts or bruises. "This is not your case and it'll do no good."

"I want to see her."

"Carver."

"Just for a minute. What are you playing?"

"Dexter Gordon."

"Lemon incense?"

"You shouldn't be here, man."

Lester points to the third slab and steps away. I walk over. A sheet is folded beneath Lily's chin. Crisp and smooth, as if attention had been paid. Her lips are vein blue, eyes closed, black hair pushed back. She is gone, leaving this mask of who she was. This forever stillness. I kiss her forehead. A small act, but it is all I have. I want to draw the sheet back and see her wound. Pull the bullet from her heart. Lester will. He will be tender. She will be diagrammed, clues lifted, a scalpel through her skin. I kiss her again. She is disappearing in increments, tissue retracting, molecules vanishing, so many intricacies on the way to no more. That's what my mother said when we stood over my father. "He is no more." But we must be more than this. I stroke Lily's hair, put my lips to her ear, and tell her about the time we danced in an empty bar up north as snow fell and roads closed and the old barkeep brought us blankets and played Sinatra and we camped by the window, the snow blowing thick through the dusk and us laughing and making love in the hours after the barkeep shut off the lights and found his own shelter for the night. Lily liked to tell that story to bring us back from a fight. "Hey, Carver," she'd say, "you remember that time . . ."

One more kiss. I step back.

"I'm sorry, Sam," says Lester.

"Bryant been here yet?"

"On her way."

"You know her?"

"Good cop. She'll get it done."

I nod toward Lily.

"Call me, Lester."

"I shouldn't, but I will."

I leave. Dexter Gordon plays low behind me and goes silent as I head down the hall and out the door.

"I knew you'd come," says Ortiz, leaning on my car.

"I needed to see her."

"Not your case."

"This case is all about me. You can't separate me from it."

"You want a clean arrest that'll hold up, then you don't be involved in the investigation. If it's Dylan Cross—"

"If?"

"Seems so, but we don't know for certain."

"You sound like Bryant."

"We gotta look at everything. You're tired, Carver. Go home. Sleep. We'll give her a good send-off in a couple of days."

"I'm not going to a cop funeral."

"It's Lily's funeral."

"Don't want to see that."

"Think about it."

I lean beside him on the car.

"Why did you come back from Costa Rica?" I say.

"It was paradise, no shit. We rented a bungalow on the beach. Fished, drank rum, watched soccer. I thought, I'm here, this is it, this is what cops like me do when they're done being cops. But I wasn't ready, you know. Hell if I know why, especially after last night and today. But it hit me on the beach one day. I felt unfinished."

He shrugs, looks west.

"More rain coming," he says.

"What about Bryant? She good for this?"

"She's solid. Smart. Like you a little. Bit intense. She's got a good sense of humor, though."

"I have a sense of humor."

"I never noticed," he says, glancing sideways at me. "Her husband's a famous painter guy. Trevon or Triad or something."

"Trey."

"Whatever. His paintings look like black-and-white photographs. All slave scenes. Slaves looking out at you with eyes that won't let you not look. I went to his show at the Broad last year. Bryant invited me. Pretty big deal. A lot of serious art types. The mayor. Brad Pitt. That Gustavo Dudamel conductor guy from the orchestra. It was the weirdest damn thing, Carver. Place is packed, people sipping white wine. But no sound. Quiet. Everyone looking at these slaves like they were at a crime scene."

"Hundreds of years of a crime scene."

Ortiz puts an arm around me. We say nothing for a long while.

"Lily was good for you, Carver. She had that thing some women have."

"What thing is that?"

"Hard to say what it is, but you know what I mean. That thing."

"Yeah."

His arm falls away.

"Get some sleep, Sam."

He walks up the steps and into the morgue. He's slower than before, graying mustache, blue blazer shiny at the elbows and shoulders. He should have stayed in Costa Rica, reeling in fish from the sea, dancing with his wife in the sand. My phone rings.

"Hello."

"Detective Carver?"

"It is. Who is this?"

"Manny."

"Manny?"

"The guy from over on San Pedro. You gave me your card. Told me to call if anything suspicious happens. Well, you know, man, all kinds of suspicious shit be going on down here. Hard to tell what's serious suspicious and what's bullshit suspicious." He was breathing hard. "But I've been watching, you know, since they torched that poor motherfucker. Poor man did nothing to nobody. Just be there with his heroin and his horn, well, you know, you was here, you saw, that's when you gave me your card. Would have called sooner, but, you know, I don't have a phone. Had to borrow one from Wanda. Stingy bitch, but I told her I had to call a detective. Important. She looked at me like I was making shit up. Had to give her two dollars. That bitch won't do nothing for nobody without collecting two dollars. Minimum."

"Slow down, Manny. What have you got?"

"Two dudes rolled by here in a car. Nice car. Big one from olden times. Like *Serpico* car times. They were wearing bank-robber masks."

"Ski masks?"

"I don't ski, but maybe. Masks with eyes and mouths cut out. They come rolling by and I think, what the fuck, time to call the detective."

"What did they do?"

"Went by real slow. Guy who wasn't driving took pictures of the burned place."

"Then . . ."

"Then nothing. They rolled away."

"You get a license plate number."

"That's the thing. I didn't."

"You there now?"

"I stay over here. In the gold tent next to Wanda."

"I'm coming."

CHAPTER 4

The air changes. Piss, tents, and cardboard. Garbage blows past abandoned buildings. Spools of razor wire glint in the sun. Dogs roam. Street preachers circle, scream, shake fists at invisible tormentors, chase angels down alleys. Blocks and blocks of discarded humanity, as if a battered and crazed army were camped on the outskirts. Scabbed arms and rheumy gazes. I park on San Pedro. A woman pulls at her hair. A one-legged man with a crutch edges into traffic; a junkie, leaning on a streetlight, finds a vein and goes slack. I get out.

"Jesus send you?" says a face peeking from a tent flap. "You a Jesus man?"

"No," I say.

"Shame," she says, her face receding. "We need a Jesus man."

I didn't want to go home and think about Lily or Dylan Cross, so I followed Manny's call to my unsolved case: a man torched three days ago on a Skid Row sidewalk. No ID. Nothing in his pockets but an old bus pass and a newspaper clipping about Miles Davis. The vic had on one shoe and no shirt. He had a gold tooth, and a rose tattooed on his back. Two men doused his tent with charcoal fluid and lit a match around three a.m. No one saw much else. The homeless gathered around the fire as if it were an oracle. Fire trucks came and went, and life edged on. I found the black mark on the sidewalk and waited for Manny on the corner. A guy played a battered guitar on a scratchy amp. He swayed in the breeze, long fingers dancing over the frets, eyes closed, repose on his face, as if he had flown far away, leaving his body behind, skimming the city and returning, the way they do down here, making imagined escapes. The guy is working through "Electric Ladyland" by Hendrix. The notes are manic and disjointed. Papers swirl at his feet. He stops and opens his eyes, slides his pick into a pocket, slings the guitar behind his back. Walks toward me.

"Detective?"

"Manny?"

"You don't remember. This is my sixties look, that's why. I change fashions all the time. I'm like one of those changing lizards, you know, those chamomiles. That's me, a quick-changin' chamomile."

"A chameleon."

"Some shit. Shelters got all kind of shit to pull from boxes. Rich people throwaways. Found a silk shirt once not even ever worn. Tag still on it. What kind of man leaves a tag on a silk shirt?"

"How long have you been down here, Manny?"

"Way too fucking long."

"You on meds?"

"Why you say?"

"You're talking fast and your eye's twitching."

"You want twitching eyes, look at *these* motherfuckers," he says, waving a hand over the sidewalk.

"Where do you live?"

"Third tent down, by that bitch Wanda."

"I'm trying to know a little bit about you, Manny," I say.

He goes quiet, rubs his twitchy eye. Looks at me as if I were daft.

"I would like to declare my right to privacy," he says.

"Fair enough, Manny. You said you saw two guys in a car."

"In masks. That's some odd shit, even for here," he says, again waving at the sidewalk.

"You said the car was . . ."

"Vantage."

"You mean *vintage*," I say.

"Whatever the fuck old is."

"Color."

"I want to say red, but it was almost night so could have been purple."

"You didn't get the license plate number?"

"Fucked up on that, Detective. Sorry."

"So, what are you thinking, Manny?"

"Guy got burned was a white guy."

"We haven't ID'd him yet. But he was white."

"I think they wanted to burn a Black dude but fucked up."

"How so?"

He steps closer to me, lowers his voice. Sweat, whiskey breath, cologne. He lights a slender used cigar.

"That wasn't the white boy's tent," he says. "That was Marcus Robinson's tent. That boy and Marcus played music, sometimes with me. Boy plays trumpet. Marcus plays sax— not as good as he thinks, but who the fuck is, right? He's okay. Marcus left to see a woman he knows over in . . . now, what's that fucking place. Shit, I can't remember. Some fucking place. So he lets the white boy have his tent for a few days. White boy didn't have a tent. He was living in a box over by Whole Foods. You been there? Whole Foods? It's like Ralphs for rich people."

"What's the white boy's name? You played with him, must know his name."

"White boy didn't speak. Only to Marcus, whispered to him. That white boy was fucked up, but he could play."

"Who'd want to kill Marcus?"

Manny laughs.

"Long list, Detective."

"You know a lot."

"Soul got to keep his eyes open down here. Look at these motherfuckers," he says, sweeping his hand over the street.

"When's Marcus coming back?"

"Maybe now, maybe never. I ain't his keeper. That man got his own time."

"I'm glad you called, Manny. You see anything else, or if Marcus comes back, call me again."

"Kinda like a job. Like a thing a man might get paid for."

I hand him a twenty.

"I'll be in touch," he says. He walks to the corner, puts his amp down, swings his guitar across his chest, and plays slow, static chords. Fresh clouds roll in from the west and the air cools. I walk to my car. "You a Jesus man?" says the voice from the tent. I am not. I hand her a five. She takes it, closes the flap, and zips back into the shadows. I head home on Third, take a left on Hill, pass the Grand Central Market and Angels Flight, and pull into my building, wondering what I'm going to do with Lily's clothes and the things she's left behind.

CHAPTER 5

I throw my shield and gun on the counter. Two p.m. I shower and make coffee, sit at the piano, and play. Lily liked when I played. She'd stand behind me, slide her hands over mine and follow my fingers over the keys. "I'm your shadow, Carver," she'd say. I improvise off an old Evans tune. The notes circle and fade. Go nowhere. I rise and stand at the window. Rain. Clouds press down on Pershing Square and the jewelry district. I lie on the couch and listen to a million drops, falling hard and soft between gusts. I look to the record player and the bookcase, empty glasses on the sill, and the framed photograph of an African tribesman standing alone on a ridge, a river flowing below. With his spear and markings, he is complete, ancient, at one with the universe. Slender and tall and certain of who he is. How does a man get that way? I close my eyes. Rain blows against the window; Nicaraguans march on Fourth Street, banging drums and chanting for the undocumented. I think of the unmade bed down the hall, the scent of Lily, her powder and perfumes, although she wore little of either. And then I think of nothing.

I awake in the dark, on the couch. One a.m. The rain has stopped. I drive to Lily's and sit outside in my car. A half-moon shines. I feel like a night watchman, a soldier on a borderline. I pull up a Chris Smither playlist. Turn it low. Headlights creep closer in my rearview. A BMW stops beside me. I see the silhouette of a woman, cigarette in her lips, the spark of a lighter. Her face aglow for a split second. She turns toward me and speeds away. I follow. She hits the 101, heads north. I can barely keep up—my Porsche is old and needs work. I don't call for backup or put the blue light on the roof. I'm one hundred yards behind her, but the highway is nearly empty and she's in my sight. She slows, speeds up, slows. Taunting. She weaves between two cars and veers off at Sunset. She rockets through a red light, turns a corner, and pulls into a 7-Eleven. She shuts the car off but doesn't move. I park beside her. Her head is resting on the steering wheel, her face hidden in a swarm of black hair. I reach for my gun and get out. She doesn't look up. I cross the front of her car, draw my weapon. Two skateboarders hurry into darkness beyond the gas pumps. The cashier inside dips below the counter. No one else is around. I walk to the driver's side. Her hands on the steering wheel, her face still hidden. I tap my barrel on the glass. Take aim.

"Get out, Dylan. Now."

A face streaked with tears and mascara turns. Lips red, skin so white, just like Dylan's. The profile sharpens in the night, just like Dylan's. I open the door and yank her out. She screams and sobs and fights me. She slides on her high heels, catches her balance, and stands. I release her. She steps back with fear in her eyes. It is not Dylan Cross. Dylan is tall and shows no fear. This woman is small and frightened. I lower my gun.

"What the hell are you doing!" she says.

"Stay calm. Everything's good. I'm a cop," I say, showing her my shield. "I thought you were a suspect."

"I thought you were a stalker," she says, catching her breath, wiping tears, shaking. "I saw you when I stopped to light up in Boyle Heights. You scared me. Guy sitting in a parked car in the dark. I took off and you came after me. I didn't know what was happening. I pulled in here after I thought I lost you."

"Why are you crying?"

"Is it against the law to cry? You're crazy, man. This is harassment."

She leans into the car and pulls a tissue from her purse. She wipes her eyes. The skateboarders roll closer.

"Not that it's any of your goddamn business, but my husband's having an affair," she says. "I knew forever, but tonight I found out."

"In Boyle Heights?"

"Some Moldovan bar singer. I didn't know that was a type. Apparently, I didn't know a lot. I was trying to get home and got lost."

A patrol car screeches into the parking lot. Two uniforms hop out. I flash my shield.

"I'm Detective Sam Carver."

They walk toward me.

"What's going on, Detective?" says N. Reyes, holstering his gun.

"I thought she was a suspect in a murder investigation."

"Whose?"

"Lily Hernandez."

The uniforms look at one another and back to me. Nothing more has to be said. They walk to their car. Reyes turns.

"Sorry, Carver. Lily was good people. We went to the academy together. We rookie patrolled for a few weeks back in the day. I heard she was going to get her detective shield."

"She would have."

"We good here?"

"Yes. My mistake."

The cheated-on wife leans on her BMW and lights a cigarette. She offers me one. I take it.

"Who was Lily Hernandez?" she says.

"A cop. She lived on the street where I saw you."

"I'm sorry."

"Sorry I scared you."

I look to the street, back to the parking lot. I run a sleeve over my eyes.

"Lily Hernandez was more than a cop, huh?" says the woman.

I don't answer. The skateboarders glide away. We smoke in silence. The woman doesn't want to go home; nothing will be the same when she gets there. She lights another cigarette. She looks at me and nods, gives a half smile, as if we two strangers are bound by things that have fallen from our grasp. She smooths her black dress and yawns. "I went to the club and saw the singer," she says. "She's what you'd expect a man might want. The kind of thing I had—still have, but he doesn't see it. You ever think about why that is? The fucked-up end of something." She watches a passing car. She says more rain is coming, and how unusual it is, even in winter, for so much rain to fall. "Whole planet's messed up," she says. She looks to the sky and back to me. She drops her cigarette, crushes it out. "Jackie Criswell," she says. "My name. Aren't you guys supposed to ask?" She gets in her car and leaves. A man walks a dog into the 7-Eleven. Two motorcycles pass. I turn. Alicia Bryant is standing at my car.

"We going to have a problem, Carver?"

"I don't see one," I say, walking toward her.

"Not your case, Carver."

"I thought I saw—"

"I know what you thought you saw, but you didn't. Don't jeopardize my shit, Carver."

"You like my last name? You keep saying it."

"It's an okay name."

Bryant walks around the hood and stands on the passenger side, arms folded on the roof. I go to the driver's side and mirror her pose. She's wearing a Dodgers cap and a tailored black leather jacket. Soft leather, not the kind that keeps you warm. She has a rousted-out-of-bed look. Not much makeup. But there's a gleam to her. Her eyes stay on me, not letting me in, not keeping me out. Inviting, but at a cost. I remember seeing those eyes years ago at a gallery in the Arts District, way before that neighborhood drew in start-up money, licorice ice cream, valet parking, and falafel trucks. I didn't know her then. It was before Lily, too. I had read an article in the *Times* about a Black artist on the rise. Trey Bryant. I went to the gallery after work with a cellist who has since fled to Chile. The air was charged with whispers and promise, inklings of what might come, the hype that attracts critics and money. One of the paintings was called *Woman*. It was Alicia—not completely her, but a composite of the real and the imagined, a man's distillation of a woman who is at once a stranger and a keeper of secrets. It was a painting of a marriage and the deceptions we allow ourselves. I remember those eyes. They are looking at me now.

"Why are you here?" I say.

"Got a call."

"I'm not going to wreck your investigation."

"That's for damn sure, Carver. I said it again. It's those syllables. Catchy, you know. *Car-ver.*" She shakes her head, takes the blade out of her voice. "You're hurting, I know, but you have to let this alone. If it's Dylan Cross, I'll find her. If it's someone else, I'll find them. Someone's going down."

"Could be you. You don't know her."

"That a threat? I know she killed two guys and tied your ass up and left town," she says. "I know that you think she's back."

"She is," I say. "What else you thinking?"

"Looking at guys you put away. Robbery on up. See who may have done their time and gotten out recently."

"What do you have?"

"It's been less than twenty-four hours. It's cross-referencing, Carver. It takes time. Jesus."

"Lily was a cop."

"I'm red-balling it. Fast as I can."

"You know what was written on Lily's mirror?"

"'Hi, Sam, I'm back.' In lipstick."

"Pretty specific."

"Con could have done that just as easily as Dylan Cross," she says.

"Didn't look like a con's writing."

"You a penmanship expert?"

"No."

"All right, then. Let me play it all out, Carver. Okay? The con angle. The Dylan angle. Everything."

"Fair enough, but—"

"Don't say it, Carver. Let's pretend we agree."

"One more thing," I say.

She rolls her eyes.

"Why does a con kill Lily and not me?"

"Whoever did it wanted you to suffer," she says. "Getting killed isn't suffering."

"That something you picked up in Compton?"

"Look at you, Carver. Talking tough. You getting in my face? A white boy from Newport, Rhode Island?"

"It's tough in Rhode Island. Have you ever been?"

"All kinds of tough, Carver."

She smiles, steps back, turns toward her car.

"Don't get me up again tonight," she says. "Go home."

"You ever think . . ."

"Think what?"

"About all the shit out there we'll never stop."

"Don't have time for it, Carver. It's one up, one down. Don't be getting all existential. Ortiz told me about you."

"What did he say?"

"That you're trying to figure it all out."

"What?"

"The whole cosmic thing. The shit that can't be figured out. The abstract mess of us."

"You ever try?"

"Get some rest, Carver."

She looks at me. I think she might say more, but she drives east toward the 101 and the skyline.

CHAPTER 6

I don't go to Lily's funeral.

I want to keep her for myself. She'd understand. The best way is alone. I imagine the gloves, salutes, and eulogies. The polished shoes. The creak of holsters. The myth of "protect and serve." The fallen officer. The finest among us; the dead are always the finest. In war, life, and love. It is the dead who are absolved. I can see the framed picture of Lily in her blue uniform, smiling over cop faces, all of them wondering what it's like to catch a bullet in that place beneath the badge.

I drive to Point Dume and stand on the cliffs, looking out to the ocean. Green waves and darker water toward the horizon, where tankers, way out, sail south toward Long Beach and Mexico. The clouds are spread low; two surfers lift like birds in brief flight and disappear in white spray. I breathe in deep. Again. I close my eyes, open them. She is out there. Dylan Cross. She may be watching me now. She thinks I am damaged like her, that I can understand the voices that scurry and howl inside. She has told me so in untraceable emails. They are signed "D." They fill my inbox: screeds, love letters, incoherent ramblings, her thoughts on architecture, including the church she designed in the desert near Joshua Tree—its simple angles, cracks of light in stained glass, the way it rises from the land, as if part of it. I have often gone to Dylan's church, sat in its pews, looking for clues and, at times, I suppose, even sanctity, although that seems the wish of a boy long since gone. Dylan knows me. The night she broke into my apartment, knocked me out, and tied me up, in the hours before her dawn vanishing, she told me she had hacked my laptop, read my diaries, case files, and bank accounts. ("Boy, Sam, overtime really racks up for cops.") I have not built firewalls. I let her in. If I let her in, I will know her. I will find her. But I didn't see what was coming for Lily. I didn't protect her. Dylan had killed for vengeance— two fellow architects who drugged and raped her—but Lily had done nothing. I understood the vengeance but not Lily. Dylan has gone quiet. She has chosen silence. For now. But she is out there.

My phone rings.

"Carver. It's Ortiz."

"Is it over?"

"You should have come."

"I couldn't."

"It was a good send-off."

"Did you say anything?"

"I said she was wonderful."

"That's true."

"A man shouldn't lie at a funeral."

"I think that's when they lie most."

"Where are you?"

"Point Dume."

"Raining?"

"Getting ready to start again."

"You should have come, Carver."

I don't answer. In Ortiz's phone I hear footsteps, passing voices, and cars.

"Has it just finished?" I say.

"I'm leaving the chapel now. The mayor came."

"I'm heading back."

"Listen," he says, "we finally got an ID on your homeless torch job. James Fincher. Twenty-five-year-old schizophrenic from Carlsbad. Ended up on Skid Row a few years ago. I talked to his parents. They hospitalized him a couple of times but couldn't handle him. Lost touch and disappeared."

"Played the trumpet."

"They didn't say anything about a trumpet," says Ortiz, taking the long, burdened breath I am used to when he senses a case will not be quickly put down. "Hey, Carver, we need an arrest on this. Mayor came over to the chief before the funeral—like he does, you know, all crisp and clueless—and says, with all the negative shit the *Times* has been writing about how fucked up the homeless thing is, we can't be having some crazy running around burning people in tents. 'Optics,' he called it. 'Bad optics,' or some shit." Another long breath. "You good with this? Maybe you need some time off."

"I'm good."

"Work is the best to, you know, get through things."

"I was at Skid Row a couple days ago. Talked to a guy named Manny. He says Fincher may not have been the intended target. Fincher was staying in another guy's tent. Black sax player named Marcus Robinson."

"Is there a Skid Row band I don't know about?"

"Two guys rode by the scene the day after in a vintage car.

They wore ski masks and took pictures. Didn't get out, just rolled past."

"What the hell is that about? Anyone get plates?"

"No. I'm heading over there now. I know a doctor at a clinic on San Pedro. He might have heard something."

I get off the 110 at Sixth and drive through the financial district. I cross Broadway, heading east toward train tracks and the river, skimming Little Tokyo, passing windows of piñatas, bongs, and Jesus candles, and then to broken buildings and men slumped in doorways like misplaced, shoeless dolls. I park. A man with the jitters, bruises, and matted hair of an addict rolls an old woman wearing a hospital gown in a wheelchair. He stops at a tent and sits beside her. They share a cigarette. He talks about lottery tickets and wild dogs; his words blur, and I can tell he's coming down from a fix. The woman listens like a mother, nodding, stroking his back. They finish the cigarette. He rubs lotion on her arms and hands. She laughs and says how cool it feels, that she would like to take a bath in lotion, to let it cover her like a ghost and make her soft all over. He stands and lifts her out of the wheelchair. He kneels with her in his arms, kisses her on the forehead, and eases her into the tent. He folds the wheelchair and slides it in behind her. He looks up and down the street as if waiting for the return of something that passed this way long ago. He bends into the tent and zips it shut. I walk to the Lost and Found Clinic.

"Hey, Carver, long time," says Dr. Michael Ruiz, peeling off gloves, staring down a row of faces, and waving his hand across a wall. "You like our new mural? Spirit women rising from the earth to reclaim LA for the old tribes. Good luck, right? A Chicano artist from the seventies did it. Guy's still alive. Showed up out of nowhere one day and started painting."

"You've got a full house."

"You name it, we've got it. The ones who aren't on methadone are on meth. A fentanyl overdose this morning. Psychotics. Two schizophrenics had an argument over a bed. Four voices came out of them. Weird, man. Never get used to it." He hits on a vape, nods for me to follow. "The recession ones get me most, though. Families with nothing wrong except no money. Pushing shopping carts and sleeping in boxes. Kids running through the streets like sparrows. That's what they remind you of, you know. Little sparrows. Feels like end of days."

"You've got issues."

"Sorry, man. I'm preaching. Occupational hazard," says Ruiz, leading me into a small office, all eyes in the hallway on him. "I have to testify tomorrow before a city homeless commission. Another one the mayor set up to fix shit he knows nothing about. Christ. I told them, just play me on an endless loop. I've been saying the same thing for years. It's paralyzing. It's so big and scary. I don't know if it can be fixed. We've accepted it. We've said it's okay for people to live like this. It's who we've become."

"Didn't they have a march against homelessness a couple weeks ago?"

"One hundred and seven showed up. Thirty-one signs. I counted."

"Problems out there for everyone, maybe. Whole country feels squeezed."

"That's the rationale. What's that saying, though, from the Bible? The least among us . . ."

"You sound like an altar boy."

"Saint Benedict's."

"A lot of people feeling they're the least these days."

"True. But not like down here. Nothing's like down here."

He sits behind a desk. Quick and trim, dark curly hair, hands fidgety and eyes hard blue and tireless, Ruiz was an east-side kid who went to UCLA medical school, and instead of setting up in Brentwood or Santa Monica, he opened the Lost and Found Clinic, tucked between a women's shelter and a factory that once made yo-yos and spinning tops. I met him ten years ago. He showed up at the Little Easy on Fifth one night. We shared half a bottle of scotch and talked about this city's beautiful habit of betrayal. "LA's a lunatic's dream," he said, pouring a round and noting, "I read that on a wall beneath an underpass. No shit." He talked and talked, bleary in the mirror behind the shelves, saying he preferred Lana Del Rey to Madonna, the ocean to the mountains, and wildfires over earthquakes. We stayed until Barkeep Lenny sent us on our way, me walking toward Hill and Ruiz stumbling to his loft on Spring.

"I know why you're here, Sam," he says.

"Tent fire. You know the vic? James Fincher."

"He'd come in with his trumpet. He'd sit out there and play and wait for his methadone. A spidery guy. Sick with a dozen things."

"Someone told me the tent he was in wasn't his, that it belonged to a Marcus Robinson."

"Marcus is the big man on the block. Vietnam vet. Mildly screwed up but mostly sane. He found his place and shrunk his life a long time ago. That's the key to surviving here: shrinking who you are. Marcus plays sax and has women all over the streets. Comes in here for STDs and PTSD. Must be at least seventy but doesn't look it."

"He have enemies?"

"The normal number."

"A guy name Manny."

"I know Manny. Wired all the time, accelerated heartbeat. Like a motor."

"He told me a car rolled by the day after, with two guys in ski masks taking pictures."

Ruiz opens a drawer, pulls out a paper, and slides it across the desk. The top line reads "The Flag" in big letters, and beneath: "The Time to Act Has Come."

"These flyers have been tacked up all over Skid Row," says Ruiz. "Started about two months ago. You know the Flag?"

"No."

"A white supremacist group. Started about five or six years ago on the internet. They've grown fast. They despise immigrants and all the usual suspects, but they have particular hate for the homeless. They call them 'rats,' 'a scourge,' 'infection,' and my favorite: 'cancer on the American soul.' Who talks like that?"

I raise my eyebrows.

"Okay," says Ruiz, "besides our president."

"Have you seen them?"

"Just these flyers. But somebody's putting them up."

"Why a down-and-out heroin-addicted trumpet player?"

"Who was in the wrong tent."

"I'm thinking maybe Marcus was the target."

"Everyone knows Marcus. Charismatic. Black. Homeless. Makes a statement, right?"

"Could be."

"It's not just the fire. There have been beatings, too. I've set a broken arm and stitched up a few people. At first, I thought it was territorial tent stuff—always that kind of battle down here—but two of the beat-up guys said the attackers wore masks and came late at night."

A man screams in the hall. Chairs clatter.

"I better get back," says Ruiz.

"I'll keep this," I say, folding the flyer into my pocket.

"Let's get a drink sometime," he says, hurrying toward a sea of eyes. "It's been a while."

CHAPTER 7

The Flag started in Oregon and has chapters across the country. Founded by skinhead brothers Charlie and Bill Crenshaw, the group's crude 8chan Aryan ideology has evolved into euphemisms masking hate and calling for a pure white society. The writings veer from Charles Manson's apocalyptic vision of a race war to *The Turner Diaries*, a novel celebrating a white supremacist rebel army, to tweets about walls and refugees, to the musings of QAnon, a mysterious right-wing internet peddler of conspiracy theories that the FBI lists as a terror threat. The Flag's website evokes eerie nostalgia—faint imprints of swastikas and Nazi brown suits, a time of ash and snow. It opens into portals, chat rooms, and message boards, a parallel galaxy of prophets and foot soldiers rallying around xenophobic prayers for a promised land of guns and bunkers. One writer, Goebbels32, types in caps: "REGARDING HOMELESS THREAT TO BROTHERLAND: TIME TO SCOUR STREETS. WILL RESUME THOUGHTS ON IMMIGRANT INVASION AT LATER DATE. AMERICA UNDER SIEGE FROM ALL SIDES. THOUGHTS?????"

It is tough reading. I pour a drink and stand at the window. Midnight. The Hotel Clark glows. A couple, one dressed in the flowing robes of a *Star Wars* character, the other like Tinkerbell, race down Hill on Birds toward Pershing Square. I catch my reflection in the glass: eyes far back and hair wild—the pale, unshaven face of a man who has let things slip. I haven't thought about Lily in twelve hours. I don't want to think about her now. I sit back at the laptop and drift into the ether of hate.

The Crenshaw brothers sell mail-order T-shirts streaked with quotations from the Bible and the Constitution. They offer black boots, protein powder, and a natural-ingredient Viagra knockoff. They are developing "with esteemed scientists" an inoculation against *auslanders* (outsiders), who "we all know carry untold diseases." I scroll and stop at a headline: THE COST OF THE HOMELESS HORDES ON OUR GREAT CITIES. Written by a guest columnist who goes by the alias PureLand, the piece is intelligent and articulate, though also elitist and racist and filled with statistics that conclude that homelessness on city streets, particularly in Los Angeles, will bring ruin or, more likely, "retaliation" by developers and a new generation of right-wing politicians. "When the price per square foot reaches a magic number, the homeless will be expunged, and progressive libtards silenced. It is the way of the world, but we must accelerate it." He doesn't say how they will be "expunged." The trick of the writing is its ambiguity—let the rabid and the sane fill in the blanks as they will. I skim through the piece again, tracing its logic, studying its academic phrasings and the bite of its zealotry. I write "PureLand" on a piece of paper.

I push the laptop aside. I shower and let steam fill the bathroom so that I am invisible—a game I played as a child, thinking I was hiding from my parents, a spy in the fog. I turn off the water, towel the mirror dry, and come back into focus. I shave, comb my hair, and see one of Lily's earrings, a silver stud with an onyx inlay, near the sink. I pick it up and prick my finger with it. I want to feel the sting. A bead of blood rises. I return it to its place. Noise at the door.

"Carver. Carver, open up."

The banging echoes down the hall.

"Carver . . ."

I open the door. Ortiz barrels in, holding a small box tied with gold ribbon.

"Jesus, Carver."

"I was in the shower."

"Everything good?"

"What do you think?"

"You look like shit. You're relatively handsome, but this look, I don't know. I need a drink. How's the torch-job case?"

Ortiz follows me down the hall. He takes the seat he likes by the window; he told me once it made him feel princely, looking out over the city at night. He places the box in his lap. I hand him a scotch and tell him about the Flag.

"So we got a bunch of white supremacist wackos in ski masks running around Skid Row. The *Times* is going to be all over this."

"I don't know if they burned the tent and killed Fincher, but they're there," I say, handing Ortiz the flyer Ruiz gave me. "They're putting these up."

"Could be a movie. You check on that? Some dystopian shit they might be filming down there. One of those X-Men, superhero, comic-book things."

"Marvel."

"Yeah, Marvel. Whatever."

"It's not a movie."

"What about this Marcus Robinson, the guy whose tent it was?"

"Can't find him. He may have had his own enemies."

"Which means it may not be the Flag. It'd be good if it's not. That'd be nothing but trouble head to toe. City's got enough problems. Corruption. Incompetence. It's a broken place. Don't need a pack of neo-Nazis running around with lighter fluid."

"You should have stayed in Costa Rica."

We sit in silence.

"How was today?" I say.

"You should have been there."

"I couldn't."

He lifts the box from his lap and hands it to me.

"She left a will," says Ortiz. "One page. It was in her file. She wanted you to have her ashes. She said you'd know what to do."

I hold the box. Not heavy or light, a weight between air and sand. I put it on the table and sit back and stare at the gold ribbon, as if this were a box from a gift shop, packed and tied by a woman with careful hands. It is small. Death is small. I wipe back a tear. Ortiz stares out the window. A siren rises and fades. Another. The room goes quiet again. I fill our glasses. We drink to Lily, half expecting that she will appear from the hall with a story of a perp or how good her run was on the canyon floor, past chaparral and rock, sky blue, wind at her back.

"What time is it?" says Ortiz.

"Late."

"I don't want to drive home. Let's sit here until morning. It's gotta be close."

"How's Consuela?"

"Stayed behind in Costa Rica."

"Is it over?"

"Nothing like that. We're good. She wanted more time. She thought we were staying forever, but I changed the game on her."

"Men."

"Fucking men." He laughs. "We kick a lot of shit over that we don't clean up."

"She'll forgive you."

"I may have used up all my chits. But she will. I think."

"You hope."

"I wonder what I'd do if she didn't—you know, if she never came back."

"Like Lily."

"Don't say shit like that. Not now."

He stands, takes off his jacket, loosens his tie, lays his gun on the table. He sits back down, the bulk of him easing into the chair. Ortiz is not big, but he seems so. There's an air of resignation to him—not morose, but lived-in and knowing. A man who has not underestimated the world's capacity for cruelty yet waits for its moments of grace. He never misses mass. Years ago, shortly after I started in homicide, he told me to meet him late one night at a downtown church. We walked alone beneath the eyes of saints, lighting candles like men lost in a catacomb. I told him I had been raised in the church, in the time before my father died, but had left it long ago, not out of rebelliousness or sins gathered, but out of a diminished sense of wonder. He told me that was impossible, that even if religion had left me, there was something beyond it that stayed. I answered that the church brought only the ritual of memory. He smiled and said, no, it was more. "Don't be a cynic, Carver," he said. "Cynicism will solve a case, but it won't get you through a night." He crossed himself with holy water and we went separate ways into the dark.

"I haven't heard from Dylan," I say.

"When did she last email?"

"Couple months ago. 'Hi, Sam, It's me. Not much to report, feeling lazy. Sad.'"

"That was it? Doesn't sound like her. She's an expounder."

"A what?"

"Talking shit all over the place about all kinds of things."

"She hit a low, maybe. Crazy ones do."

"Sane ones, too."

Ortiz sighs, leans forward and back.

"You know," he says, "Dylan's MO was a knife, something sharp. Her kills were intimate. A gun's not intimate."

"Those were revenge kills. Lily was different."

"Still."

"Lily could have taken her."

"She did that Iron Man shit, I know. But Dylan's a psycho. Whole different equation. If it is her, she needs to hear the last breath, slow and up close. Gun doesn't do that."

"It's her."

"You gotta let Bryant into this case, Carver. I heard about your chase the other night. Reckless. The department could take a hit if you go crashing something up. You're lucky that woman didn't file a report."

"She looked like Dylan. I thought it was her."

"Let Bryant work it. Let her know if Dylan contacts you. Give her the emails."

"It's my case. My life."

"No, it's not, Sam. It's too personal. Let's stop having this goddamn conversation." He lifts his glass, sips. "Work this Skid Row thing. That's your case."

He quiets, closes his eyes. I reach for Lily's box. I pull the gold ribbon, but not all the way.

CHAPTER 8

I drive past the Midnight Mission to Gladys Park, where booze boys shoot hoops with a half-deflated basketball and old men play backgammon for quarters and dimes. Dogs run. A kid races with a Batman kite that rattles and spins but does not soar. I park and walk over to homeless men camped behind a fortress of cardboard, blankets, and shopping carts. Manny, who had again borrowed Wanda's phone, costing him "two goddamn dollars," had called and suggested the men might know how to find the elusive Marcus Robinson.

"Marcus," says one of them. "Who's Marcus?"

"You know Marcus, fool. Vietnam Marcus."

"Big guy with the horn?"

"That's him."

"Thought he died."

"Somebody else died."

"Mmm. Always happening that way, I guess. Maybe he moved to Denver."

"I saw Marcus yesterday," says a third man with swollen

ankles and cracked skin, clothes hanging off him like ancient tapestry. "He was with a woman."

"Truth in that."

"Marcus always got a woman."

"Over by the river."

"River with no water in it."

"My head hurts."

"Lie your ass down."

"I seen him by the river."

"What'd he do?" says the third man, looking at me.

"Just want to talk to him," I say.

"Man like you ain't just a talker," he says, tipping the last drop from a bottle. "Maybe the whale swallowed Marcus."

"Yea, that river whale," says the first man, laughing.

"Some fool did get swallowed," says the second man.

"That's in a movie," says the first man.

"Shit's in the Bible," says the third man. "Jacob got swallowed by a big fish."

"Jonah," I say. "Jonah was swallowed by the whale."

"Who's to say it was a whale, exactly, I mean?"

"Fake news," says the first man.

"Fuck Jonah, anyway."

"Fuck the whale, too . . ."

I drive past the Arts District. I stop and walk along railroad tracks and the thin thread of a river. A marsh bird lifts to flight. I wonder what it was like before the city was settled by men driving stakes and laying claims and thinking this land of oil and deep cracks would touch the divine in them. Long gone. Now it is the domain of hipsters, coders, gaffers, ruined hearts, reimagined faces, Eggslut denizens, Guatemalans, Hondurans, East Coast escape artists, gallery wives, and lost men like Marcus Robinson. I scan tents, lean-tos, and campfires, but

Marcus does not appear. I walk a while longer, the city pushing up against me, mountains rising north and west. I take off. I run as fast as I can, chasing no one, setting my sights on a light pole about a hundred yards away. My lungs feel stretched and brittle. But I settle into a rhythm, as Lily taught me, and my pace smooths. A man in pants, good shoes, and a jacket running toward the outskirts, like a thief with a diamond or a madman escaped from an institution. I touch the pole, turn, and walk back through fresh rain to the car, searching weed and rust for any moving thing. I drive deeper into Skid Row, beyond San Pedro, and stop at an underpass where Michael Ruiz told me Kiki Brown keeps a mattress and a hot plate beneath a tarp on a sidewalk across from a row of tweakers. I park and walk beneath the underpass, giving off a cop scent that sends whispers among the meth heads. They stagger away, one of them lost in staccato words, another clawing the air. I turn and see a woman sitting against the wall. Glassy eyes, slack face, runny nose. She's stirring soup, shivering, braless in a tank top, needle tracks in her arm.

"Kiki?" I say.

"Could be," she says, not looking up from her soup. "You a cop or dealer? You want pussy? My soul don't need saving, if you're one of those."

I step closer.

"Why you looking at me like that?" she says. "Staring. It's creepy, man. Stop it."

She sets the pot on the hot plate, turns off the heat.

"You're trying to figure it out, right? Like what the fuck," she says. "Kiki Brown should be Black. Name's as Black as a Black woman gets. Soul-singing Black. You look mind-blowed, whoever you are, like who is this face that doesn't fit the name? Perception's all fucked up." She laughs, rolls her head back, coming off a high, trying to stay awake, a spoon in her hand. "I'm white as my daddy who gave me the name. He liked them singers, I guess."

"You've got an accent," I say.

"It ain't French."

"Where?"

"A long-ago place."

"Where?"

"Go away, Mr. Twenty Questions. No time for you. Let me have the last of my high."

"I'm looking for Marcus Robinson."

"Name fits the color. That's all I'm saying. Go away."

She jabs the spoon toward me, tries to stand but can't. She catches her breath and wraps herself in a blanket that looks newly washed. She pulls her legs up, perches her chin on her knees, hisses like a cat. She has a bruised cheek and dried blood on her forehead. Her hair is long, red, and tangled. She's an addict, but unlike most, she has not all the way succumbed to the streets or gone mad. She has her teeth and an old bottle of perfume. Clothes are folded in crates around her mattress. A flower pokes from a small, battered kettle. A book with a torn cover lies beside her.

"What are you reading?"

She hisses again. Pushes the hair back from her face. She looks early thirties but could be younger.

"Marcus gave it to me. It's about a man in war. In a jungle. He can't get out."

"Is it good?"

"What's good about a fucking war, man? The writing is horrible but pretty. A soldier man just got killed. His blood squished into the mud." She looks up, one eye half closed. Her head bobs, rolls. She nods off but catches herself, snapping back, startled. Goes numb again, words slow. "My baby died a while ago. They took it away. Fell out of me one day, like a bird from a cage. Came into the world and died. You ever hear of something like that? Baby just dropped out dead, like it wanted no part of nothing. Go back to where he came from. It was a boy. I saw. A gray little blue thing. Didn't even cry."

She wipes her cheek. Traffic passes in the distance. New storm clouds roll in with the dusk.

"I'm sorry," I say. "I'm not here to cause trouble. I need to find Marcus."

"You're like a cockroach, won't go away. I'll scream," she says. She leans against the wall, sways her head from side to side. She coughs, scratches her arm. She looks at me, thinking maybe I'm the one somebody sent to bring her home or at least ease her with a fix, let her feel another warm tide in her veins. Her words blur into silence. I'm not the one, but she wants to pretend, to play the broken game a little longer. "What'd Marcus do?"

"Someone burned his tent over near San Pedro. He wasn't in it, but somebody was. I'm trying to figure it out."

"I don't know about that. Marcus came a few days ago. He stayed the night. He left. I don't know. He comes and goes."

"Any idea where?"

"Who are those guys who don't want a home? They live in the desert, like, you know, in Jesus times."

"Nomads?"

"That's Marcus," she says.

"How long have you known him?"

"People just meet, man. Ain't nobody marking a calendar. He sat down one day and started talking."

"He was in Vietnam."

"He was all over."

"What about you?"

She looks at me, looks away. A tear comes to her eye but doesn't fall.

"I ain't for sale."

"What are you on?"

"Whatever comes this way. Marcus don't like it, but he's a nomad."

She lights a half-smoked cigarette.

"I'm thinking of moving," she says.

"Where?"

"Venice."

"Too many in Venice."

"You can always find a spot. Smart ones can, anyway."

"LA's all about real estate."

"You fucking with me?" She reaches over and touches my hand. "You got a phone?"

"Yes," I say.

"Play me a song."

I open Spotify and scroll. I click. "Golden Slumbers" by the Beatles. She closes her eyes. Her face relaxes.

"My daddy played this all the time," she says. "He'd sing it in my ear, real soft—like words made of fog, that's what he'd say. He could say things like that, just out of nowhere. He'd sing it when I couldn't sleep. He'd kneel beside me and brush my hair and say, 'sleep, little girl.' He got killed in a mine. Covered in coal." She swallows, wipes her eyes. "Anyone ever sing to you?"

"My mother."

"What'd she sing?"

"'Summer Wind.'"

"Don't know it."

"You think Marcus could come by tonight?"

"He's like fog." She laughs. She lights a candle; we become

shadows on the brick wall. "Marcus got beat, you know, real bad. Two men in masks came to his tent. Late one night. He was all cut up. Lost a tooth. They kicked him. He said they wore big, hard boots."

"Were you there?"

"No. He told me about it. I saw the cuts. He came the night after."

"When?"

"A month, at least. I'm not good with time. People always want to know when. *When* don't matter to me. They held him down and drew a flag on his forehead."

"What kind of flag?"

"I don't know, a flag. I helped him wash it off."

Lightning flashes beyond the underpass.

"It's like a picture frame," she says.

"What?"

"Seeing the world out from under here."

"It won't stop raining."

She lights another candle, pulls her blanket tight. Wind blows, swirls papers, and dies.

"You got ten bucks?" she says. "I'm cold and need something."

"You just had something."

"Shit quality," she says.

I hand her two fives and my card.

"If you see Marcus . . ."

"I know," she says, "but Marcus, he doesn't always listen."

I walk to the edge of the underpass. Protected. The rain falls in sheets. I cup my hands and hold them out. I splash my face, run fingers through my hair, my scalp cooling, beads running down my back. I turn. Kiki stands with the tweakers across the street. She collects her fix and goes back to her mattress. I see a needle, a match strike. She eases against the wall as if her bones had been pulled from her. A fallen girl in candlelight. I am in no hurry to leave. I belong among the lost. I walk to her mattress and sit beside her. She looks at me, drooling, hazy-eyed, a sleepy smile. She pulls her blanket tight. Another day has kept its sparse promise. She says nothing. She leans into me. I don't know why, maybe a reflex, but I put an arm around her, smell her wild hair. Ginger, sweat, and smoke. Night comes. The darkness beneath the underpass mixes with the rest of the world. Everything is one. I'm cold. My father taught me to endure the elements, but as a boy I was curious why he could not endure himself. "He has lost all his answers." My mother told me that once when my father locked himself in a room for days. But my mother doesn't recognize me anymore, curled in a bed in her sister's house in Boston, bit by bit losing who she is, not knowing she gave me life and told me stories on a coast and in a time far from here. I should leave this place, but there is nothing for me at home, except the small box with the gold ribbon that holds Lily. Kiki presses closer. She'll be out for hours. Maybe Marcus will wander in from the rain with his washed-away tattoo and his soldier stories. I'll wait with Kiki. The tweakers are fixed up, slumped, and quiet. More men come from out of the wet. They wrap themselves in blankets and huddle together. They pass a cigarette. The ember dies and they sleep. A siren rises and fades, and the night goes quiet.

I awaken against the wall. Kiki is stretched out and sleeping. I check my gun, wallet, phone. Two a.m. I rise. The rain has stopped. I take a few steps.

"I don't know you," says a man. He flicks a lighter, holds it to my face. "This ain't your place. Go." He is squat, bearded. A pit bull on a thick chromed chain pants beside him. "You hurt Kiki?"

"No. I'm a cop."

"Strange for a cop to be sitting on a mattress next to a junkie under an overpass."

"Difficult case."

"Lucky for you Kiki's cleaner than most."

He laughs; the dog relaxes.

"You live here?" I say.

"Me and Jake come and go."

"I'm looking for a guy named Marcus Robinson."

"He comes here for Kiki from time to time. Big man, keeps himself clean. Mostly."

"Any trouble?"

"Nah, he's one of those who's figured it out. You can do good on the streets if you learn that."

"Have you seen him lately?"

"Nah."

"Would you tell me if you did?"

"Nah."

"Why are you up?"

"I'm bipolar with sleeping issues and a weak fucking bladder."

"You seem . . ."

"Almost normal. I get that a lot. I stay in that RV down on the corner. It don't run anymore." He pets Jake, lights a cigarillo. "You like cartoons?" He doesn't wait for an answer. "I love 'em—the old ones, you know. Short stories with morals. Something meaningful about Bugs Bunny. He's like a parable, a thing of universality. All kinds of meanings in Bugs Bunny. Full of instruction. They're not just for kids, cartoons. They speak on a whole other level. You've got to find the buried messages, that's all."

"The ironies," I say.

"They're voices from another planet, trying to tell us something. I think the cartoons are real and we're not. You get what I'm saying? All this ain't real. We're cartoons for the cartoons. It's a fucked-up, tricky thing. But I've figured it out." He looks to the street beyond the overpass. "All this rain. When did it ever rain so much in LA? Never, that's when. What's that tell you?"

"Climate change."

"We need more goddamn cartoons. That's what it tells me."

"They'll fix things?"

"Or explain."

"I don't know."

"They're perfectly apt. Cartoons know about destruction. That's where this shit show is headed. Poof. We're gone. The whole thing. Like we were never here. Wiped from eternity."

"You believe that?"

"I see the logic in it."

"What did you do before this?"

"Before what?"

"Before your RV died on the corner."

"Irrelevant."

We stand in silence. He's in bare feet, shorts, and a jacket with ripped patches. A tweaker stirs, then another. I look back to Kiki. Still asleep. A car with a loud radio and laughing girls passes. It heads toward the 10. No one knows where I am, and I wonder what it would be like to vanish.

The man flicks his lighter again; holds it to my face.

"I gotta go piss," he says. "You take care. Something ain't right out here. Jake feels it."

CHAPTER 9

Alicia Bryant walks in off Fifth Street and sits across from me. She orders a latte.

"Didn't know this place was here," she says. "Questionable location. Two blocks from Skid Row."

"The owners are from Lisbon."

"So, they didn't know better."

"City's changing, Bryant."

"Not that fast."

"You have to be—"

"I'm open to new shit, Carver."

The waiter slides the latte in front of her. Bryant and I are the only customers here. Fado music plays. The tables are draped in white linen; the floor is tiled. Mirrors line the wall, reflecting a polished bar, espresso machine, rows of glasses, and Sylvia, the manager, a tall transgender woman with swooped-back rainbow hair and an apron tied at the waist. She crushes out a joint and walks to the window with a paintbrush to finish a picture of sailors tangled in a mermaid's hair. Bryant watches, then turns to me.

"I don't get it," she says.

"Portuguese folklore. It's about a shipwreck. You should bring Trey. He might find a kindred soul in Sylvia."

"Trey's got enough kindreds."

"What do you have?" I say, nodding to the files.

"Three guys you put down. All out recently. None of them liked you very much."

"You're still going that way, huh?"

"I'm working all angles, Carver. Just look at the shit."

She pushes the files my way.

"That's some color," I say.

"Purple midnight."

"They real?"

"Of course they're real," she says, holding her hands to the light.

"Never understood about nails," I say. "How do you draw your gun?"

"Read, Carver."

I open the files. Three faces from the past stare up at me—men I locked away and long gone. They look young: tats and smirks, perps photographed hours after the deed, their eyes expectant, mean, scared, and seeing, in the flash of that moment, the future. Willie Slocum, gangbanger, script dealer, custom car detailer, shot two rivals on Broadway, stuffed the gun in his pants, went to have a soft serve at McDonald's. Fifteen years ago. One of my first collars. Dustin McNally, landscaper, meth-head, curly-headed psycho, stabbed his hooker girlfriend in a loft on Eighth Street. He blamed it on a burglary, then blamed me for finding the murder weapon hidden in his freezer. A real not-so-smart-guy. Angel Castillo, drug runner, scion of Boyle Heights, clever but too ambitious. Shot his boss in a power grab, not knowing that the boss,

Enrico Fuentes, who wore dark suits and tan shoes and drove around in an ancient black Fleetwood, which earned him the nickname "the Undertaker," had been a CI of mine. I hold up the pictures, match my lost youth against theirs, remembering the ways we collided and the things I took from their vics— bullet, bracelet, ring, and from Fuentes, an uncashed poker chip—and put in my inlaid box for the dead.

"Some crew," says Bryant.

"How do guys like this get out?"

"C'mon, Carver," she says, laughing. "Overcrowding, bureaucracy, appeals, reform. All kinds of ways to get into prison, all kinds of ways out. You know that."

"What are you thinking?"

"They talked shit about you inside."

"Denial before acceptance. All cons talk that game. Part of the act."

"They do. But we have Lily . . ."

I flinch. Bryant catches it.

". . . and that changes the equation."

Sylvia paints another sailor face in a crack of sunlight.

"Slocum comes up clean," says Bryant, hurrying things along. "He found Jesus inside and just moved in with his mother. McNally was released two months ago. Got his truck out of storage and went back to landscaping. Just went back to doing what he was doing, like nothing happened. His parole officer says he passes his drug tests and lives in a one-room apartment in Lincoln Park, the part they haven't gentrified. Which leads us to Angel."

"Mr. Castillo."

"Had a particular hate for you. Wrote emails about payback. Interrogation tape and trial transcript show you went after him hard. Like, maybe, too hard."

"I know what they say."

"Tell me about it."

I push the files aside, finish my espresso, and nod for another.

"Castillo hooked a girl I knew on meth. Molly Serella. Late twenties, from the valley. She worked as a temp in the federal building across from my apartment. I ran into her a lot. We went out a few times. Nothing serious. Different interests, but we liked each other's company. She played guitar and accepted the world the way it is. That fascinated me. She was guileless." The waiter brings the espresso. I stir in sugar, lean toward Bryant, who is like a statue looking at me, chin in hand, betraying nothing. "One night in Boyle Heights, we're at a taco place and Fuentes comes in. He's startled to see me. Doesn't want his cover blown. He looks around, relaxes, starts talking. But then Castillo comes in. Fuentes turns back, tells Castillo I'm a cop and that they better watch themselves." I sip, stir, glance to Sylvia, back to Bryant. "They joke about it. Fuentes is getting real anxious. He starts talking shit on cops. I let it pass. Understand his predicament. Castillo is into it. Why not, right? Harmless fun. We all swim in the same pool. He sits down next to Molly. He's got a strange charm, you know—street kid in silk kind of thing, but quick. I let him feel big."

"I know the type," says Bryant. "We call it 'greasy cool.'"

I finish the espresso, pour water from a carafe.

"Fuentes sits next to me, playing along. I go to the counter to get our tacos. I come back and Castillo and Fuentes are standing, saying goodbye to Molly. A couple more jokes about cops. Castillo winks at me and out they go. It was obvious that Fuentes had no chance against that guy. Fuentes was a crook, but not full-blown. You know the type—liked the allure of it but not doing the hard shit that needed to be done. Castillo was smart, vicious, complete."

"Molly found that out."

"I don't know what was said when I left the table. But Molly and Castillo started seeing one another after she and I ended. We stayed in touch, though. I didn't know at first. I couldn't figure the connection. Was it part of her acceptance of the world? The allure of the dangerous? I warned her. I drove to her house a couple of times. She stopped coming to work. Didn't take my calls. It became the shit we know. Meth. Heroin. He keeps her for a while, gets bored, starts hooking her. She ends up dead in a bungalow in the valley. I tried to help but not enough."

"You did more than try, Carver."

"I kicked the shit out of him one night."

"He filed a report."

"Internal Affairs cleared me."

"You said he was resisting arrest. What was your probable?"

"Could have been anything. Thought I saw a gun."

"Bullshit, Carver."

"Maybe, but I was cleared and that was it."

"Six months later," she says, "Fuentes is dead."

"Point-blank to the forehead. He had just bought a new suit and was getting dressed to go out."

"You go right for Castillo as the doer."

I nod yes.

"Word on the street said he was," I say. "Wanted more power and bling, took out his boss, laid the message down. It caused a storm in his organization, but the big guys let it pass. It was a ballsy act. They like that, to a degree. Some of them suspected Fuentes was a rat. They never could prove it, but the whiff was enough. Castillo gets a pass, rises in stature. I had two eyewitnesses who put him in Fuentes's apartment right before the hit. See him coming out right after. I had another CI testify that Castillo bragged about it and bought night rounds at some dive off Fourth."

"Then all of a sudden, the gun turns up."

"In a dumpster off Alvarado."

"You'd think a guy like that would be smarter," says Bryant, relaxing her statue pose, leaning back in her chair, checking her nails.

"Maybe. I would have picked someplace else. Who knows? His prints were on it."

"Interesting about the prints," she says.

"I know what he claimed."

"He said when you picked him up it was just you two. You drove him around. You drew on him and forced him to hold a gun."

"Jury saw it another way."

"Let me ask you, Carver, cop to cop, 'cause we've all been there. You do it?"

I sip my water, look right at her.

"It was a good case, Alicia. Castillo knew what he did, and I knew what he did."

"Question is, which crime are we talking about."

I let it pass. She's doing her job.

"Castillo has been out three months," she says. "No one's seen him. Not at his given address. His PO has a warrant out."

"He did Fuentes, but he didn't do Lily."

"I want to find him. Cross him off the list."

"Dylan is the doer. Simple."

"She needs to be crossed off, too. I'm not having any loose ends, Carver."

"Fine. Chase all the bullshit leads, but don't get sidetracked for too long. Lily deserves better."

Bryant jumps up; her chair screeches on the floor. Sylvia

and the waiter turn. Bryant glares at me. She steps toward me, bends down, puts her lips to my ear.

"Lily's getting the best I have, asshole," she says. "Don't come at me with that shit. You're hurting, Carver, but there's a limit."

A lot of cops would have walked out. Bryant sits and orders another latte. The anger in her eyes fades. She collects the files and stacks them before her. I wonder what secrets she has—the cop-life things that gather inside, missed leads, overlooked clues, lost evidence. Her color is a double weight. It runs beneath the cool smoothness of her, rattling deep down, making her doubt what she should be most sure of. Reminding her every day that despite her prep-school diploma and detective's badge, she's a Black kid from Compton. Living with it on the streets and in the office and at home with Trey, whom I never met, and his paintings of slaves old and new. They are works of defiance and grace, but they are also Alicia's history, hanging, watching, pressing down so she is haunted by those who came before her. It's what I will never know: the feeling of being a suspect in your own skin, seeing two faces in the mirror. What you see versus what the world outside your door sees. Bryant sips her latte. We sit, not talking, listening to music in another language, about lost sailors and sunken ships. Bryant starts to say something but quiets. She grabs her files and leaves. She crosses Fourth, gets into her Mercedes, slides on sunglasses, and heads west.

I wave for another espresso. My phone flashes. It has been a while, but I know. I lift it and read Dylan's email.

Dearest Sam:

I'm soooo sorry. I heard about Lily. You poor man. What kind of world do we live in? I hope you find peace. Do we ever? I wonder. We just say it, like it will appear out of thin air. Like magic. I suppose that's how we get by. Believing in wished-for things. Like children. We are all poor, confused children. It's tiring trying to believe. But I believe, Sam. Don't get mad, but I have to say something. Lily wasn't right for you. You do know that. Sweet little Lily. She didn't fool me. A clever, coy one. I know her type. Oh, yes. We girls know. But, still, I hope she didn't suffer. Was it a robbery? The news wasn't clear. The news is so unclear these days. It makes you wonder, though, huh, Sam? About us. How we belong together, even after so much time. I have so much to tell you. The places I've seen. The old continent. Ruins and ghosts. Stones that speak. Oh, yes. I will tell you all. Not now. You must grieve. Did you know Jews grieve for a whole month? Who has that capacity? But soon I will tell you. I am not as far away as you might think. The other day we breathed the same air. Tingle. I am too bold, I know, but I wanted to see you. Can you guess where? Guess. Guueeeess. I like games. I am good at games, you remember. I kept leaving you clues, little fairy-tale bread crumbs. I'm on-again, off-again meds. Zoom-zoom, then fall-fall. I glide and crash and fly again. Some days I don't know who I am. My mother was like that before she burned our house down when I was a girl. Poof. I am not like her. But still. I'm drawing like crazy. So many buildings inside me. The architecture of the self. It comes down to that, doesn't it, Sam? The cracked lives within, the divided selves that will not mend. You are like that, too. Oh, yes, I think so. We are one. See you soon.

Love, D.

She's back, her words glowing in my hand. I was scared she might have vanished after what she did to Lily, just as she did after killing the architects. But she is coming. Closer. I knew she would. Dylan can't resist the endless temptations she creates in all the strange designs she has fashioned for us. I read the email again, knowing that soon I will put her down or she will do the same to me.

CHAPTER 10

I walk north on Spring to headquarters. I never liked it here—
too many cops and bureaucrats scheming in back offices and
hallways. Badges and politics, and the scents of careers rising
and suddenly ending. Ortiz isn't around. I take the elevator to
tech forensics. Jimmy Knight is scrolling on three laptops, long
fingers swift over keys. He has the pale skin of an insomniac,
a young man who lives in blue glow, chasing code through
cyberspace. He was a Sherman Oaks teenage hacker—stole
credit card numbers from coffee shops and worked his way up
to corporate accounts—but in a plea agreement, he switched
sides and went to work for the LAPD, which for the past ten
years has provided him with state-of-the-art technology, a
steady salary, and a fridge full of Red Bull. He looks at me, hits
a vape, turns back to his screens.

"Are you playing or working?" I say.

"It's all play to me, man."

"Find anything?"

"C'mere, look at this."

I step behind him. Images on screens, like rivers, race, slow, and blur.

"It's amazing what's out there. It's ridiculous, Carver. All the shit going on in these cyber wrinkles. Black holes of infinite idiocy. Nazis and alt-right bullshit, and then you've got the left-wing shit, but they don't get it, you know. Don't know the language. Don't know how to talk to the edgelords. Internet's got its own vernacular, man, like *Game of Thrones*. Basic." He laughs and leans closer to the screens. "The Right's got that shit down, though. Trolling around gamer sites looking for lonely Harry Potters. Planting little messages. The right-wingers say shit like they're winking at you all the time. They love that vague shit. But there's double meanings in the vagueness, you know. They know it; you know it. It's all wink-wink. All those incels pecking away, just looking to be angry at shit, just wanting to be part of some ether tribe. I mean, damn. You can get *lost* in this ocean."

"I caught sixty percent of that," I say. "You better cut back on the energy drinks."

"I'm like this all the time," he says. "This is my resting state. You should see me on vacation. The point is, look." He points to the middle screen. "This is your guys, the Flag. Hateful fuckers, but Bill and Charlie Crenshaw from Oregon come across as real folksy, out to save the white race from the scum poisoning America, which now, as we know"—Jimmy *wink, winks*—"is being invaded by immigrants, enslaved by Jews, polluted by Muslims and libtards, and infested with the homeless on our city's streets. These assholes don't even like the Dalai Lama. I mean, shit, Carver, really, who doesn't like the Dalai Lama?"

"The Chinese."

"Fuck the Chinese."

"How big is the Flag."

"Their site claims they have two hundred thousand followers," says Jimmy. "Hard to tell, could be bullshit. The site's retro. I can't tell if that's by design or just shitty coding. I think, by shitty coding. It's not intuitive, but these guys run on different intuition, which is why, look, they have a picture of Hitler morphing into the face of this white guy in the mountains with camo and gun. Oddly hypnotic. Not bad tech, actually pretty good. But it's not consistent."

"What about the guy who posts under the name PureLand? He writes a lot about homelessness. LA-specific."

Jimmy rolls to another desk, clicks a few keys, and rolls back.

"Name popped up on 4chan and 8chan," he says. "Relatively new. He started posting on the Flag about a year ago. He's a prophet looking for a flock. My guess, smarter than most of the National Alliance and Stormfront types. Probably from LA, but don't know. No bio. He doesn't have Twitter or a Facebook page, at least not under PureLand. He could have another alias. Hard to tell. I'll keep cross-referencing. The homeless are his thing, though, right? Hates 'em."

Jimmy sips a Red Bull, chases it with coffee.

"Where do you stand on immigration, Carver?"

"Jimmy . . ."

"Okay, okay. No politics."

He offers me pizza from a box. His lair is cool, dim, quiet, almost lulling, despite the hate and screeds on the screens.

"What about the tent burning?" I say. "Any mention of that?"

"Just cryptic shit on 4chan. Chats back and forth. Here's some: 'See LA had a little campfire last night.' 'Yeah, one less rat.' 'Is that the way?' 'Someone's got to do something?' 'Can't burn a city.' 'Why not?' 'Dude, you're sick.' 'Maybe time for some kinda sickness. I ♥ whoever did it.'"

Jimmy hops up and gives me his seat.

"I collected a bunch of shit for you," he says. "Scroll."

Pastoral images flicker. Mountains, streams, dazzling blue sky. An idyll. Families, all white, picnic in the grass beneath a towering cross and an American flag with swastikas for stars. The images accelerate and the sky darkens. The grass turns brown; mountains are stripped of trees; streams flow with garbage and poison. Refugees in boats, faces pressed against border fences, lines of dispossessed pushing through jungles and forests, all with their eyes on the cross and the flag, as if a black- and brown-skinned army were marching in endless numbers. They are joined by bearded Muslims, black-hatted Jews, homeless rising in rags from sidewalks, drug addicts and psychotics screaming from alleys. All hurtling toward the heartland. The families at the picnic gather their guns—children aim Glocks and AR-15s—and huddle beneath the flag and cross. They wait as the hordes advance. Then a bright flash streaks the sky. Hitler appears with eyes of fury. A messianic messenger. Klansmen from D. W. Griffith's *Birth of a Nation* gallop in wearing white robes and hoods. David Duke, William Pierce, neo-Nazis, jackboots, black boots; Aryan legions, dressed in camo, rushing to save the families. On and on it goes, a torrent of images, scrolling with no beginning or end. I feel like the sociopath in *A Clockwork Orange* who has his eyelids pinned open and is forced to watch the world's atrocities until he is catatonic and numb. Until he becomes a believer. Or is cured. I lean back from the screen.

"Wicked, huh? Apocalyptic. And that's the *mild* shit," says Jimmy. "I turned the sound off. I couldn't listen to any more Wagner, Landser, or Skullhead. You ever listen to neo-Nazi punk rock? That shit'll kill you."

"You're up on these guys, huh?"

"It's where it's all being fought, man. Not on the streets. Not in Charlottesville or those mosques in New Zealand, but on the web. It's the future, Carver. Hell, it's the *now*, man."

"Keep trying on PureLand," I say.

"You got a thing for him."

I pull the Flag flyer from my pocket, hand it to Jimmy.

"These have been showing up on Skid Row. Then a guy gets torched in a tent and guys in ski masks roll by and take pictures. You come across any pictures like that?"

"No. But I'll do a wide sweep."

Jimmy holds the flyer up.

"'The time has come to act.' Sounds just like these wackos. Vague but creepy. That's their shtick."

He hands back the flyer.

"You want pizza?" he asks. "You know, I ate, like, twelve hundred dollars' worth of pizza last month. Expensed it all. The sergeant got on my ass. I told him I was a high-level asset, Jason Bourne kind of shit."

He laughs.

"I gotta go," I say. "Let me know what you find."

"Be cool, Carver."

I head down the hall. Jimmy's tapping fades. I leave headquarters and walk over to a bench in front of city hall. I sit. A hawk circles. I've read where they have come back, nesting in unfinished high-rises and skimming over the city, swooping down on pigeons. I take my notebook out and write: *Marcus Robinson.* I draw lines of suspects who would want to kill him. Jealous lovers. Street guys. Dealers. Stray crazies. Neo-Nazis. Why the masked men in the car taking pictures? That's planned, or is it? I close the notebook and walk past the old *Times* building. I head up Spring Street and take a right on Fourth.

My phone hums.

"Didn't I just talk to you, Jimmy?"

"Yeah, but listen, man, I jumped into a few more channels and chat rooms. A lot of chatter."

"What kind of chatter?"

"Noise, like they do. Nothing specific," he says. "But something's going down. You can feel it in the noise. Like hornets all stirred up."

"Where?"

"I don't know where, Carver."

"What are you saying, Jimmy?"

"Expect some shit."

CHAPTER 11

"Rain won't stop."

"How many weeks?"

"I lost count."

"Sorry about Lily."

Richard Greenberg hands me a cup of coffee, pours in a thimble of whiskey. He caps the bottle. We stand on his Laurel Canyon porch, watching rain fall in rows across the thicket.

"No mudslides yet," he says, arching his eyebrows. "Sometimes, I can feel this house move under me. Like someone's tugging on a rug I'm standing on."

"You've got luck."

"For a time, I did," he says. "You, too."

"Not long enough," I say.

"Too bad we don't get more of a warning before it goes to shit."

"We're not that bad off, Richard. On most days."

"I know. It's the weather talking. Commiserating kind of day."

I met Richard when I was an undergrad at Berkeley. His son, Ben, a geology major, was my best friend. We would come to LA on breaks and weekends to stay with Richard and his changing constellation of women, who ranged in age between early twenties and late fifties, each having a quality specific to something Richard felt he lacked at a precise moment. Ben used to say the women could be cataloged like library files: Art. Music. Psychology. History. Romanticism. Erotica. Miscellaneous. Some were striking, others less so. One was a guerrilla from Central America, another a painter from Slovenia. They would each last about six weeks, departing when Richard would awaken to a "shift inside," which Ben would explain to his father in geological terms as similar to an earthquake that starts deep and shudders to the surface. Richard would reply, "Ben, it's hardly that dramatic. It's just life." They never spoke of Ben's mother, and I never asked, but once I saw a picture in a closet, of a dark-haired woman with Ben's eyes, in a silver frame. Ben died our senior year in a plane crash. He was piloting a small Cessna with a bad fuel line that went down in Tarzana. I stayed close to Richard when I moved out here to join the LAPD. We remind each other of lost things.

"I finished my twenty-fifth film, Sam."

"I don't know how you got in and out of Yemen without getting killed."

"Shame what the world let happen there. The bad guys can do a whole lot of bad when no one's looking. America certainly looked the other way. Let the Saudis do what they wanted. The place is a land of graves. A lot of *small* graves, Sam."

"When's it open?"

"In a few months, at the Laemmle in Pasadena. I'll get you a ticket," he says, pulling his wool cardigan tight. His face is unshaven, his hair long and white, brighter than the mist around us. He's compact, strong, aging, and on many nights since Ben died, he sits on the porch, listening to birds and lizards rustling in the brush.

"Have a bit more whiskey, Sam."

He pours.

"So," he says, "I've been thinking about your case. These white supremacists are nasty bastards. I got a lot of threats after my film on the Aryan movement. Must be ten years now. We traveled all over the country for that doc. They're everywhere, you know. Police, churches, schools, government. Everywhere. Scared, mean little people thinking they're owed. That's a dangerous creature."

"Some people have been forgotten."

"I know. The world changed on them. But that doesn't make the hate right."

"Did you run into any of them out here?"

"Like this PureLand guy you're looking for?" he says. "We did a few interviews around LA. One guy called himself 'the White Preacher.' Another one called himself 'the Avenger.' I went back after you called and looked at the footage. The White Preacher's a carpenter from Calabasas who puts the Bible, *Mein Kampf,* and *The Turner Diaries* into a fanatic's blender and spews whatever bile comes out. He might still be around. I have an address. He's small-time, though. A garage prophet with bad lighting. Not very smart."

Richard offers another pour. I wave him off.

"Aim higher, Sam," he says. "A lot of rich guys into white supremacy. How do you think they got rich in the first place?"

"You're not going to get political, are you?"

"The personal *is* political. Can't separate them."

I cut him a glance.

"Okay, okay," he says, "but this country is based on white supremacy. The whole structure is built around it. Slavery was more about economics than race."

"I don't even know if we're dealing with that. I've got a burned white guy in a Black guy's tent on Skid Row."

"You've got those flyers and those guys taking pictures from a car."

"If it's them, so far they haven't done an ISIS. No one's claimed responsibility."

"Maybe they're waiting," he says, setting his glass on the rail.

"Could be—and I think it is—someone attacking homeless to make a bigger point. Start a movement. I know a lawyer, well connected in Hollywood. Represents a lot of politicians and developers, too. He told me a few months ago that the powers that be—and I don't mean our vacuous mayor—are worried. Lot of bucks, foreign and otherwise, pouring into downtown. Buildings going up. Risk and money bring out bad shit in people. This lawyer says no one knows what to do with the homeless. It's like, and I quote, 'uprooting an ant colony.'"

"Meaning?"

"You need an exterminator."

"Is this guy . . ."

"No. He's not alt-right or anything. That's not his sentiment. He's a pragmatist, but like I said, he knows everyone. Bills like the devil himself."

Richard walks down the steps and stands in the rain. He spins like a child and walks back up to the porch.

"Stay for dinner," he says.

"I thought you'd have a date over."

"I'm between moods these days. I wake up and don't know what I want."

"Celibacy can be enriching."

"Okay, Mr. Guru."

Richard makes pasta. We drink wine on a candlelit porch as night falls and rain turns to drizzle. I had often thought that Richard and my mother would have made a good pair—intellectuals, kind, wry humor, each having an acerbic side, which my father, even though he battled in and out of the ring, could not tame in my mother, although I don't think he tried. He loved her as she was and knew that the chronic disappointments between them—disguised often with a tenderness that could make her cry—came of his flaws and were of his doing. I don't have much from my father—an image, bruised and solitary, a caricature in my mind. But that's not fair. He bled and felt hard in his own way, and it was the loss of him that let me fill in what was missing, this figure punching his way through the morning fog.

"The ones that stay inside us, Sam, are always the ones who go before they should."

"I miss Ben," I say.

"Sometimes, a small plane will fly over the canyon. Its little engine humming. I think of him up there. A light moving in the night." He sips his wine, holds the glass by its stem, close to his chin, as if warming himself. "How close were you and Lily?"

"We were cops, so we understood."

"Can't get too close."

"You can, but it becomes something else."

"You love her?"

"Yes."

"Tell her?"

"I think once. I hope she heard."

"She did. They always hear. That's our redemption."

I forgot how quiet it gets in the canyon, the way the winds surge and die, leaving an empty-church stillness. Richard pulls his sweater tight and bundles in a blanket. He clicks on a playlist of Melody Gardot, a recent obsession whose voice

and piano make you think of somewhere far away—perhaps
a cellar bar in Paris at three a.m., after the lucky ones have
departed for the night and all that's left are those who want one
more song to carry into the darkness. Richard sleeps. I clear the
porch table, wash the dishes. I throw another blanket on him,
go to my car, and drive home.

I'm on the 101. My phone buzzes. Ortiz.

"Got two others, Carver. Just now. Get to Skid Row."

The blazes burn about fifty yards apart on different sides
of the street. I catch the last glimmers before the fire guys turn
them to smoke and steam. Homeless wander along sidewalks
and zigzag in the street. Agitated, laughing, crying, a man in a
ripped cap and knee socks yells that it's all a movie. "Wonder
Woman is coming. Suicide Squad, too." Cops are streaming
out yellow tape. TV crews are roaming. I see Ortiz in the red
flash: loose tie, too-small raincoat, phone to his ear. I walk
toward him and glimpse Manny, dressed in sweatpants and a
T-shirt, his hair matted and wet, so unlike the Jimi Hendrix he
was a few days ago. I put a finger up and nod for him to wait.
I slip under the yellow tape to the first tent.

"These things go up like paper," says Ortiz. "Nylon."

"What do we know?"

"Life sucks," he says. "Couple of these people say they
heard a car going by. Cars don't come by here this time of
night. Then they heard two pops, small explosions. I smell
gasoline. You smell gasoline? My guess, it's a Molotov cocktail
or some shit."

"Dead?"

"The guy at your feet."

I look down to a burned face, the pink of a tongue slanting
through lips, blackened hands, knuckles bright white, turned
up like claws.

"Probably stoned out of his mind and didn't feel a thing," says Ortiz. "Look at the burn radius. Looks like the cocktail ignited a cooking stove or some shit he had inside. Double explosion. Guy burned fast."

I bend down over the body. A Black man, but too short and lean to be Marcus Robinson. I turn to a uniform.

"Anybody know this guy?"

"A junkie," says the uniform, holding a flashlight over a half-charred driver's license. "Get this, it's from 1985—says he's Warren Simpson, last known address Three-Fifteen Elm Street, Cleveland, Ohio."

Crime scene guys arrive in white, clicking on floodlights. The scene takes on an incandescent moon glow, a scouring kind of light shining across torched bits and pieces—an overturned shopping cart, a clump of clothes, a tin cup, a toothbrush, meds melted into a rainbow puddle, tatters of a green tent clinging to its brittle bones. Ortiz and I cross the street to a half-burned yellow tent on the corner, where paramedics are tending a man with singed hair and a blistered face. Eyes wide with shock.

"Looks like whatever was thrown didn't hit the tent direct," says Ortiz, pointing to the curb. "See this black. Must have hit here and flashed to the tent." He nods to the burned man. "Another junkie. Looks like he'll make it. Wonder where he's from."

"They come from all over," I say.

"To the Promised Land. You ever wonder who they were before?"

"This town is full of befores and afters," I say. "You talk to him?"

"Guy's not ready to talk. Look at him. I'm not thinking he knows much."

A cut of sirens. SUVs. The entourage stops.

"Fuck," says Ortiz. "It begins."

The mayor gets out wearing a blue zip-up jacket. TV lights beam on him. Tanned, impeccably coiffed and combed, he has the somber, angry, worried look of a man engulfed by unexpected forces of the kind that spoil a career. Microphones jut toward him as aides press in. It is a small cabal of our current times: media and politician on a landscape of desolate faces, a dystopian clusterfuck far away from, yet oh, so close to, the crystal skyline, where the mayor, I'm sure, wishes he were now, thirty floors up, drinks flowing, donors writing checks, clouds rolling past. He waves the cameras away and walks along the street. He stops at the first burned tent, looks over the linen-draped body, and says the city and its most unfortunate will not be intimidated by these "vicious attacks."

"Any idea who's behind this?" asks a reporter. "It's the third one in a week."

"The investigation is ongoing," says the mayor.

"What precautions—"

"I've talked to the chief," says the mayor. "We're stepping up patrols in Skid Row."

"This feels targeted," says another reporter, Mariana Sanchez, a onetime BBC war correspondent who covered gangbangers and ICE raids before ending up on the city hall beat for KABC News. "Do you think some individual or some group is making a statement? Or is there a turf battle going on down here? And what about your homeless policy? It's been a failure. You could fill Dodger Stadium with all the homeless in this county."

The mayor glares at Sanchez, who, a few years ago, was rumored to have had an affair with him. Nothing was ever proved, but photographs of a dinner on a boat in Newport Beach appeared on the internet, made a stir, but were forgotten when news turned to wildfires flaring in Bel Air and the Palisades. "Do you know," Ortiz said at the time, "how many political careers have been saved by wildfires and earthquakes?" The mayor relaxes his gaze, lowers his voice to a mournful, determined pitch.

"We don't know everything yet," says the mayor. "As I said, the investigation is underway. We'll get whoever did this."

A few homeless men walk toward the mayor. His aides part. He waves the men closer, huddles with them. TV cameras edge in. His aides and two uniforms hold them back. The mayor and the men step beneath the eaves of a shuttered shop. None of us can hear what they're saying. The mayor stays with the men for a minute or so and then slips through the crowd toward his SUV.

"Mr. Mayor," yells Sanchez, "what can you tell us about the investigation into the killing of Police Officer Lily Hernandez?"

The mayor stops and turns.

"We have leads," he says. "The loss of a police officer to a city is like the loss of a family member. Justice will be served."

"But . . ."

The mayor slides into the back of his SUV. His black, shiny, soaked entourage drives away. Sanchez shakes her head and walks with her cameraman to their van.

"This goddamn thing's going national," says Ortiz. "We'll be on the news nonstop."

"You should have stayed in Costa Rica."

He turns to me, lets it pass.

"I've got to talk to this guy over there," I say.

"I'm heading back to the station," says Ortiz.

Manny stands shivering on the corner. The fire trucks have rolled away and the crowd is thinning. Scents of gasoline, ash, and sodden clothes and blankets fill the air. A wisp of dope.

Tents zip shut, voices murmur. The street is calm, like a jungle in the quiet before dawn.

"You okay, Manny?"

"Shit's bad, man. Someone burning homeless people. Crazy fuckers," he says, walking in tight circles around me. He's either off his meds or on too many. "Like we ain't got enough shit coming down on us. I'm watching all the time now. Nerves acting up. Got my pills all mixed up. What day is it? Feels like a Wednesday. Gotta be Wednesday. Wanda won't let me use her phone no more. Not even for two dollars a goddamn minute. Bitch. I'm cold. You cold?"

"You see anything?"

"I saw that same fucking car as the one before. The old-time Serpico car. Vantage."

"*Vantage.* Old is *vintage.*"

"Yeah, some shit."

"Three guys. Masks on. Coming real quiet. Car growling, soft-like. You know those vantage cars. Dark color like night. They threw out bottles. Big flashes. I'm talking big motherfucking flash. Little atom bomb flash. *Pop. Pop.* Then the car took off. Gone. Taillights like a demon's eyes." He pauses as if he were seeing the scene again. "Tents went on fire, people running and screaming. Scary shit, Detective. Wanda on her knees in the rain, calling out for God. Shit makes crazy people crazier."

"You see anything else?"

"That's a lot I just seen. You listening?"

"They never got out?"

"The men in the car? Nope."

"You get a license plate number this time?"

"You got twenty dollars?"

I hand him the bill. He recites like a third grader unsure of an equation.

"Manny, there's seven numbers and letters on a plate."

"Not on this plate."

"Maybe you didn't get them all. It was dark."

"I got 'em. Kept 'em right here in my head."

"You sure?"

"Sure as I'm out here like a fucking drowned cat."

He stops his circling and looks at me.

"How about another twenty?" he says. "Overtime."

I hand it to him.

"I gotta go find a warm place," he says. "Not staying in my tent tonight."

"Where?"

"I know a guy over near Pico. Meth-head security guard. Let's me sleep inside one of those storage sheds. Amazing shit in those things. People got all kinds of shit they can't fit into their houses, so they take the shit and shove it somewhere else. Fucking crazy, right? Why have shit you can't use? He opens one of these sheds up and I find a couch or some shit. Sleep real fine, like you're in an attic surrounded by furniture. Can't do it all the time. But he'll let me in tonight, once I explain."

"You still have my number?"

"I'll find a way," he says. "Catch these masked-men-devil fuckers. You got any pills? I need pills."

Manny disappears down the street into darkness. I call in the plate number. Tell dispatch that I know it's a partial but to run it and see what comes up. I hear a sigh on the other end and hang up. I nod to a uniform stationed on the other corner. He's smoking. I walk over and bum one and head to my car.

"Sam."

I look left down an alley, slide a hand toward my gun.

"Who's there?" I say.

Dr. Michael Ruiz steps closer.

"Get under," he says. "Your cigarette's getting wet."

I slip beneath the umbrella.

"What are you doing here?" I say.

"I was working late at the clinic. I heard the sirens. Got here as they were putting the fires out. What happened, Sam?"

"Masked men in a car tossed Molotov cocktails. One guy in a tent dead; another's burned but is going to make it."

"Same as the other day?"

"Probably related."

"Hold this," he says.

I take the umbrella, toss my drenched cigarette away. He pulls a flask from his pocket.

"Sip?"

"On duty."

He tips it, a glint of silver in the night.

"You okay, Michael?"

He doesn't answer. Rain rattles the umbrella. I glance west; the skyline is in mist.

"It's that white supremacist group, isn't it?" says Michael. "The Flag."

"The dead guy is Black, but the one who survived is white."

"They don't care what color when it comes to the homeless."

"Have you seen Marcus Robinson?"

"No." He sips, caps the flask, pockets it. He lights a cigarette. We share it.

"I thought you vaped."

"Both."

"Something wrong, Michael? Besides this?" I say, nodding toward the burned tents. "You don't seem yourself."

"I testified before the Homeless Commission yesterday. Same every time. Ridiculous questions from clueless people. Nothing changes. Just more money for more studies to keep everyone in business. Politicians. Activists. These homeless activists rake in a lot of cash. Homelessness is big business. No one's going to do anything to fix it. I've been at the Lost and Found Clinic—you know what they call it on the street, don't you? 'The Lost and Fucked Clinic'—for ten years." His face lightens and fades in the ember light. He passes the cigarette to me. He wipes back a tear. Maybe it's rain.

"It's funny, isn't it?" he says. "We can both walk home from here. But here feels like another country."

"You still in that loft on Spring? I thought you moved last year."

"I decided to stay."

"On the borderline."

He laughs but doesn't mean it. I step out from under the umbrella.

"We should meet for drinks again at the Little Easy," he says.

"I'm a regular."

I walk to my car. Michael heads toward Main.

"It can't keep going like this, Sam," he yells over his shoulder.

The rain stops. He folds down the umbrella, sips from his flask. He lights a cigarette and blows smoke beneath a streetlight. He walks on like a wanderer with no fixed destination. I turn toward my car. The street is empty, the big show over. I hear footsteps. Someone presses up behind me. A forearm clamps across my throat. It tightens. I try to pull away, but the guy's too strong. He rushes me into an alley, my feet barely touching the ground. He squeezes. I try to push him back into a wall, but he doesn't budge. Another man appears, wearing a black ski mask. He snatches my gun. He holds a lighter to my face. He leans in real close. I struggle to breathe, but the man is in no hurry. He flicks the lighter on and off a few times. He's there and not there. He laughs.

"It won't end, you know," he says. "They'll keep burning till we run them out of here. Clean this place of the filth. Hate 'em. Got to hate 'em. My advice: stay out of it for a while, Detective. Don't look too hard. Might not like what you find. Could be bad for your health, kinda like terminal. Just thinking out loud mostly, but, you know, word to the wise."

The guy behind me loosens his grip a bit. I gasp, gulping in big breaths.

"Who are you?" I say.

"I'm kinda like a messenger. Message delivered. We gotta go. Feels like more rain's coming. Not a very pleasant night. Odd weather we've been having. My friend here's gonna tighten a little harder so you'll go to sleep—you know, pass out. He'll lay you down real soft. He's a kind of expert. Probably be out a few minutes. But, really, Detective, listen to the messenger. Stay out of the way. It'll all be done soon."

"Are you part of the Flag?" I say.

He laughs. The air goes out of me. All goes black.

I wake up in the rain. My gun is in its holster. I slowly come back to myself. I get up and drive to the station. I crack my window, smell the scorched night and the cut flowers on trucks bound for warehouses across the railroad tracks. I click on Melody Gardot and for a moment pretend that all that happened before Lily died was from a borrowed life.

CHAPTER 12

Alicia Bryant sits in candlelight at the head of a long table. No badge, no gun. She's wearing a saffron-colored sleeveless shift, gold necklace, her hair down and long. Two waiters skim past, pouring water and wine. A chef in a puffy white hat shimmers in the light of swinging kitchen doors. Tall windows look over the Arts District. The sky is moon bright. The sixtyish woman with the buzz cut beside me owns a gallery. She pats my hand and tells me in a voice that invites and commands, "You must come, darling." The man to her left is a sculptor. He's talking to a once-famous model sitting next to the showrunner of an Amazon hit series about zombies and interstellar texts hidden in a bank vault in a Minnesota town. "Is it surreal?" says the model. "I can never tell these days." A conductor from Hungary sits across from me—fierce eyes and wearing an ascot, her accent conjuring centuries. Her date is a hip-hop singer from New York, a man of bracelets, tattoos, and swift, barbed sentences. Other faces hang in soft light as if conspiring. The wine is good. Vagabon's soft cosmic music is playing in the speakers. To my left, facing his wife at the other end of the table, is Trey Bryant, who returned the other day from the London opening of his new show, *Slave Gaze*. He's tall and thin, hands like wings, shaved head. His words are sharp and unhurried. He has the assured manner of a celebrated Black artist from a Cleveland slum, who has risen beyond what he was told he must endure. He holds up his water glass.

"Thank you all for being with Alicia and me tonight," he toasts. "Your company graces us. Each of you is special, each a sacred world. Let's enjoy and value one another and, for a few hours, leave the troubles out there (he nods to the windows) for another time."

He lowers his glass to light applause. Alicia cuts him with a glance.

"Horrible case you have, Sam," says Trey. "Alicia told me you're working the homeless murders."

"We still don't know much."

"Hate," he says. "It will come to hate and privilege."

"We don't—"

"Yes, Sam, I know. I'm married to a cop. Can't talk about it. I understand." He sips his water, glances down the table and back to me. "These last four years have damaged us. The country, I mean. No limits anymore. No one is editing their hate. How many Black men must asphyxiate? How many sisters can't have their dreams? The hate of the white man's making— it marks us all, one way or the other. Burning homeless people is the latest trend."

"The victims were Black and white."

"The homeless are just another despicable race to the haters."

"How was the opening in London?" I say.

"I'm sorry, Sam, I don't mean to offend. We just met and here I'm ranting," he says, touching my arm. "The opening went well. Early reviews are good, but, you know, I'm a bit young to have a retrospective. I'm Black and suddenly a commodity. You wouldn't believe what people will pay. Does that make me a capitalist at heart? I never know."

"Does it trouble you?"

"Not so far." He laughs, waving a hand over the room. "As you can see, I've succumbed. A privileged Black man. Now, that is a rare, confusing species. Eat your eggplant and polenta, Sam. I'd rather have an In-N-Out burger myself, but things being things, well, you know."

"A lot of square feet here. What was this before?"

"A sugar warehouse. I appreciate the irony. I spend most of my time in a studio downstairs."

"Your work makes us look at what we'd rather not."

"Does it make you uncomfortable, a white man staring at paintings of slaves? Old ones, present ones? You know, Sam, the plantation and the slave ships never stopped. They just disguised themselves for a new century. Black lives dead. Black Lives Matter. It's all about Black bodies, isn't it? A question of economics. Black bodies broken and stacked like fuel for this thing we call America."

"Your painting of Obama doesn't strike me that way."

"How does he look to you?"

"Transcendent."

"Yes, almost, but look closer. Deep into the eyes. You can see the plantation. Even he, eloquent and human as he is, can't escape it."

"Maybe. But . . ."

"But what?"

"Your work has meaning."

"Schooling white people is not my job," he says, his eyes hard in candlelight. "Sorry, there I go again."

"Anyone looking at your paintings will understand."

"Understand what?"

"The shame is not the slave's, but on those looking at him."

"That's art." He laughs again. "Alicia told me you were clever."

"She didn't tell me you were condescending."

"Ahhhh. The white—"

"Don't say it. It'll be too predictable."

He glares at me, lets it pass. Smiles.

"Touché, Sam."

Our gazes meet and hold. We can't cross too far into each other's world. He knows no more about me than I about him. We are composites. The color of our skin marks us in different ways. I see the beauty and horror of that in his paintings. They come from an anger that has been sharpened with time, and I can't help but admire it. But the artist himself is another matter. Too ready to fight, but he would say I'm too easily unnerved by truth, that I have benefited from history's privilege. Perhaps. But he assumes too much. My eyes slip away from his, his from mine. We clink glasses. A truce.

"Alicia's a good cop," I say.

"There are other things . . ."

He stops midsentence. He turns to the sculptor. They talk of Basel and galleries in Europe, sublimity and failure, the near genius of a Somali man who paints saints on the wood of broken boats. I wonder how Lily might have liked this scene. "Come on, Carver, let's roll. If I hear one more thing about Mahler and the anti-Semitic press, I'm going to shoot someone." That's what she would have said. We would have laughed, sneaked a kiss in the bathroom, and stood at the windows, pointing to crimes across the city. She would have worn her blue dress and denim jacket, and on the way home we would have stopped at the Little Easy, and Lenny would have put on something soft—Dinah or Frank—and we would have danced until last call and watched Lenny count the night's receipts.

A hand slides across my shoulder.

"How's it going, Carver?" asks Alicia.

"You've abandoned your end of the table."

"Host's prerogative," she says. "C'mon, I'll show you around."

We walk past the kitchen to a vast sitting room, where the furniture seems to float beneath the eyes of slaves.

"These are his early ones," she says. "They're cruder. I like them better. The newer ones have too much dignity. That sounds strange, probably, and I can't explain it, but they're too hallowed—at least, for a girl from Compton."

"What does he say about that?"

"I keep it to myself. What do you think of my husband?"

"He's . . ."

"You don't have to say," she says. "I live with him."

"Things not good?"

She looks at me, startled.

"Sorry," I say. "None of my business."

"The only person more consumed by their work than a cop is an artist."

"Thanks for the warning."

"We live separate lives," she says, fingers sliding over her necklace. "You know, expectation and all that bullshit. We're not who we were. You never think that will happen. But it does. It's quite real," she says, her words trailing and then picking up again. "Success came so fast for him that I don't think he's adjusted. To be nobody and then somebody makes him wonder if he's just a new slave for the same master. His words, not mine."

"What about you?"

"I know Master's game."

"You winning?"

"I think I am, but I don't know. Black woman with a badge and a gun. Gotta count for something." She laughs. "But maybe I'm a little like Trey."

"You seem different here."

"At home? Aren't we all, Carver?"

I step closer to portraits of two young Black men: a gangbanger scrawled in tattoos, a silver chain around his neck, and a man in a suit, holding a child whose face is turned away.

"Why am I here, Alicia?"

"I feel bad about the other day at the café. I'm not ruling out Dylan Cross. But we've got to look at everything."

"It was my fault. I was an asshole. I shouldn't have questioned your resolve toward the case."

She steps closer, so hard and lovely in saffron and gold, a cop like me but nothing like me at all, a woman with fine things and doubt, far north of Compton.

"Listen, Carver, we've got a lead on Castillo. He's been on the move. Place to place. We're not there yet, but we're close. We think he's holed up in Long Beach."

"Not his territory."

"He skipped out on his parole officer when he got out. Maybe he knows people down there. If we find him, we'll know if he killed Lily or not. We can cross off another box one way or the other."

"Dylan Cross is your killer. Not fighting you, just letting you know."

"Let's leave it at Castillo tonight, okay?" she says, turning toward the window. "Look outside, Carver. The rain's stopped and we're having chocolate soufflé for dessert. Let's be normal for a few hours. Put on airs and trick life." She takes my arm and leads me back toward the dinner table. "How's your case?"

"If we're going to be normal," I say, "let's not get into my case."

"Perfect."

I take my seat. Trey and the sculptor are talking about ancient Greeks. The Hungarian mentions Michelangelo and the *Pietà* and the draped pain of a mother's sorrow and burden. The model appears bored by the showrunner. She turns to a hipster type who has raised millions—or is it billions—on an app that recognizes and explains every piece of art the world has ever made. From etchings on cave walls to Caravaggio, to Picasso, to Trey Bryant and his family of slaves. Old and new.

CHAPTER 13

A video of burning tents is playing on 4chan and 8chan.

"You see it?" says Jimmy Knight. "I just sent you the links. Where are you?"

"Home on my laptop," I say. "I'm watching it now. Looks blurry."

"Low-res, man. Image quality sucks," he says, tapping away and sipping Red Bull in his office at HQ. "But it gets the point across."

"Must have been three guys in the car."

"Driver. Bomber. Videographer. What a crew," he says. "The video was shot from the back seat on a smartphone. Not much from the inside of the car. Only the bottles being tossed out and the tents going up. Looks like they drove down one side of the street and up the other. Cocky fuckers."

"Can you pull anything useful?"

"No sound. Only briefly see the backs of two guys wearing masks. I'll play around with it. Slow it down, see if I can get shit from inside the car."

"We've got a partial plate," I say.

"There'll be something here. Always is, Carver. Just gotta work it, man. Break the pixels down. Sifting for gold. Shiny things popping up."

"How long have you been awake?"

"Thirty-six straight."

"Cut back on the Red Bull."

"Don't mom me, Carver. Let me get to this."

"Hey."

"What?"

"Who posted the video?"

"Finally, the man asks the sixty-four-thousand-dollar question. You must be a detective. Scroll down, Carver. Jesus."

My eyes stop on eight white letters, two capitalized.

"PureLand," I say. "That's him. Can you trace him?"

"Don't be obvious. It's boring. I'll call you when I get something."

I hang up and watch the video again. Fifty-seven seconds. One bottle, a flash. A tent in flames. The car moving. A stretch of dark sidewalk. The car U-turns. Another bottle, another flash. Another tent in flames. The last image is taken from the end of the street, through the car's rear window. Two tents burning. Figures running in the night. Shadows and flames. Silence. I watch it again. It seems in slow motion, but it isn't. The pace is steady; the car accelerates. The camera doesn't jerk or waver. It knows its intent. It's omniscient and voyeuristic how our times see the world, broken into fragments—slivers of lives uploaded and sent into the ether. I call headquarters and check on the partial plate. "Two digits shy, Carver, and the last number your guy gave, I think, is a wrong one. Maybe not, but if it is, that's three digits off," says Officer John Moon. "It'll take a while."

"My guy says it's an old car. Maybe from the seventies," I say.

"We're running everything," says Moon. *Click.*

I close the laptop, finish my coffee. I head out the back stairs, cross the street, and take the escalator to California Plaza. Tourists are drinking Starbucks and taking pictures at Angels Flight, looking over the city, which from up here lacks symmetry, as if no one had thought about how it all might appear—a jumble of art deco, Gothic Revival, and Beaux-Arts pushing against the aloof splendor of the San Gabriels. The weather calls for rain later, but the sun is out for now. The air is fresh. I don't know why, but I feel repose, a brief gift even as I whisper Lily's name. I don't want her to disappear. As long as her name is spoken, she is still in the world. Lily. A woman is playing a violin. A child is singing. I walk to the café at the Colburn music school. A man in a blue suit, white shirt, and muted red tie waves. Norman McNulty is the aging-athlete type: trim, long jaw, black-silver hair, gold cuff links—a man intimate with the tidy and illicit intricacies of life. He stands, shakes my hand.

"Carver?"

"Yes."

"How's Richard?" he says. "His new film about Yemen is coming out soon. That bastard never stops, does he? An insatiable need to document."

"He does brave work."

"Don't let him fool you. He's a madman, too. Loves the adrenaline rush and righteousness of exposing the world's ills."

"There's a lot of them."

"I took the liberty," says McNulty, pushing a double espresso toward me. "If you don't like it, we'll get something else."

"This is good, thanks. Richard thought we should meet."

"Listen, Sam, before we get started, let's get things straight. I'm a lawyer; you're a cop. The two don't mix so well. I prefer discretion, if you know what I mean. But Richard's a good man and he says you're one, too. So I'm here. I won't tell you anything about my clients. I can talk in general, tell you what I know. What I think you're looking for." He glances at me to make sure I'm following. "I have relationships all over the city. Movies. Music. Developers. Tech gazillionaires. Relationships I don't want damaged." He stirs two sugars into his espresso, sips. "That barista's good. You ever been to a concert here? One of the best conservatories in the country. Big kids, little kids, prodigies from all over the world, playing Bach and Beethoven. Prodigies are strange flowers, you know. You have to be careful with them. I'm on the board." He takes another sip. "Anyway, you ask questions and I'll see if I can help."

He smiles. Veneers. A hint of cologne.

"Have you been following the homeless tent burnings?" I say.

"Can't miss them. All over the news. The *Times*—by the way, I've sued them a couple of times—started writing about homelessness in a big way about six months ago. I'm sure you know that. Made it a national issue. Then this. The mayor must be shitting himself. He's in way over his head, but that's another story. This will kill him. Politically, I mean. Of course, the Dems need Latinos, and he'd love to be on somebody's ticket, so maybe he survives. Who knows?" He scans the room, runs a hand through his hair. "But masked men tossing Molotov cocktails at tents? Not good for anyone concerned."

"A video of the last burning went up on 4chan."

"The *Times* mentioned it. I didn't see it."

"It was posted by someone whose alias is PureLand," I say.

"Sounds Aryan," he says. "Like that crowd from Charlottesville a few years ago. So much hate in those faces, remember? White shirts and hate. Those stupid torches. Terrible for the goddamn country."

"PureLand has also posted on a white supremacist website called the Flag. He writes a lot about homelessness, particularly in LA. He's not a nut—well, he might be a nut, but he's smart, educated. Less a ranter than a man with purpose."

"Mhm, an intelligent guy with hate and purpose. Not good."

"I'm looking into a possible connection to the tent burnings and the alt-right, neo-Nazi crowd."

"Those attacks could have been pranks. Stupid kids in a car. The kinds of kids who drown hamsters."

"Doesn't feel that way," I say.

He finishes his espresso. He sits back, looks out the window to the steel bones of a new hotel designed by Frank Gehry. Cranes swing; yellow hats glimmer. Hammers blur; sparks flash. A new piece of LA, rising on the dust of torn-down Victorians that sat atop Bunker Hill in the days of Mary Pickford, Douglass Fairbanks Jr., and that writer who knew it all so well—desperate men in flophouses, carrying hip flasks and paying a nickel for a haircut. What was his name? John Fante. Long gone like the rest—a scurrying of ghosts in the dirt.

"Big changes," says McNulty, still gazing out the window. "We won't recognize downtown in another decade. Money's flooding in—Korean, European, even Russian until recently. A lot of vision. New Yorkers are moving here, finally discovering, I guess, that you don't need snow and twenty-degree days to be creative. To get rich. Tech people are taking over Playa del Rey. The economy's changing. It's a Netflix-streaming-gig-dream-up-any-kind-of-shit-before-global-warming-sets-it-all-on-fire world. So goddamn glad I'm not a Gen Z or a millennial or whatever we're calling the young and doomed these days. Traffic's gotten worse. Is that even possible?" He looks away from the window to me. "If this thing doesn't bust—and it could—the homeless will be on prime real estate. Skid Row is, what, fifty square blocks? Almost sixty thousand homeless in the county. People with blueprints don't like that. Spoils the dream."

"What are you saying?"

"A lot of pressure being put on the city to fix it. But it's not being fixed. People might be looking for other ways. PureLand ways. LA's a liberal town." He laughs. "But not when it comes to money. What place is, really? You know how many closeted right-wing fanatics are out here? Going to museum galas, pretending they love their gardeners? Forget about the grievances of the coal miner in West Virginia or the factory worker in Ohio. What about the one percent? Hell, the half percent. The quarter percent. Call it alt-right or call it pragmatism—it's a mix of both, in my opinion—but they've decided the homeless have to go."

"The deplorables."

"Don't miss the point, Sam," he says. "These guys incite from a distance. Behind hedgerows. Let the Flag and that ilk handle the messy stuff. Just like always." He spoons the last of the foam out of his espresso. "Let's go with your theory about this PureLand, whatever he is. Could be one of them, sitting in one of these high-rises, giving money to the Philharmonic and the Hammer while peddling right-wing crap on Facebook, funding survivalist camps in Idaho. All anonymous. Wealth can make you invisible. It fucks with you."

"No one like that is one of your clients," I say.

He lets the sentence hang for a moment.

"That's right. But we're not talking about my clients."

"We're talking about what you know."

"Put it like this," he says. "If I were a detective investigating the angle you're looking at—and I still say it could be stupid kids—I'd probably want to look at Milton Archer." He sits back. "You don't know him, do you?" He doesn't wait for me to answer. "Made all kinds of money in hedge funds in the eighties—a big giver to Reagan back in the day—then got into development and real estate. Guess where a lot of that real estate is?"

"Downtown. Skid Row."

"Archer was one of the guys who put up money to swiftboat John Kerry. You remember that, right? He spreads a lot of money around to these fringe groups. Most of it anonymous or under aliases. I can't tell you how I know this, but I do. I've heard—haven't seen—there's pictures of Archer with David Duke. I don't know why he'd pose with a Klan leader. He's smarter than that. I doubt he did, but that's what I hear."

"Why are you telling me this?"

"Simple answer. I don't like him. He's toxic."

"And not a client."

"Hell. No."

"Any of your people connected to him?"

"You got this funny way of edging toward my clients. I told you I'm not discussing them. Everyone at that level is connected in some way. But no, not like that. I wouldn't represent anybody like that." McNulty taps his phone. "I've got to go. Deposition."

"Can we meet again?"

"Let's not plan anything, Carver. I gave you what I know." He stands, shakes my hand.

"Give Richard my best," he says.

He steps through the door and out to the sidewalk, passing children with violin and trumpet cases, and a girl in a tux pricking the air with a baton. I order another espresso and watch them. So young and small with their big talents, oblivious to PureLand and Archer, living in rehearsal rooms and concert halls, waiting, poised, in that transitory silence in the air between sacrifice and expectation, before the first note is struck. What will become of them? A few will make it. Some will be corrupted; others will break. It is the way of things. I finish the espresso and leave. The miniature symphony fades behind me.

CHAPTER 14

"What are you doing here, Carver?"

"I heard."

"You shouldn't be here," says Alicia Bryant. "Stay back."

"What do we have?"

"Shut up, Carver. You're not going to mess this up. We got him."

She glares at me. Lets it pass. Hands me binoculars. It's near dawn. Creosote, crude oil, and jacaranda hang in the Long Beach stillness. A mist rolls in from the ocean. The street—chain-link fences, clapboard houses, toys in front yards—is blocked by patrol cars on both ends. A SWAT team snakes up the sidewalk toward a darkened house with a couch on the porch. A helicopter hangs quiet in the distance. Bryant talks into her radio. Voices return. All is set. She waits, grips her weapon. Takes a breath. She pushes the radio button. "Go." The SWAT team bursts through the front door. The helicopter skims closer, circles, its light beam dancing over rooftops and yards. Two children in pajamas are hurried out of the house; a woman in a nightgown follows. Screaming, crying, faces toward heaven. They are hustled through the fence and down the street to an operations van, blankets thrown around them. A man bursts through a second-floor window. Glass glints the air. He hits the ground hard and rolls. He's barefoot, shirtless, wearing jeans. He sprints, tries to jump a side fence but is tackled by two SWAT guys. Bryant runs toward him. The SWAT guys cuff him, yank him up, shine a flashlight in his face. He's bleeding from the shoulder, broken glass in his cheek. I walk to the edge of the fence. Bryant pulls the perp toward her. She studies him like an insect she has trapped. She's amped up, talking cop shit at him. Trying to rattle him. The guy spits toward her. She dodges it. "Fuck you, bitch," says the perp. She steps back. She turns, looks at me, shakes her head. She does not have Angel Castillo. House lights click on. Neighbors step outside, squinting and wondering what went down in the cold darkness. The helicopter circles once more and flies away. The mist recedes toward the ocean; a tanker sails south on the horizon.

"Bad intel," I say.

"The guy's Castillo's second cousin or some shit," says Bryant, stopping beside me near the SWAT truck. "Low-level dealer. Fentanyl, oxy, a little heroin."

"Not a total loss, then."

"All this for that? Shit."

"It happens."

"Castillo was here two nights ago. Asshole's been in the wind."

"Cousin know anything?"

"He wants a lawyer."

She watches as the cousin is folded into the back of a cruiser.

"Goddamn it!" she yells.

She kicks the SWAT truck. Slams it with her hands, cracks a nail. A finger bleeds. She curses. Her eyes are red. Rage lifts off her like heat. She tries to push it down, but she can't. She turns away.

"I needed it to be him. Castillo," she says, "I gotta put this case down. Everyone's watching. Got a cop killer out there and it's on me to bring him in. You know how many people hope I screw it up? They're waiting for it." She turns back toward me. "Don't look at me like that, Carver. I know your theory—your Dylan Cross thing—and I know how broken you are. But you don't show it, man. Is that some Rhode Island stoic bullshit? Lily's dead and you're like a flatliner obsessed with one suspect. I wanted Castillo. I needed to cross him off or not. That's how you get Lily's killer. Police work." She steps toward me. "Get mad, Carver. Do something."

I stare at Bryant a long time. She's a breath away, not blinking. I close my eyes. I feel the morning cool, the ocean air. I want it to take me away from Bryant, this street, this failed raid, this ruined dawn parade. But it doesn't. I see myself pulling the gold ribbon on Lily's box of ashes. I don't want it to open. If it opens, another piece of her is gone. I can't have that. Not yet. I open my eyes. Things move in blurs. The jolt happens before I know it. I punch the SWAT truck. I punch it again. Again. Two officers tackle me. I feel their bulk and holstered guns as we hit the pavement. They pin me down for what seems like forever. I resist but then ease. I feel like a boy in a lost playground battle. They grab me and yank me up.

"What's your problem?" one of them says.

I swing and hit him. Three more guys, all big, young, and SWAT-suited, jump on me. I go down. I hear voices and radios and Bryant yelling for them to stop. They get off me. I roll to my knees and rise.

"Get the fuck out of here," says the one I hit. He's bleeding from the lip. "I'll cuff your ass if you're not gone in thirty seconds. I don't care if you're a cop or not. You're fucked up, is all I know."

They shove me away. Bryant talks to them, calms things. She comes back to me. She nods and walks ahead. I follow and catch up with her. She stops.

"I'm impressed, Carver. You beat up a truck."

"You kicked it."

"Yeah, but that's not surprising."

She raises a hand to my face and brushes away a tear. I should turn away, but I don't. She is the first woman to touch me since Lily. She glances down at my hands.

"They don't even look hurt," she says.

"My father taught me how to give and take a punch."

"You're messed up, Carver. But you're not as much of a flatliner as I thought."

"Don't tell me how to feel," I say.

"Noted."

We walk on.

"You okay?" I ask her. "You're still shaking."

"I wanted him bad."

"Just like I want Dylan."

"Carver . . ."

"It's what I know," I say.

"You think she's coming for you?"

"Been heading at me for a long time."

"Keep your piece by the nightstand, then."

"Won't be that simple."

"You sound like you need it."

"I need it to be over one way or the other."

"You let her in too deep," she says. "Never let the bad ones in too deep. Cardinal sin."

Bryant looks at me. The storm of her rage stills.

"Dylan Cross is a suspect, Carver. You know I know that, right? I'm looking at her like I'm looking at everybody else."

I don't answer. I don't want to talk about Dylan now.

"You'll get Castillo," I say, nudging Bryant. "Did you notice I stayed mostly out of the way?"

She smiles.

"You pick now to have a sense of humor, Carver. I'm pissed. You shouldn't have been here."

"Coffee?"

"You got this thing about not listening."

"Coffee?"

"This really annoying thing."

"Coffee?"

"Yeah," she says, shaking her head. "I'll do the paperwork later."

"Long Beach SWAT is pretty good. They hit hard."

"You deserved to get your butt kicked," she says. "It was their op. I asked for help and they set it up. I know a lieutenant on the force."

"So, where are we going?"

"A Cuban café a few streets over," she says. "Guy's probably up."

The SWAT team drives away. The street reopens as if nothing happened. Bryant and I walk to our cars.

"So clear and quiet," she says, looking to the sky and then down the street. "Like it's too early for anything to be wrong. My father used to sit on our porch in the morning dark and wait for first light. Did that every day. I used to think he didn't trust that it would happen. He wanted the magic of it."

"I get that."

"Do you?"

"A man needs his time before the day's shit settles in."

"He didn't want to be messed with on that porch. Never said it, but you could see."

"Leave him be."

"That's exactly what my mom said," says Bryant. She stops shaking. She seems a girl in the dawn. "I went by Compton the other day. Strange seeing that house without us in it. It's been painted and has new windows. Still felt like mine, though. I remembered every crack and fine line."

"It once held all you were."

"My whole world was between those walls. Someone else's world now."

She takes off her ball cap and cop jacket, throws them in her car.

"How you holding up, Carver?"

I look at her but don't answer. She doesn't press.

"Follow me," she says.

The Cuban is half awake. He pours two black, sugared coffees, puts pastries on a plate, and disappears into the kitchen. Hiss and steam, the rip of a stove flame. A skillet rattles; a radio plays. I consider telling Bryant about Dylan's email, but I don't. Let her find Castillo, check a box off. Methodical. She'll see where it ends. "It changes, doesn't it?" she says.

"What?" I say.

"Going after who killed a cop, one of us," she says. I don't answer. "Lily was a good cop," she says. "I saw her file."

"She was learning," I say, "like we all do."

"Tell me about her, Carver—just one thing," she says.

"There's too much for one thing," I say. "Drink your coffee, Alicia."

The Cuban comes out of the kitchen in an apron. He sets egg burritos on the table, pours refills, slides the check toward me. "Thanks for asking about her, Alicia," I say. The sun is a quarter of the way up the window. A man enters with a little girl; she twirls on a counter stool, blond hair swaying, a balloon tied to her wrist. It's her birthday. They're going to Disneyland. The Cuban brings her a candle in a pancake. We sing "Happy Birthday," and the girl stands on the stool and jumps into her father's arms.

Bryant has never been to Disneyland. I ask how that can be. "Compton's not that far from Anaheim," I say.

"Farther than you think, Carver," she says. She sips her coffee, shakes her head. My phone buzzes.

"Detective?"

"Manny?" I say.

"You better come," he says. "Marcus Robinson is with Kiki Brown."

"Where?"

"That place Kiki stay with them tweaker fuckers."

"You there?"

"Was there."

"I'm on my way."

"You owe me twenty."

Click.

I take the 110 north, passing ghosts of oil derricks and pump jacks, speeding through the industrial fringes. LA stands in smoggy distance. I exit, run a few red lights, and come to the underpass where Kiki Brown and the tweakers lie in dimness. I park and walk in, the air cool and foul. A candle flashes. A big man in camo pants throws off blankets and rises from Kiki's mattress, unfolding himself piece by piece. Belt unbuckled, cigarette between his lips, he stretches, steps into boots, swigs from a bottle. His gaze cuts toward me.

"Are you Marcus Robinson?" I say.

"People been asking me that my whole life," he says. "Must be."

"I'm Detective Sam Carver."

"Don't like cops much."

"I don't either, sometimes."

"This one of those times? Sure is for me."

He walks toward me. Around six feet two, lean but muscled, eyes sharp. Hair cropped, coiled, gray.

"You stay in shape," I say.

"Hold my own."

"I'm investigating the tent fires."

He looks down and then to the tweakers.

"Your tent was the first one burned," I say.

"Wasn't in it. Feel bad for Jimmy. Real bad. Man was scrawny as shit but played good horn. I'd let him stay there when I'd go on the roam."

"You think anyone was targeting you? Came the wrong night and got Jimmy instead?"

"How the hell would I know sump'm like that?"

"I'm only trying to figure out what's going on."

"A few people don't like me, but none would do that. Don't think so, anyway."

"Kiki said you were beaten up not long ago. They gave you a tattoo."

He looks back at sleeping Kiki. Shakes his head.

"When that girl ain't high, she talks," he says. "Too much."

"Is it true? I'm not looking to bring trouble, Marcus. But I've got three torched tents and two dead men."

He walks to the edge of the underpass, warms himself in sunlight. I follow. He offers me a cigarette.

"I was in Nam," he says, "probably before you was born. I liked the jungle, you know. It was wet and scary but a lot of places to hide. Lot of killing. Real close, but you never always saw, you know. Just heard a rustle, a leaf shake, and you blasted

that big fucking wet leaf and the rustle stopped. Death hid
from you in the jungle. But it was out there. A whole other
place, man. You sat still long enough, mold would grow on
you, creep right over your skin."

"How'd you end up here?"

"We ain't got time for all that," he says. "Man ends up
where he's supposed to."

"Tell me about the guys who beat you, Marcus."

He lights another cigarette, closes his eyes, draws in the sun.

"I was walking over near Pico on a roam. Sometimes, I gotta
wander. Life small on the streets. People don't think that, but it
is. I roam, stay here, stay there. Met Kiki on a roam. People all
over know me. 'Here comes Marcus.' 'Hey, Marcus.' That kind
of shit. Where I stay over near San Pedro, they all come to me,
like I'm somebody. Like I know shit they don't know."

"Why do you roam?"

He opens his eyes.

"Voices," he says. "Jungle voices. Real quiet, nothing crazy.
I don't take meds. Doctors always want to pump you on meds.
Not for me. Look at all these fuckers out here on meds—you
think anyone of 'em better? Hell no. They worse. I just roam.
Voices get softer, go away."

"You were near Pico."

"Yeah," he says. "Car pulls up beside me. Old car, like the
car I had before Nam. Big long steel."

"What kind?"

"I don't remember names anymore. An old one. Two guys
get out. They got bats and they're wearing masks. They start
swinging. I try to punch one, almost caught him but missed.
They just kept swinging. I go down. They still swinging. They
say I'm trash. Ruining the country. A rat living on the street.
One of 'em pins me down. The other takes out a marker. Starts

writing on my face. Pushing in hard, like he wants to write on my bones. They get up. Spit on me and drive away."

"Anyone help?"

"What fucker down here can help? C'mon, man, don't ask stupid shit. I got up. Never bled so much, not even in the jungle. I went to a gas station. Into a bathroom. Wiped away the blood and saw in the mirror one of those stika things on my face."

"A swastika."

"A Hitler shit stika. Right on my goddamn face, man. I tried to wash it off, but it wouldn't go. Waited until night. Went to Kiki. She had rubbing alcohol and soap. She washed it off, but not all of it. It was deep-like, but after a few days, gone."

"Then . . ."

"Motherfuckers burned my tent. Killed poor Jimmy."

"Made you an example, maybe. Everybody knows you. Respects you. Good way to scare people."

"I don't know about that."

"Anything you can remember about the guys in the masks?"

"They hit hard."

"Could you tell what color they were?"

"Man, ain't no Black man writing stikas on people's faces. They was white. Mask can't hide the whiteness."

He reaches into his pocket, lifts a folded paper.

"They jammed this in my mouth," he says, handing it to me.

"The Flag."

"What kind of shit is that?"

Kiki steps out from the underpass into the light. She's wrapped in a blanket, hair matted and wild from sleep. Edgy, twitchy, needing a fix. She squints, points at me, a cloudy memory messing with her.

"Girl like a cave bat," says Marcus, taking her in his arms. "Been in that tunnel so long, can't figure the light."

Kiki soft-punches him in the chest, rises on tiptoes, kisses him. He releases her. She walks toward the tweakers, a five-dollar bill in her hand.

"Thought she might make it," he says. "There's a turning-back point for some."

"What about you, Marcus?"

"I stay on the roam."

"I hear you play sax."

"A little, yeah. Not lately."

I hand him my card.

"Just in case," I say.

He slides it in his pocket.

"You know," he says, "this place been like this forever."

"People want it to change."

"People who don't know better. People say all kinds of shit."

We share his last cigarette.

"Sorry about what happened, Marcus."

"People been saying that all my life. Fuck 'em."

He tosses the cigarette and drifts back into the dim. A flame, a needle. Kiki's head droops. She lies on her mattress, calling his name, losing syllables. He stands over her, puts on a camo shirt, a hat. He bends down and kisses her on the forehead, strokes her hair. He grabs a small duffel and a sax case and walks out the other side of the underpass.

CHAPTER 15

Hi, Sam.

Me again. Still haven't found the perp, huh? I like
that word. A cop word. I'm borrowing it, but I'll give
it back. Haha. Is Alicia Bryant a good detective?
Why isn't Lily's case solved? I wonder, wonder,
woooooonder. I saw the mayor on TV. He looks
worried. Eyes darting all around. I saw you, too,
Sam. Tingle. In the background while the mayor
was talking to the cameras at those tent fires. You
get so many sad cases, Sam. I worry for you. I know
you are good and see the best in things, but it
takes a toll. It must. The world's depravity. People
are vile, Sam. I have learned this. But there are parts
of us that love. I bet you know where I'm going with
this, huh? YOU. ♥ I hope I'm not that kind of girl.
You know, the cloying, what-are-you-thinking-about

kind. But you are my unvile (is that a word?) thing,
Sam. You know this. You have always known. It feels
good to write it, too, see the words. To send them
to you. Like a little valentine from a secret crush.
Oh, those days. Wondering if we'd be picked.
Who would kiss us and run away? Remember that
feeling of wanting to be chosen? I better stop
writing or it'll be a book. Ha. Just wanted to drop
you a note. Bye, for now. Oh, almost forgot. I was
in the mountains the other day. It was pouring. I
was alone. I took off my clothes and stood on a
ridge. The rain was soooo cold. Like an icy baptism.
It didn't bother me, though. I didn't even shiver. I
didn't want to leave. I wanted to disappear into the
rain. To be gone from the vile things. The things no
rain can clean. I cried. But then I thought of you.
How you need me. How we belong together. I ran
under a tree and dressed. I never felt so alive.

Love,
D.

I read it again. Put it in my Dylan folder—not the official
one about her crimes, but the one with emails like this. The
folder no one has seen. I scroll. A text from Ortiz: "Mayor
pushing hard. Media all over him. Get something fast." The
plane banks east. Sunlight through the window. A catch of air.
The sky is blue and cold; the land below a ripple of hills and
green, bordered by farms and roads. A lake shines like a mirror,
geese soar over a forest toward the coast. We descend. Capt.
Barry Wilkins—an Oregon state trooper Ortiz met years ago
at an FBI training camp in Quantico—waves in his uniform

by baggage claim. He leads me to an unmarked car and we head northeast out of Portland.

"About a two-hour drive," he says. "Nap if you want."

"You know these guys?"

"Bunch of them up here. Survivalists. Armageddonists. Nationalists. White supremacists. You name it. Proud Boys and frontier of wackos." He puts a pinch of Skoal between his lip and gum. "Thing is, most of them are just lost, you know, pissed off and confused like those guys who join ISIS. Except for the masterminds. The ones programming the worker bees. But mostly these guys eat Spam, dig bunkers, shoot squirrels, and ride off-road." He runs a hand through his graying crew cut. "Not saying they're not dangerous. They are. They've made patron saints out of Timothy McVeigh and that shooter from New Zealand, the guy who rained hell on the mosques. Only takes one or two like that. But . . ."

A brown blur. The car swerves.

"Sorry, Detective, lot of deer up here."

"What about the Flag?"

He cracks the window, accelerates.

"Charlie and Bill Crenshaw," he says. "Your basic *Turner Diaries* variety. Aryan brand. Want a white-European-stock America—you know, put a fortress around us and let the rest of the world go to hell." He clicks on the wipers, cleans the windshield. "They're good on the web. Sell mail-order shit, too. Protein powder, T-shirts, camo shit, survival manuals, end-of-days go bags, alt-right punk rock CDs. A little Nazi Amazon. A few years ago, they even peddled cryogenics—you know, freezing yourself to come back later. Who the hell would want to come back later? Can you imagine what this world will look like *later?* I don't want to come back to that mess. They gave up on it, though. Too expensive and scientific for their crowd. But the brothers—their father was a Bible-pounding polygamist, dead now—are entrepreneurial."

"How long has the Flag been around?"

"At least ten years," he says. "Brothers must be in their forties. Charlie worked on a fracking crew in North Dakota for a while. Drifted back. Bill dropped out of some college or other—I think Baylor. Always politically minded, that one. Got it from his dad."

"Were they ever arrested?"

"I checked after Ortiz called," he says. "Charlie was picked up once for drunk driving. Way back. That's it." He spits into a foam coffee cup. "They're on all the lists, though. All the ones that list hate groups. Simon Wiesenthal Center, Southern Poverty Law Center, FBI. You name it, they're on it."

We leave the highway and travel a two-lane road for a few miles. Wilkins turns left onto a cinder road lined with evergreens that opens to a clearing. A stone farmhouse with rust-red shutters and a slate roof rises behind a split-rail fence on a slight hill near a pond. An American flag and a "Don't Tread on Me" banner fly over a barn. Wilkins slows. Three men in camos—one carrying an AR-15—walk toward us. Wilkins rolls down his window. Nods. The men wave us through the fence.

Two men come out of the house.

"That's them," says Wilkins.

The shorter, muscular one—Charlie—wears jeans tucked into black boots, a T-shirt, knit cap, and a holstered Glock. He has the quick eyes of a mercenary. A tattoo of a snake coiled around a dagger runs up his left forearm. His face is pale and flinty but young, as if it got frozen somewhere between fourteen and forty-five. The pimples on his chin are scrubbed and raw in the late-morning light. His brother, Bill, is dressed in a blazer and a button-down white shirt. He could be a deacon or an actuary with a fresh haircut, a man who doesn't so much take up space as slips into it. He shakes my hand, his gaze long and deep. The brothers lead us to the barn, a converted high-ceilinged open office of exposed wood and brick with cathedral windows. Five men and two women, all millennials, sit at Macs, tapping keyboards and drinking canned espresso. TV screens with the volume low slant overhead. Fox News. BBC. CNN. ISIS videos on YouTube. Mexicans at the border. A Rambo movie. A chorus of dissonant whispers. We sit in a glass-walled conference room. A woman wearing a long lavender dress and a Jesus bracelet brings coffee.

"Welcome," says Bill. "This is a little curious, if you don't mind my saying." He sips coffee. "I don't know how we can help you, Detective . . ."

"Sam Carver."

"You're far from home, Sam Carver," says Charlie.

"As Captain Wilkins may have explained, I'm investigating attacks on the homeless. Tent burnings. Two dead."

"Saw it on the news," says Charlie, glancing down and back up to me. "Gotta do something with the homeless. I mean, who needs 'em."

"Charlie," says Bill, "let's hear what the detective has to say."

"I'm just saying," says Charlie. "They're ruining the country like the Blacks, spiks, gooks, towel-heads, queers, and libtards. All of 'em. Hillary, too."

"You'll have to excuse my brother," says Bill.

"Why?" says Charlie. "That's how we feel. No need to put a disguise on it."

"Or a sheet," I say.

Charlie glares at me. I should have stayed quiet. I went at him too early. Silence.

"Let's not get off track here, gentlemen," says Wilkins. "Detective Carver has a few questions. Let's get this done."

"Are they the we-gonna-need-a-lawyer kind of questions?" says Charlie.

The brothers lean in and talk to each other across the table from Wilkins and me. Charlie is the easy read. He's agitated. He wants to walk out. Bill is calm, measured, accustomed to defusing things with a confidence that is at once smug and ingratiating. I have seen his kind many times. Charlie pushes back in his chair, thumbs his holstered gun, not threatening but making a point. Bill straightens his blazer and turns toward us.

"I'm sure we don't need a lawyer," he says. "Go ahead, Detective."

"The attacks appear to have been targeted," I say, pulling the Flag flyer from my pocket. "These have been tacked up around Skid Row. One was stuffed into the mouth of a homeless veteran who was beaten by men in masks."

The brothers look at each other.

"What does it mean? 'The time to act has come,'" says Bill, reading the flyer. "It's obtuse and foreboding. Rather ridiculous. What time is it? Act on what? It's like a Nike ad. A slogan you could plug into anything. It's certainly not us, Detective. We don't do flyers." He waves a hand toward the millennials at the Macs. "You might find our message crude— as my brother has already displayed—but we are high-tech. This is not us. Not our style."

He pats his lips with a napkin, reaches over, and grips his brother's arm.

"Is someone hijacking your brand and turning these out?" I say.

"The Flag is hardly copyrighted," says Bill. "Who knows

who could have printed these. We don't have an office in Los Angeles."

"You have followers there."

"We have followers in many places," says Bill, "but I'm sure you know that."

"I am curious about the two guys who jumped me the other night after a tent fire," I say. "You wouldn't happen to know who they might be, would you?"

"Los Angeles sounds like a dangerous place," says Charlie. "You should be careful. I never go there, myself. Too many libtards and loonies."

He bites his lip and looks at me as if he might come across the table.

"Do you know who posts under the alias PureLand?" I say.

The brothers smile at each other.

"We know PureLand," says Bill. "Well, let me rephrase. We don't *know* him or her. PureLand sends us posts. I think we've put up two or three on the site. I'm sure you've read them. He's quite intelligent. He sees the dangers inherent in what liberalism has created."

"He's fixated on the homeless," I say. "He wants developers to retaliate. He wants a class war."

"He's a Nietzsche capitalist," says Bill. "The homeless destroy investment, ruin neighborhoods. For what? So crazies, drug addicts, and the lazy can live on land they don't own, and suck up tax dollars. Is that fair?" He pauses. Takes a breath. "You might find us reprehensible, Detective. I don't know. We just want a white, hardworking America. No dregs. What's wrong with that? Illegals come here; the homeless roost here. It's like one disease after another. They all want to change us. They want to put us in their image. To make us acquiesce. Why?"

"Fuck 'em," says Charlie.

"Why do you think Trump won?" says Bill.

"Fuck Trump, too, until he builds the wall," says Charlie. "He's a pussy when it comes to getting shit done."

"Americans don't want America overrun anymore," says Bill. "We were once exceptional. We need to get back to that."

"Through hate," I say.

"That's predictable and reductive, Detective," says Bill.

"Fucking reductive," echoes Charlie.

"PureLand," I say. "I need to find him. Can you go in your data bank and pull his email and IP address? I can get a warrant."

The brothers laugh.

"I'm afraid that won't do you much good, Detective," says Bill. He nods to Charlie, who leaves the room. "PureLand is not high-tech. He's more of a snail-mailer." Charlie returns with a shoebox, puts it on the table. "This is how PureLand corresponds," says Bill, pushing the box toward me. "Letters."

"I like the guy," says Charlie, "Whoever he is."

"You've never spoken to him," I say.

"Never spoken to or received an email from him," says Bill. "Just these."

"Why do you post them if you don't know his identity?"

"It's what he's saying, not who he is," says Charlie. "I like the alias."

"Yes," says Bill. "Cool name."

"Video of the last tent burnings was posted on 4chan and 8chan," I say. "By PureLand."

"I wouldn't know," says Bill. "Maybe PureLand's joining the New World. We have nothing to do with who or what posts on those sites. Just because he posted it doesn't mean it's his." Bill lifts a letter. "But as I said, he only sends us these."

"These are copies," I say. "Where are the originals? The envelopes?"

"Well, Detective, I'm afraid—oh, this is embarrassing—the originals were inadvertently destroyed," says Bill.

Wilkins edges in, crosses his hands on the table.

"How'd that happen, Bill?" he says.

Charlie stares ahead. Still.

"Burned," says Bill. "We make copies of all correspondence so we have an original and a backup. The problem is—was—the originals weren't filed where they should have been and were wrongly put in the discard bin. They were burned a few days ago."

Wilkins shakes his head, runs a hand over his mouth. He glances at me—letting me know he wants in—and back to Bill.

"See how that might seem suspicious?" says Wilkins. "This PureLand all of a sudden posts nasty shit on 4chan, and *poof,* his letters to you get flamed. See how that might bother the detective and me?"

"I assure you," says Bill, "it was an accident."

"Leaves a funny taste to me," says Wilkins. "How about you, Detective Carver?"

"I'm happy to make copies of these copies to give you," says Bill. "But everything PureLand has written to us, we've posted. It's all on our site."

"I think Bill and Charlie are hiding something," I say. "How about it, Charlie?"

"My brother told you the truth," he says. "That's what happened."

"You look like something else happened," I say.

"What are you talking about?"

"You look smaller," I say. "Like you're trying to shrink. Don't want a part of this."

"Fuck you, Detective," says Charlie. "My brother's telling the truth. He always tells the truth."

"No need for vulgarity, Charlie," says Wilkins.

Charlie stands and points a finger at me. Bill reaches up and pulls him back to his seat. Charlie glares. Bill strokes his brother's back as if he were a dog off its chain. We sit in quiet. Let it sink in. I swivel my chair, looking away from the table to the Macs, millennials, and TV screens. Trump is on Fox, reporters around him, his hair blowing in the breeze, making an address on the White House lawn. Syrian refugees are crossing a border on CNN. The BBC is stuck on Brexit. A Chuck Norris movie has replaced Rambo. I swivel back around to Bill and Charlie. I take my notepad out, flip through pages. Hold the moment. Decide on a gamble.

"Do you know Milton Archer?" I say.

Bill's jaw tightens. The slight blush on his cheeks is so quickly there and gone, I barely catch it.

"Mmmm," says Bill. "Milton Archer. I don't think so. Who's that?"

"Developer in Los Angeles," I say. "Very rich. Very connected to causes like yours."

"I don't think—"

"Has he sent you any checks, donations?"

"We do receive donations, but they're private. I can't share those. But I don't know a Milton Archer."

"I can get a warrant," I say.

"Get a fucking warrant, then," says Charlie.

"Excuse my brother's language," says Bill, "but I must agree with him. We've been cooperative. Trying to help you. But I don't like your tone, Detective. What you're presuming." Bill turns to Wilkins. "Does Detective Carver have jurisdiction here?"

"No," says Wilkins. "But I do. So does the FBI. Any money crossing state lines makes it federal. Gets serious."

"Well," says Bill, standing, his composure restored, "you'll have to talk to our lawyers."

Bill holds up a hand and waves. The men in camo who met us at the gate earlier appear.

"They'll show you out," says Bill. "We've tried to be helpful."

Wilkins and I walk to the car. The camo men hang back, gun muzzles angled at the ground. I turn. Charlie paces in front of the barn. He yells something at Bill, hops on an all-terrain vehicle, and speeds over the rim of the hilltop. Out of sight. Wilkins and I drive away through the pines, to the main road.

"I don't get it," says Wilkins. "Why produce copies of letters whose originals you then burn? Doesn't make sense. Why produce anything?"

"He had to give us something," I say. "PureLand going viral on 4chan changed the math for them. The originals and the envelopes had fingerprints, so they did some quick thinking."

"Poof. Maybe PureLand did only send letters."

"That's my guess. Makes him harder to track."

I crack the window.

"What did you think of their response to the flyer?"

"Honestly, I don't think the flyer is theirs," says Wilkins. "Didn't register on their faces. They were surprised and curious. But who knows? The burning of the letters bothers me. They're up to something." He pinches another bump of snuff into his lower lip. "What really freaked Bill, though, was when you brought up this Milton Archer guy. That got to him. You see him tense up?"

"Just for a second," I say.

"All you need."

"What did you make of Charlie?"

"He's a twitchy trigger of a man anyway. Hard to say."

"His face doesn't hide much."

"Certainly doesn't like you. Sorry you got jumped the other night. You okay?"

"Yeah. Happened real fast. No leads."

"Who the hell is Archer?" says Wilkins.

"I have to get back to LA and find out."

"I bet Bill's already on the phone to him," says Wilkins.

"It could be nothing. I brought his name up to get a reaction."

"You got one."

"But to what? I've got a feeling about Archer or someone like him."

"I guess we'll see."

Wilkins spits in a coffee cup.

"Can you get a warrant for the files and computers?" I say.

"They're probably deleting and scrubbing now, but yeah. I'll get one tomorrow and run back out here with a crew."

"Thanks. We worked them like partners."

"It's always a rush, isn't it?"

We reach Portland at dusk. Wilkins drops me at the airport, shakes my hand. I write the details of the day in my notebook on the flight back. The glass-walled office in the Crenshaw barn. Eyes and faces. The way men play off one another; the twist, hide, and deceive; the balance of power shifting and changing; and how a man starts off sure but then loses himself, his eyes betraying the artful lie he thinks he's constructed. I tilt my seat back and hold a scotch. The cabin is mostly dark, an indigo glow of screens. There is no sensation of speed or distance when flying through the night. Only the engine hum and shudders of air beneath the wings. You feel the world's gravity, but you're immune to its cruelty. A glimmer in ink. Until the descent, when clouds thin and vanish and the earth takes shape again, like a painting rushing toward you. The plane banks, and Los Angeles spreads across the window in a net of lights.

A text from Ortiz:

I'm at the curb.

I hurry through the near-empty terminal.

"What are you doing here?" I say, sliding into the car.

"I checked to see what flight you were on. Thought I'd meet you."

"Like a married couple."

"Yea, kinda like that. Screw you, Carver."

He laughs.

"Bad situation," he says. "Mayor's outta control."

"It's all over the news."

"TV crews invading skid Row like they're on safari."

"Have you been drinking?" I say.

"Just a beer. Stopped off at a place before I picked you up."

"It's late."

"Eleven thirty."

"Trip went well. The Crenshaw brothers know something. Don't know what yet, but something. I'm going at Milton Archer tomorrow."

"You have enough to go after him? A rich right-winger. Lot of those. But what connects him to torching homeless? Can't go too early and miss. Not smart."

"Maybe nothing connects him," I say. "But he gives a lot of money to these fanatics. I'm thinking, under an alias. But the Crenshaw brothers had a reaction when I mentioned him. I threw it out there on a hunch and it hit something with them. I'm going to have a friendly conversation with him."

Ortiz tamps his mustache. Yawns.

"Don't talk to any reporters," he says.

"You always tell me that. I never do."

"You slept with one."

"She's long gone."

"They're never long gone. Reporters are like stains."

He takes the on-ramp to the 105 and cruises into the fast lane.

"I like LA when it's late like this," I say.

"You can breathe. Rain stopped a couple hours ago. More's coming."

"Who's this?" I say.

"Rosalía. Spanish singer. She's got that kind of voice you can listen to low."

He sings a few words in Spanish.

"Why did you pick me up, really?" I say.

"Bryant went after Angel Castillo again. She got a call a few hours ago from a CI that Castillo was in that dive near the old Rosslyn Hotel. You know the place. She sends a patrol car over and tells the uniforms to sit outside until she gets there. There was a miscommunication or some shit. The uniforms went in. Castillo pulls off two shots and bolts out the back door. The uniforms chased but lost him. Guy was way jumpy."

"He skipped out on his parole officer and disappeared."

"Could be more than that, Carver."

"You're thinking he's extra nervous because he killed a cop."

"I'm just saying. A guy who skips parole doesn't shoot up a bar. Why risk going back to prison when you just got out after fifteen or whatever years? Something's going on."

"I thought he was in Long Beach."

"Bouncing all over, I guess."

"What about Bryant?"

"Talked to her before you landed. Pissed, obviously. No, make that very pissed. She got there three minutes after it went down. Reamed the uniforms. She's been working this thing hard, Carver. A lot riding on this for her."

"She's going after the wrong person."

"Doesn't feel that way to her. And if it is, she'll get the right person."

"Dylan Cross."

"Could be. Probably even likely. I'd gladly put a bullet in Dylan Cross if she did that to Lily. I can't get over the anger. Burying that poor girl. But Castillo has motive, too."

"I can't see little Angel Castillo writing with lipstick on a mirror, saying, 'Hi, Sam, I'm back.'"

"I've seen stranger shit."

We bend toward the 110. Palms in silhouette, the skyline bright against the mountains.

"You know," says Ortiz, nodding at the windshield, "a third of that wasn't even there six years ago."

"Everybody's moving to LA."

"For now."

We sit in silence. The city presses closer. Homeless tents are strung along overpasses. Beams of unfinished buildings shine in construction lights. A Maserati zips past.

"Asshole's gotta be doing one-twenty," says Ortiz.

"Let's chase him."

"Fuck that."

He rubs a hand over his face, wriggles like a man in a too-tight suit. Yawns.

"Cut Bryant some slack," he says. "She's a good cop. I like her. You know, she carries a picture of Lily around. Small one in her pocket."

"She had me over to dinner the other night."

"You meet the husband?"

"Trey, yes. Wouldn't have put them together."

"I wouldn't put half the people I know together."

"This felt different, though. Like a low-grade war."

"Whatever," says Ortiz. "Just let her do her job."

He pulls up in front of my apartment building.

"You want to come up for a drink?"

"No," he says. "I need sleep."

He drives south on Hill, turns right on Fifth toward the Biltmore. I walk half a block to Angels Flight. I stand in the darkness, wondering what my neighborhood looked like back when trams clattered and the city was coming into itself, spreading in all directions, a puzzle of orange groves, dry winds, and fantasy. I walk back to my building, take the elevator up, enter my apartment. Keeping the lights off, I pour a drink and sit by the window. The rain comes.

CHAPTER 16

The solitary surfer lifts. He gains speed, skims along the white, then pulls up, letting the dying wave slide beneath him and break near the shore. He paddles back out. It is minutes after dawn. His wet suit mixes with the last bits of dark. His gray hair is a sheen in the distance. He catches another wave, his body not as limber as it once was. His rise on the board is less graceful than methodical and determined. But there is a cut to him, a tautness. The wave collapses early. He goes down, lost in the surf, momentarily gone from the world, then reappearing, wiping back his hair, gathering his board in the shallows. He walks to the shore, drops the board in the sand, sits like a guru beside a towel. I wait a minute and walk toward him.

"Milton Archer," I say.

His eyes are closed.

"Be still," he says.

"I'm—"

"Shhh," he says. "Still and quiet."

He breathes in rhythm, serene in the cold air. I sit a few

feet from him, say nothing. The beach is empty. Cars with boards are parking along the road. The sun cracks the sky.

"You've disturbed my peace," he says, "and you don't even have a surfboard."

"Milton Archer?"

"Yes."

"I'm Detective Sam Carver."

"I have an office, Mr. Carver. Much better to meet there," he says, glancing at me and back to the ocean. "A detective on the beach. You'll get sand on your badge. How did you know I was here?"

"I read this was your spot."

"Oh, that thing in the *Times*. Ruined my surfing for a while. All kinds of people showed up on the beach after that. Wanting a donation for this or that. Shouting business ideas at me." He laughs. "One poor fellow hauled down an architectural model of how he wanted to redesign LACMA. As if that museum didn't have enough design problems. That was years ago. People forget. Yet here you are."

"It's not that secluded."

"It used to be. All along here. Up to Oxnard."

"Is that your convertible up there?"

"Nineteen sixty Thunderbird."

"You collect?"

"Many things, but not cars. I rebuilt one when I was younger. Some things stay with you, I suppose."

Surfers pass us. A few nod to Archer. They slide into the water. We watch them glide beyond the break.

"You don't surf, I imagine."

"I have a few times."

"A few times does not count. You should try it, though. Away from land. All that power beneath you and the board.

The aloneness of it. It's when I'm most myself." He shakes his head. "I must sound like St. Augustine or some mystic. You caught me at a sacred moment, Detective."

"It is magnificent."

We both stare at the horizon.

"Yes, yes, it is." He takes a deep breath and lets it go. "I'm sure you didn't come here to talk about my car or the glory of nature." His voice drops a shade deeper; his calm disappears. "I have a busy day. How may I help you?"

He stands, unzips his suit, peels it to the waist. His skin is brown from years of sun; his muscles solid, like a man now in his seventies who has worked the weights all his life. He dries himself. His hair is tossed and wild. He picks up his board, washes it in the surf, and nods for me to follow. We walk over the sand toward his car.

"Are you looking for a donation for the policemen's fund?" he says, winking. "I suppose that's politically incorrect, isn't it? Should I say, 'the policepersons' fund'? Is there such a thing? I never know what to call things anymore."

"It gets confusing."

"It's numbing," he says, not slowing his stride. "First, you have *homosexual*. Then *gay*. Then some other thing. And all of a sudden, you have *LGBT*. You're just getting used to that and they add a *Q*." He glances sideways at me. "You're not one of that capitalized-letter crew, are you? If so, my apologies, although, I must say, I'm sickened by that whole alphabet soup of identities."

"You seem angry."

"My wife says that, too. It happens the farther I get from the shore."

"Maybe you should only surf."

"Don't think I haven't thought about it. But too much to

do, Detective. Too much to do. Now, please, let's get to it." We arrive at the car. He slants the board into the back seat, opens the glove box with a key, pulls out a phone, scrolls, drops it on the front seat. "C'mon, what is it?"

"I'm investigating the homeless fires on Skid Row. I'm sure you've heard about them."

"Yes. Tragic. How does that possibly concern me?" he says, walking around the hood of the car to the driver's side. "What's the question, Detective?" He opens the door, settles in, slips on sunglasses. "Please."

"We think white supremacists might be behind it."

"I'm perplexed, Detective. What does that have to do with me? Has someone sent you? Is this part of a joke? I have friends famous for this kind of joke. Are you really a detective and not an actor? They're quite elaborate in their tricks, my friends."

"You fund a lot of right-wing organizations."

"Ah, so, therefore, I burn tents. Are you serious? Your appearing here is ridiculous. Let me tell you, Detective, and I've never hidden this, I am conservative—right-wing to the core, if that's your label. I despise what liberalism has done to this country. I don't hide my disdain for this nation's diminishment. I fight against it. But I'm not a rabid Fox Newser or a white supremacist, nor are the organizations I fund."

"What about this one?"

I walk to the driver's side, show him the Flag flyer.

"These have been spread around Skid Row."

He takes the flyer, scans it, hands it back. He starts the car.

"I know nothing about this, Detective."

"You have no connection to the Flag?"

"I just answered that. Do you have more pertinent questions? You're wasting my time. I really must go."

He shifts the car into drive. Holds the brake, looks up

at me. I can't see his eyes through the glasses. His mouth is pressed hard, his hand tight on the steering wheel. "Next time, Detective, don't spoil my morning. Call my lawyer. He handles silly intrusions." He guns the car and streaks toward Malibu.

I call Ortiz.

"You up?"

"I'm always up," he says. "You didn't push him too hard, did you?"

"I don't think so. Enough to rattle him. I showed him the flyer."

"And?"

"Same reaction as when I asked the Crenshaw brothers about him."

"I don't know, Carver. You may have gone after him too soon."

"He didn't deny it."

"Deny what?"

"I asked him if he had a connection to the Flag. He never answered."

"He said nothing?"

"He said, 'I know nothing about it.'"

"That's an answer."

"It's not the right answer."

"Semantics."

"They're important."

"Jesus, Carver. This guy might just be another right-wing billionaire. No crime in that. World's crowded with them."

Ortiz doesn't say anything for a while. I hear him breathing. I look to the water. Five surfers ride the same wave. Two of them fall; another cuts back. The two others race at perfect angles, slicing through the water as if on wings.

"So what now, Carver?" he says "You could have blown it. He knows what you're looking for. Tipped your hand."

"I want him to know."

"You think a guy like that is going to make a mistake? He's talking to his lawyers right now. Probably dialing the mayor. Christ, that's all we need."

"They all make mistakes."

"So does a detective who goes for too much too soon. What if he *is* connected to the Flag? Gives them money or some shit. Doesn't mean he's part of some wacko tent-torching operation. That's a big gap to fill. What have you really got? A big developer who owns property on Skid Row. So what? How many people own buildings down there?"

"Maybe. But he's connected. I feel it."

"Don't say shit like that. I don't want you to feel it. I want you to *know* it. Don't let this get away from you."

CHAPTER 17

MacArthur Park. An old boardinghouse a few blocks from the lake. Curious junkies and gangbangers stand at the edge of blue flash and yellow tape. Cops all around. I follow Alicia Bryant up three flights, down a hall, and into a two-room apartment that was furnished in the 1930s. A dive Black Dahlia could have called home. Worn-out lace curtains, overstuffed chairs, a foldout dining table near an open window with a fire escape. Bryant nods to a syringe and a few packets of what must be heroin or meth on the floor. I step over them. I see him lying near the kitchen. Angel Castillo. White T-shirt. Two shots to the chest. A nine-millimeter lies next to him. One shoe on, one shoe off. A man in a hurry. Surprised. Dead. Bleeding into an ancient carpet. I bend down and look into eyes I last saw more than fifteen years ago. The gleam and menace they once held is gone. They are black and still, looking up at a water-stained ceiling in a building of ghosts. He is slighter than I remember, but years in prison can compress a man. His face is smooth, though, no wrinkles, no scars. I kneel closer. My eyes pull toward a glimmer. I reach for it but do not touch. The locket on the chain around his neck is the one I gave Lily—a gold-winged shoe of Mercury engraved with the letter *L*. My breath leaves me. I feel dizzy. I look up to Bryant and back to the locket. It shines in the glare of police lights—a small thing, a gesture, a surprise wrapped months ago and left on a nightstand until morning, when Lily opened it and slipped it onto a chain. She asked why. I told her I saw it and thought of her. "Because I'm fast?" she said. "Yes," I said, "because you're fast and I want you to win." "Okay, then," she said. "I will." She put it on and said the best presents are given on ordinary days. She never took it off.

Bryant taps my shoulder. I rise.

"You okay?" she says.

"Yes."

"Look at this," she says, handing me an evidence bag holding a picture of Lily and me on the beach at Redondo.

I lift it to the light.

"Lily took it as a selfie a few months ago. She had it printed and kept it on her dresser mirror. Where did you find it?"

"Next to the drugs."

"What's going on?"

"Sit down, Carver."

I sit in a hardback chair next to the open window and the fire escape. I look into the night. The skyline presses close. A breeze cools the sweat on my face.

"Dispatch gets an anonymous call around eleven p.m.," says Bryant. "Caller says Angel Castillo is at this address. Gives the room number, everything. Hangs up. I get here. I mean, look at this place, right? A halfway house of dopers and misfits and little old actors who never made it. Goddamn sad. A perfect place to disappear. I show the guy at the front desk

Castillo's picture. He doesn't want to, but he confirms. I call for backup. Go upstairs and stand outside Castillo's door. I hear low music coming from inside. The uniforms arrive—I didn't want to wait for SWAT. I go down. Tell one to wait out front and one to cover the back. I bring the two others up with me. Music's still playing." Bryant pauses, swallows, calms her shaking hand. "I knock. Yell 'LAPD.' Nothing. Just music. I knock again, hear something moving inside. We kick the door open. Castillo is staggering like he's stoned or startled or some shit. He's waving his gun. Slurring his words. He keeps waving the gun back and forth at us. Keeps looking back at the fire escape window. I tell him to drop the weapon. He slurs some more. I can't make it out. He pulls off a round. I fire twice." She steps to the window, stares out, and looks back at me. "He went down fast, Carver. I never shot a perp before. Didn't know they went down so fast."

"Sounds like a clean shoot," I say. "The uniforms will back you up. Man waving a gun, that's you facing deadly force. You'll be cleared."

She wipes back a tear.

"You okay?" I say.

"It happened so goddamn fast. Just a blur and light and a jack-off with a gun."

"You come out of yourself."

"It felt like that. Like you're standing next to yourself, watching."

"You did right."

"Yeah. But I never shot anyone before."

"It stays, but not like you think."

She looks at Castillo and back to me.

"The locket around his neck," I say, "I gave it to Lily."

"There's more, Carver."

She nods toward a camera on the couch. I slide on gloves. "He was stalking you," says Bryant. "Scroll."

I peer through the viewfinder. Pictures of me coming in and out of my apartment building, walking on Hill Street, entering the Little Easy, meeting with Ortiz at Demitasse, sitting alone in my car in the rain outside Lily's house on the night she died. It is a diary of my life recorded by another, so close as if taken by a shadow self. Hundreds of images, some so candid they seem not me, but they are. The tilt of my head, a hand sliding into a pocket. The way you never see yourself. I speed up the images. They run like a short film of a man alive in a world that doesn't notice him. Alone in his anonymity. I lay the camera on the couch.

"I don't know," I say. "The locket, the pictures. A little convenient."

"He took the locket and the selfie picture when he killed Lily."

"Why take them? That links him."

"Castillo wanted to be linked. He wanted you to know. My guess is, he was going to confront you. Play it all out for you and then take you out."

"Why follow me around with a camera?"

"The guy was obsessed with you. You put him away for a long time, Carver. It was revenge time. A man's got to taste it. Didn't you say this guy was like that? A hard guy. Took out his own boss. What was his name?"

"Enrico Fuentes."

"Yeah. Takes out Fuentes and then takes over his drug territory. A real comer. Guy like that carries a lot of meanness. Lot of patience."

The curtain blows in the window over the fire escape.

"More rain's coming," says Bryant.

I stand over Castillo.

"You said the tip was anonymous?" I ask.

"Yes. A woman speaking Spanish."

"A woman?"

"Correct."

"You said he was staggering."

"Staggering and slurring. I'm sure tox is going to tell us he was coming down off smack or maybe blasted on meth."

"He was holding the gun when you came in?"

"Waving it. Nine-millimeter. Same caliber that killed Lily."

"You think a smart guy would hang on to a murder weapon?"

"Didn't you arrest him fifteen, sixteen years ago after finding the poorly stashed gun that killed Fuentes? Some guys are smart some ways, not so smart other ways."

"I still don't know. Feels too easy. A little convenient, don't you think?"

"You must not be seeing what I'm seeing."

"I guess not."

"What are you saying, Carver? I hope you're not doubting this. This is Lily's killer, right here." She stands and steps beside me. "That's him," she says, pointing to Castillo. "He had motive. He has pictures and a locket, and my guess is, ballistics are going to match the gun to the one that killed Lily. It's a down case, Sam. Accept it. Don't spin it to Dylan Cross. She's not here. What's here, with all the evidence a good cop needs, is Angel Castillo."

She walks to the window, reaches into the rain. Wipes her face with water.

"I can't talk anymore," she says, her voice low and cracked. "I've got a lot to deal with tonight. I've got Internal Affairs and paperwork and coroners and forensics and then I've got to go home to Trey with this thing I've done. It may be a good shoot, but it's there, you know, inside me now like a picture nailed to the brain." She turns from the window. The white suits and the evidence guys get busy. Swabs and vials. "You better leave, Carver," she says.

I walk down the three flights and into the rain. The dopers have scattered. A few gangbangers stand under a tree across the street. Watching, murmuring. Eyes in headlights. I turn and glance up to Castillo's window. Shadows in curtains. Bryant won't be the same for a while; the deed will settle in, pinch at her. Trey will make it better or he won't. He won't have much say either way. What's hers is now his. A dead man's face in a recurring dream. Cop life. I call Ortiz. No answer. I walk around to the fire escape; the last ladder slants to the lawn. I turn on my phone light, check for footprints. See nothing. I rub my hand over the grass. I walk up Wilshire to my car. Homeless tents ring the park and the lake's edge. Match strikes flare here and there; silhouettes flicker and vanish. Dogs bark and quiet. The rain falls hard, and I think it all might float away, wash to the sea, and be gone. Like Gomorrah. I drive north to Third and head downtown. A few minutes after midnight. I park at my building and walk to the Little Easy.

"Sam, shake your coat out before you come in here," says Lenny, polishing the bar. "Can't have a wet floor. Liability and such."

"No one's here," I say.

"This guy's here," says Lenny, nodding to Dr. Michael Ruiz. "We've been talking about things. How humanity keeps making the same mistakes. Over and over. Amazing, really. Hubris, mostly. Never learning, you know. That's the key to us." He tosses his rag under the bar. "What are you having, Sam? Surprise me."

"Beer."

"Ah, curveball. Good call." He draws an IPA and waves me closer, lowers his voice. "I gotta leave on time tonight, Sam. No after-hours partaking. Two a.m. we're done."

"You have a date?"

"Of sorts," says Lenny, loosening his bow tie.

"Tell me more."

"Not what you think."

I take the beer, walk to the corner of the bar.

"Sit, Sam."

"Hello, Doctor. Late night?"

"Closed the clinic an hour ago. They just kept coming. Some days are like that."

Ruiz sips whiskey.

I nod to his glass.

"How many?"

"Two," he says. "Started with a martini and switched. I'm glad you came in. It's been a while since we've been with Lenny."

"You seemed distressed when I saw you at the tent fires over near San Pedro."

"That was a bad night. I gave you shelter, as I recall, let you under my umbrella."

He smiles, tinks my glass with his.

"Why you out late?" says Ruiz.

"Just came from a crime scene."

He sips.

"I should have gone into cosmetic surgery," he says. "A guy I went to med school with has a practice in Beverly Hills. Golfs in Brentwood. It's a good life."

"Can't see you doing that," I say.

"You know what it is, Sam? The faces. They never stop.

Every day at the clinic, more faces, all looking at me for some kind of miracle. Not really a miracle, just something to fix them, some little thing to ease all the shit inside them. Methadone. Tylenol, Antipsychotics. A little temporary magic. That's all they want, can't see beyond that." He finishes his drink, waves Lenny for another. "I lost a guy today. Thirty-five-year-old asthmatic. Living on the streets ten years. Came in, had an attack in the waiting room and died, just like that—died before I could do anything useful. I checked his chart. His name was Byron. No last name. Just Byron. No address. No next of kin. No one to call. He had been to the clinic twenty-nine times."

Lenny slides him the drink. Ruiz rubs a hand over his face. He looks into the bar mirror and back to me.

"Sorry," he says. "I'm sure you have your own bad days."

"Having one now."

"They follow guys like us, maybe."

"It's what we do. We get good ones, too."

"Yeah, I know. But the good doesn't feel as good as the bad feels bad."

"You see that sprayed on a wall?"

He laughs. Goes quiet. Sips. A tear rims his eye.

"How's the tent-fires case?" he says. "Close to anything?"

"Looking at a few things. Too soon to tell."

"It's the Flag. Those flyers like the one I gave you are still showing up on Skid Row."

"Could be. Still trying to figure it out." I think about scotch but order another beer. "I found Marcus Robinson the other day. He never really left Nam, did he? All that time in the jungle. Still wears camo. Looks like a lost soldier. He told me about the guys who attacked him. They beat him pretty bad."

"Marcus will be all right. He's made it through to the other side. He's survived the street. Some of them can do that. One day, though, he'll die on the sidewalk or along the river. They'll zip him up and take him away. It'll be as if he was never here. You ever think about that? Where they all end up?"

"Glad I stopped in tonight."

"I know, I know," he says. "Sorry." He looks into his drink. Sinatra is playing low, and Lenny has the *Times* spread out at the other end of the bar. "Too many homeless, Sam. No one gives a shit. Shouldn't be that way. I testify all the time before these city and state commissions. They don't know what to do. They don't understand. They're overwhelmed, incompetent, corrupt—you name it. It's worse than that, though. People don't care."

He sips his whiskey, swallows slow.

"A lot of people struggling to live in this city, Michael," I say. "Everybody's worried, looking at their own lives. Hardworking people. A lot of them think the homeless are sucking too much air."

"That's a society without compassion."

"Did we ever have that much?"

"Now who's the cynic? This is about hate, though. Goddamn white supremacists, nationalists, whatever. We can't let them get away with this. What would that say about us?"

"What have the last four years said about us?"

"Americans won't stand for people—even homeless ones—getting burned alive in their tents. It'll change. This is a moment of change. The whole world is looking at LA now."

"It's got the mayor's attention."

"That guy, jeez."

"I thought you liked him."

"You always like them when they're just starting out, you know, when they think they can make something happen.

A beautiful naïveté in that. Then they learn, and it's not so beautiful anymore."

"You should run."

"I'm where I need to be."

"You'd need to dress better anyway."

"I'll give him that. The mayor's got nice suits."

"Maybe we should move to Montana, Michael."

"I've got a friend there. Likes it pretty much. Lot of hours to fill in a place like that."

"That's the point, right? Just go walking in that scenery. Thinking shit, noticing things. Nothing waiting for you except time."

"I don't know."

"Yeah, probably not."

"It's good to think that way, though, sometimes."

"Last call, guys," yells Lenny. "Hey, Sam, play us something before we go."

Lenny likes it when I play. He thinks that's how a bar should be. A piano man in the corner. A soft pulse through the night, making people feel special; notes winding through pickup lines, politics, and confessions. But it's late and the place is empty. Glasses stand in clean rows. I take my beer and sit at the upright. I close my eyes, find the keys. I begin Scott Walker's "It's Raining Today," a song I first heard in a train station coffee shop on a winter's day outside Boston in the year my father died. It's one of the two or three songs I play well. I can feel my hands draw it into the air, letting notes breathe, like slow words gathering into sentences. A song is like a war; it must be told in details, not abstractions. It feels right. The music rising as if there's no separation between it and me. Lenny and Ruiz hear it, too. In this moment, in this city of rain, in this time of tent fires, in the troubles of Michael Ruiz, in Lenny's quiet sadness for the secrets he keeps, a song drifts among us. I want it to go on, but such gifts are rare and fleeting. They shine and slip away. I lift my hands. Lenny applauds. Michael, too. I stand and finish my beer. Lenny locks the receipt box, shuts off the lights. We are shadows. The door opens to a drizzle. We go our ways—Michael to his loft on Spring, Lenny toward Union Station, and me up Fifth, where I make a right on Hill and cross the empty street to my apartment.

CHAPTER 18

I brush away the rain, towel my hair, kick off my shoes. I turn on the lights, skim the mail. I reach for the scotch bottle but decide against it. There are nights when this happens. I don't know why; perhaps there's an allotment, a number, a line not to be crossed. I don't think so. It's more of a pause, a brief masquerade before returning to who we are. Better not to dwell. I take a breath and let it be. I make tea, stir in honey, sit at the window. I open my laptop. Know what awaits.

Hi, Sam:

What a night, huh? All this rain and cold. I don't like it. This is not LA. Ah, well, we carry on. But this weather. Something is happening in the world. How are you, my darling? I've decided sometimes I will call you darling. I like intimacy. Don't you? There's so much between us. Even now, here, in these words you're reading. It's us. We should

dance. One day, maybe. The two of us in the Little
Easy. Tell Lenny to put on something soft. It'll be
as it must be. Not now, I suppose. I'm soooooo
impatient, though. Are you still grieving, darling?
Poor Lily. Poor Sam. It would have never worked,
you know, Lily. Not to be. Not your type. Not really.
I know you thought so. Men don't understand that
about themselves. They don't know themselves
enough to know what's right for them. A flaw in the
gender. Sooooooo (Have you noticed I draw out
words for emphasis? Emphasis is important.) how
was MacArthur Park? No emoji, but you should
see my face as I type this. What a sly face it is. The
smile. You should see it. One day. Angel Castillo.
Mmmmmmm. Lily's killer. Dead. How does that feel,
Sam? To have him gone. Does retribution redeem
the aggrieved? Speaking from experience, no, it
does not. It brings temporary joy, I suppose, like
blowing out candles on a birthday cake. But then
it's over in the snap of a finger, and what was there
before, that terrible loss, is still there. I know the
feeling. That unfillable hole. It becomes you, even
with all your masks. I have many masks, but not for
you, Sam. I am as I am. Buuuuuuut. Are we sure
Angel Castillo is our man? Alicia Bryant thinks so. I
haven't made my mind up about her. I think I might
like her, but it's too early. Good cop. Isn't that what
you guys say? Good cop. Term of endearment.
All your little cop sayings. She did well for a girl
from Compton. Or is it Watts? But her husband
is the star. All his slave faces. I have seen them.
Gimmicks disguised and celebrated as art. Are you

rolling your eyes, Sam? Ha. I can be a critic too.
Anywaaaaaaay. Alicia might be wrong about Angel
Castillo. I type his full name because there's music
in it. Say it. Angel Castillo. Angel Castillo. What was
the evidence linking him to Lily? Ooooops. There
goes my sly-smile-face-that-you-can't-see again.
I'm just surmising here. Little ole me. What do I
know about police work? I'm sure Alicia has it in
hand. She put him down. Bang, bang. I bet it was
loud. I mean, I'm assuming. How would I know? It's
over, right? Case solved. Justice served. Oh, Sam,
I'm tired. I've been so tired lately. It's the on-again,
off-again meds. I can never find the right balance.
But now that Lily is behind us, I'm thinking we need
to see one another. It's time. It's been too long. Do
I sound like a pop song? Yikes. I had a dream the
other night, Sam. We were sitting on a fire escape
drinking beer. You kissed me. Just like that. Out
of nowhere. You kissed me and gave me a locket,
and then we climbed down the fire escape and
disappeared into the night. Soooooooo romantic.

Bye, Sam. Love, D

The confession is cryptic and circumstantial. Meant
only for me. Bryant won't believe it, but that's how Dylan is.
There and gone without a trace, like when she killed Michael
Gallagher and Paul Jamieson. She knew Castillo was a suspect.
She must have followed him for days, waiting, tracking him
to MacArthur Park, sneaking up the fire escape; somehow
injecting him (she drugged Jamieson, too), planting the locket,
camera (she took all those pictures of me), and then, as Castillo

was coming out of his stupor but still not himself, she called 911. She swapped his gun for the one that killed Lily. When Bryant burst through the door, Castillo was unsteady, waving the gun. That's what Bryant said. Waving the gun, slurring words, looking back at the fire escape. He wanted Bryant to check it. But it happened too fast. He was dead. Dylan was gone. I can't prove any of it. There's not enough evidence in Dylan's email to change Bryant's mind. I read it again. Taunting and elusive. A clever girl's tease. Dylan must have hacked Bryant's computers. That's how she knew about Castillo. It all fits. Intricate as a birdcage. Screw it. Let Bryant close the case, pick up a commendation. I don't feel like arguing anymore. Dylan is my phantom. She is coming. Soon. And I will find out—how did she put it?—*if retribution redeems the aggrieved.*

I close the laptop. It is nearly dawn. I pour another tea, stir in honey. I stand at the window. The light is spreading, the city revealed. *The peeling of masks*—that's what Dylan would say. Clouds blow west toward the coast. I open the window. Cold air fills the apartment. The brisk jolt of a new day. It rushes over the city, blowing papers into dervishes that spin and die as the sun crests the Grand Central Market and warms the sidewalk in front of Angels Flight. Looking out, I think, despite my many years here, I don't know my adopted city. Like me, it is ephemeral, a bit of transitory magic at the edge of an ocean pushing against sky.

A knock on the door.

"This is getting to be a habit," I say.

Ortiz steps in.

"What time is it?"

"Almost six thirty," I say.

"You been up all night?"

"What do you think? You?"

"I got to MacArthur Park after you left. I helped Bryant finish up. She's pretty shaken. Didn't expect that. You know how tough she puts on."

"Killing a man will take that away."

"For a time. She's a good cop. It was a good kill."

"I know."

Ortiz follows me into the living room. I put on water and make coffee. He stares at the photograph of the African tribesman on the wall. Ortiz has often commented on the man's serenity, how he gazes out over the land as if knowing what's to come. He thinks the man had many children but liked best to be alone, walking through high grass, waiting for the rains, for the animals moving like thunder across the earth, gathering at their watering holes. Ortiz imagines much when he stands before the man. I hand him a coffee.

"No espresso?"

"Machine's broken," I say. "French press."

"What kind of beans?"

"Sumatra."

He sits.

"After I left Bryant, I drove around for a while," he says. "Drove down Wilshire, cut up to Sunset, turned into the hills, looped back down. It's some city, you know? All these fucking strange pieces, seemingly apart but growing together. Not pretty, but beautiful, you know, especially at first light. When it's all quiet." He sips. "Listen, Carver, I thought a lot about it. All the possibilities, all the shit I'm sure you're thinking. But Castillo is our man. It fits. It just does. You don't want to believe it, I know. But it's not Dylan Cross. Don't get me wrong, she's out there, but she didn't kill Lily. Castillo did. You've got to accept that."

I take a breath. Look at him.

"I do," I say. "I don't want to, but I do. Ballistics . . ."

"They'll come back to show it was the same nine-millimeter that killed Lily."

"I know."

"So, you're not going to fight Bryant on this? We can close the case?"

"If ballistics checks out and you're sure he's the perp, close the case."

"You think it's too easy."

"It did wrap up neat. Who called it in?"

"A woman speaking Spanish," he says. "Hung up fast, no name."

"Trace the call?"

"A burner phone."

"What are you thinking?"

"Castillo had a lot of enemies."

We sit in silence. He glances at the small box of Lily's ashes near the chair.

"You should do something with those," he says.

"I will."

"I miss her."

I get up for more coffee.

"You hear from Dylan Cross lately?" he says.

"No."

"You would have heard by now if she was the doer, if she killed Lily and Castillo."

"The thought has crossed your mind."

"Yeah, Carver, but the evidence tilts the other way." He looks into his cup. "Maybe she won't come back. She'll stop haunting you."

"She'll be back."

"I want to be fucking retired by then."

"You had your chance in Costa Rica. You should have stayed."

"It was goddamn pretty down there. An hour would go by, you wouldn't even know it. Sitting there watching the waves, feet in the sand, holding the wife's hand, like when I was fucking fifteen. We found a little wooden church. Yeah, it was okay for a while."

"Not you."

"One day. When I go back, Carver, I'm going to buy a boat and fish. Just sit there floating and fishing until dark."

I pour more coffee. Ortiz and I sit in quiet.

CHAPTER 19

"Detective Carver."

"Who's this?"

"Barry Wilkins. Oregon State Police."

"Hi, Captain. It's early."

"I figure guys like us don't sleep."

"You just missed Ortiz."

"You two live together?"

"No. Late-night case. What's up?"

I twist open the blinds, let the light in. A man in an apron hustles down the sidewalk for a bus; two kids, puffing vapes and carrying backpacks, cross Fifth into Pershing Square.

"You there?" says Wilkins.

"Yes."

"Okay. We got warrants and visited the Crenshaw brothers. They had a lawyer waiting. Fat guy. Heavy breather. Nice suit. We got to business. You remember Charlie, the balled-up, tattooed angry brother. He was pissed. Started stomping around, screaming about the First Amendment. I laughed to myself when he said it. I thought Charlie was strictly a Second Amendment guy. The lawyer calmed him, sort of. We seized a few computers. Checked their office files. Talked to a couple of their data people. That's what they call them. 'Data people.' Jesus. Anyway, they must have scrubbed the computers. Couldn't find anything on PureLand. But I'm thinking they were telling the truth on that."

"That PureLand sends his articles by old-fashioned mail."

"Yeah, and the Crenshaws post them online. They're sticking with the story that PureLand is anonymous. A like-minded zealot, but they don't know who he is. Going to be hard to trace him." Wilkins must be in a car. I hear a train pass in the phone. It fades. Then the quiet of a forest road. "They had burned boxes of documents. One of their data people told us they did it the day before you and I got there. But he said they often burn papers. Nothing special. I don't know if I believe that. Amazing, the stuff they did have, though. These alt-right neo-Nazis are all over. The Crenshaws have contacts with groups in Germany, Austria, Poland, Russia, Sweden. Even Iceland. I mean, there's what, forty people living in Iceland and they've got a supremacist group. Christ. A lot of rabid shit out there. You start thinking it's bigger than you thought. Hard to get a bead, you know, like some of them revere Hitler, others hate him, seeing him as the evil embodiment of the authoritarian, big-government state. It's goddamn confusing."

"Did you find any connection to Milton Archer?"

"I pressed Bill Crenshaw again on Archer. He said he didn't know him. That Archer has nothing to do with the Flag. He was lying. Same way he did when you mentioned it to him. The lawyer fidgeted when Archer's name came up. Kind of nervousness in the air. But there was nothing about him on the computers or in the documents. We'll go through them again."

"Maybe an alias."

"See, Carver, that's why we'd be good partners," says Wilkins, laughing. "There was a name. A donor. Gives big sums a few times a year. Might not be any connection to Archer at all, but it's a name." Wilkins pauses, takes a breath. "Albert Speer. Know him?"

"Are you smiling?"

"A little, maybe."

"Albert Speer was Hitler's architect."

"Yeah, I googled him. He was going to turn Berlin into ancient Rome or Athens or some shit."

I hear brakes.

"Whoa," says Wilkins.

"What?"

"Almost hit a raccoon," he says.

"You okay?"

"Straightened back out."

"Did you run a check on Speer?"

"I'll let you do that."

"It's got to be an alias."

"I would assume."

"What did the Crenshaws say?"

"That they get a check every so often from Albert Speer," says Wilkins. "They never met him, so they say. They said nothing wrong with a guy sending in donations. They report it. It's in their financials. The brothers are good at playing dumb. Their lawyer is extra entertainment."

"Do you have the checks?"

"I'm texting you pictures of one of them now."

"Thanks, Captain."

"You want me to go back at the Crenshaws?"

"Let me run Speer first. See what comes up."

"Whole lot of bad history's going to come up. Who takes a name like that?"

"It's got to be an alias."

"Even worse."

I hear tires on gravel through the phone.

"Where are you?" I say.

"On my way to a domestic. Way out in the sticks. A county commissioner up here keeps beating his wife."

"Hate those."

"It's starting to snow. The road's empty. The sky is that color it gets up here. Orange-gray. I don't mind the drive."

"I grew up in Rhode Island."

"Same kinda sky, huh?"

"Peaceful," I say.

"Peaceful and cold. You miss the East?"

"I miss the winter mornings. Like the one you're driving through now."

"You don't want the rest of life to start, so you can have more of it to yourself."

"Take care, Captain."

"Tell Ortiz I said hello."

I click open the text and study the check. It's from a Panamanian bank. The handwriting is ornate. Cursive, slanting right. Old-school. Check number 1155. Written out to the Flag. Forty thousand dollars. The memo line reads, "For the mighty." Signed: Albert Speer. The name has stayed with me since I read Speer's memoir in a class on the Holocaust I took at Berkeley. Speer and Hitler fed and consumed one another's desires. Each made the other possible. Speer never thought of himself as evil; he was an artist, a keeper and designer of dreams and delusions. At the end of the war, when Speer was in handcuffs on a military plane, on his way to prison, he looked down over his destroyed Berlin and began to weep. All that he was going to build—a new metropolis, a reimagined Rome—lay in smoke and ruin. Ragged women in the Tiergarten tore away tree limbs for firewood; families scavenged through scattered bricks; the dead lay in stacks on the Ku'damm, where the rich once played in cabarets and everyone thought that the angry man with the funny mustache was just another crazed prophet in a beer hall.

I set the phone down. Morning fills the apartment. I lie on the couch, close my eyes. What must it have been like to be so close to your dream, only to have it snatched away?

CHAPTER 20

I lean against a back wall and watch the scene before me. Alicia Bryant stands next to Ortiz. Police Chief William Conroy is snug in dress blues and gold buttons, badges agleam. The mayor is at a podium in bright light. New haircut, tailored suit. Some good news. Finally. He reads from the script: "Officer Lily Hernandez's assailant, Angel Castillo, was shot and killed by Detective Alicia Bryant as police closed in on an apartment building in MacArthur Park. Evidence collected at the scene, as well as ballistics on the gun Castillo fired at Detective Bryant, confirm that Castillo killed Officer Hernandez in her home."

Reporters horseshoe around him, aides flitting behind, scrolling phones.

The mayor keeps on about the diligence and "painstaking" police work. Countless hours, a courageous manhunt. How justice has been done. He says *justice* many times, as if in prayer. Resolve in his eyes, empathy in his voice. He exalts Lily. The finest among us. The ultimate sacrifice. He is good at this. But there's a tricky part.

"The department's investigation has determined that Angel Castillo shot and killed Officer Hernandez because of her relationship with Detective Sam Carver. Fifteen years ago, Detective Carver arrested Castillo for the murder of drug kingpin Enrico Fuentes. The investigation has shown that Castillo, who was released from prison just weeks ago, wanted revenge. He targeted Officer Hernandez . . ."

"What kind of relationship?" yells a reporter.

"They were close," says the mayor. "That's all I'll say."

"Were they dating?" asks another.

"I'm not getting into the specifics of their relationship," says the mayor.

"Why not target Carver himself if he wanted revenge?" asks a reporter from the *Times*.

"We can't get into the mind of a crazed criminal," says the mayor. "He wanted to hurt Detective Carver. We believe that's why he killed Officer Hernandez."

"You *believe*? Does that mean you don't know?"

"As I said, Castillo was a man capable of a perverse crime."

The reporters circle closer. Questions fly. Bryant and Ortiz stand rigid. The chief pushes back his shoulders. The mayor shrinks in the bright light. Before the pack starts looking for me, I step out the door and walk across the plaza. Sun slants through broken clouds. A homeless man chases a runaway shopping cart through a red light and down the hill toward Little Tokyo. A couple kisses against a tree. Three Guatemalans wave banners for refugee children. "No More Cages." I hear footsteps from behind.

"Detective Carver."

I know the voice.

"Mariana Sanchez. KABC News."

"No comment."

"I'm sorry for your loss, Detective. Were you and Lily together long?"

"No comment."

"She was on track to make detective. Didn't she work with you on the Russian ballerina murder a year or so ago? Some case that was, huh? Spies. Movie producers."

"No comment."

She is alone. Her cameraman must be inside with the mayor. I slow my pace.

"Hey, Carver, I know what it's like."

"What?"

"To have a relationship go public."

"You and the mayor. Maybe. But from what I can see, he's still alive, so I don't think you know."

"Wasn't much of a relationship. A botched date in Newport Beach. The press turned it into something it wasn't."

"You are the press."

"We're a strange lot."

"He was married."

"Separated."

"Convenient."

"The truth."

"Isn't he back with her?" I say. "What was the attraction?"

"Now you're asking the questions? I don't know. He's got a quality, but not really my type." She laughs. "It was a mistake," she says. "What else can I say?"

"Sounds like you're working me."

"I just want to know about you and Lily. It's a story. People care about stories. I don't want to push, Detective."

"I thought that's what you people do."

"'You people.' Seriously?"

"You know what I mean."

Her black hair is tied back. She's wearing jeans, T-shirt, and a blazer—her in-the-field look. I remember seeing her on the BBC years ago, covering the Iraq war and uprisings in Africa. She was slender, wrapped in a flak jacket, but she filled the screen. Your eyes went to her. Her voice was clear, deep, and immediate. She knew things you wanted to know, and once, at a mass grave, she cried on camera—not in the false way that so many of them do these days, but because she was moved; the puzzle of bones in the dirt beneath her had taken its toll.

"Why did you quit the BBC?"

"Too long living like a nomad. I was dating a guy out here at the time. Thought, what's not to like about LA? The guy ended up leaving me."

"Men tend to disappoint you."

"I've been a cautionary tale once or twice."

"You still feel that way about LA?"

"It's like living inside a trick."

"It happens."

"It's the story of the place, no? Betrayal."

She lights a cigarette.

"I'm never going to quit," she says.

I nod. She hands me one.

"A fellow outcast," she says. "Vaping is for pussies."

"There's smoke in your voice."

"People tell me."

I cross the street to Grand Park and up the hill toward Disney Hall. She stays with me but says nothing. I stop at a railing and look down. City Hall rises like a white gravestone for a prince. The press conference must be over, the story out, Bryant and Ortiz heading for a celebratory drink, the mayor safely in his office. What I had with Lily is private no more; we have become a bit of scandal. But in time, perhaps a day or two, we will be forgotten, like all the dead bodies and lost names before us.

"It's hard," says Mariana Sanchez.

"What?"

"Being where you are now. Exposed."

"Why are you here?"

"I told you."

I turn to leave but stop. She leans beside me on the railing. We're quiet for a while.

"I'll tell you a few things about Lily," I say.

"Let me call my cameraman."

"No. This is just for you. Lily lived in Boyle Heights. In a small house with a garden she let grow wild. She could run for miles. Her father was a cop. His father, too. She would have made detective. She was smart that way. Mind always working. She wanted to be my partner. I didn't know if I wanted one. But she would have pushed, and I would have relented. She was like that." I glance at Sanchez. "This doesn't tell you about Lily. It's just details. They're not the things that make her real. Those are my things. You can't put them into three minutes. It wouldn't be fair. She was lovely. She'd dance in the rain on the porch and look up to the cross at St. Mary's and say, 'Carver, what do you think it all looked like when no one was here?' How can you fit that into your story? I know you're good at what you do, Mariana. I respect it. But I can't give you Lily. She's mine. We don't get much in life, and the few things we do get, we don't know we have until we have them no more. Understand?"

"Yes, but—"

"No *but*."

"You'll want to tell it one day, Carver."

"I don't think so."

"If you do."

"I know."

"I was in Libya during the war," she says. "A boy had been killed. His father carried him through the village. Everyone came out and followed the father down the road to a big tree that stood by itself. The father sat with the boy draped over his lap. He stroked his son's hair. The villagers sat around him. It was late morning. Wind blew through the branches of the tree. No one said anything. Not a word. They sat until dusk. A man brought a shovel. He and two other men took turns digging a grave. It was primal but tender, you know. The father laid the boy in it. They covered him, and everyone walked home in the dark. No one spoke. Not the whole day. But I felt I knew all there was to know about the boy, his father, and their village."

"You thinking that now?"

"Maybe. A little. A woman I met a long time ago told me that everyone has a search. What's your search, Detective?"

"Search?"

"Meaning. Beyond this day. Beyond Lily."

"That's not a five-o'clock-news question."

"It's the only question. There's no camera here. Two people talking."

I glance at her again. She's trying for a way in. Her eyes stay on mine.

"I don't know you," I say.

"You know what they say about strangers."

"I never thought that."

"You can tell a stranger anything. No judgment."

"Nice try."

I run a hand through my hair, look at the sky.

"I think we're done," I say.

"Seems that way. I can always tell."

"Tell what?"

"When the shade comes down."

"You must get that a lot."

"People surprise, though. We both know that, given what we do."

"You think I might surprise?"

"I didn't know. But you're not the village, the boy, or the father. You're the tree."

"Why the tree?"

"You figure it out."

"You remind me of someone."

"Yeah?"

"Susan Chandler."

"Formerly of the *Times*, now of the *Post*. Good reporter."

"We knew each other a while ago."

"Keep it cryptic, Detective. I've noticed that about you." She smiles, starts to walk away. Turns back.

"One more question."

"What?"

"You close to anything on the homeless killings? Don't look like that. It's a fair question."

"Under investigation."

"Is the Flag involved? Those fanatical Crenshaw brothers?"

"Under investigation."

"Who's PureLand? I've been reading the Flag's site. PureLand has scary social-engineering ideas. Doesn't much like the homeless, does he?"

"Under . . ."

"C'mon, Carver. One thing."

"Off the record. Background. I don't want to see it on the news. If you report it, our relationship is over."

"We don't have a relationship."

"We'll never have one if you report it now."

"When can I report it?"

"I'll give you a heads-up before the arrest."

"How much of one."

"Enough that you'll be way ahead."

"Deal."

"We're looking for PureLand. Don't know who he is. His screeds posted online are mailed in to the Flag."

"Emailed?"

"Stamp mail."

"They still have that?"

She smiles.

"What are you thinking?" she says.

"Developers want the homeless gone. A lot of money to be made on Skid Row real estate."

"Is this a theory or more substantial?"

"It's getting to be substantial."

"Might be more ideological than that," she says. "Neo-Nazi types aren't so much about the money."

"I think it's a little of both. Greed meets ideology," I say.

"That's not exactly America. Americans don't go for ideology."

"The crazy ones do."

"There's been a real pushback against the homeless. Liberal LA's getting fed up. People shitting on your sidewalk, OD'ing in driveways, and going schizoid in Trader Joe's. Not part of the dream. Maybe, someone senses the time is right."

"My guess, too. That's all off the record."

"I don't have to be told twice. I don't burn sources, Detective."

"Am I a source?"

"No. I just meant . . ."

"I know what you meant."

She looks to the skyline. Back to me.

"You must have a guess on who PureLand is," she says.

"Maybe."

I step back from the railing.

"I've got to go," I say.

"I am sorry about Lily."

"Thanks."

"I think you would have let her be your partner."

"I wonder."

"Says the tree."

I walk north toward the cathedral. I look back. Sanchez leans on the railing, wind in her hair. She takes out a notebook. Scribbles. I cross the street into the cathedral's courtyard. No one's here. I think about going in and sitting in a pew, but I have no prayers in me. I once did. They're gone, although I sometimes try to piece a fragment of one into their air. The olive trees in the courtyard remind me of Gethsemane in the Bible pictures, and stations of the cross I prayed to as a child. Suffering and blood. So much pain in the garden. A night of sorrow and bewilderment, that's what the nuns taught—a night of whips and soldiers, and a bargain that led to the cross. Such a story it is when you're young. The first time you hear it, unaware in innocence—is that what it is?—that will have you kneel and confess to the venial thoughts and acts within you. A boy runs into the courtyard with a soccer ball. It rolls and scrapes over the stones. He sees me and kicks the ball toward me. I stand and kick it back, and we play, even as rain falls. It is just the boy and me, darting, sprinting, laughing, scoring against the wall between paintings of saints and a statue of the virgin. We play until the rain seeps to bone. The boy flashes around me and scores. He throws his hands into the air. He dances and spins. A man appears at the courtyard door. He waves. The boy kicks the ball high. He catches it and runs toward the man. They disappear into the street. I wait beneath the olive trees for the rain to pass.

CHAPTER 21

The phone rings a few minutes after six.

"You up? I've been up all night. Through the rabbit hole and back."

A laugh and a slurp.

"Jimmy?"

"Who else? I got some shit. Fucking Albert Speer. What a character. The real one and the alias."

"What'd you find?" I say, yawning, rising from the chair by the window.

I can hear him typing, sequestered in his dim room, cans of Red Bull open.

"Well," says Jimmy Knight, "first of all—and you should know this if you don't already—I'm a computer forensics wizard. No shit, really. I can be amazing. Just saying. If anyone asks."

"What did you get? It's early," I say, walking to the kitchen. "I'm just waking up."

"Okay, okay. Albert Speer, as we know, was Hitler's architect. Of course, I didn't know Hitler had an architect, until, you know, this case. Anyway, you've got to go through all the real Albert Speer stuff—did you know he wrote a book about his time in prison?—before you get to the fake Albert Speers, which, and you may not know this, there's a fucking lot of. Well, 'a lot' is relative, so let's just say many. The one I think you'll be most interested in is the Albert Speer in Norway. His real name is Oskar Christensen. A very rich man, one of those old-school rich guys—family had money that Oskar invested in pharmaceuticals and vaccines and turned into, well, a fortune. He's a rabid right-winger. Aryan to the bone, one of those aloof Scandinavian types. You know, a brooder. But he keeps it mostly secret. Gives to a lot of right-wing European parties. Doesn't show up at rallies, or anything. Not that I can see."

"And?"

"C'mon, Carver, this is cool. Wait a minute and listen."

"I'm making coffee. Go on."

"You should try Red Bull. Big bounce."

"Jimmy."

"Oskar took on the alias 'Albert Speer' about ten years ago."

"I'm listening."

"I traced the check you texted me. The one with the forty-thousand-dollar donation to the Flag. We were lucky on that. Panamanian bank. All kinds of shit out there on Panamanian banks since those investigative journalists dumped all that stuff online. Massive dump. Bank accounts. All kinds of names. Dictators. Crooks. Even normal people. Anyway, Speer's name keeps popping up on checks written from the same bank to neo-Nazi wacko organizations all over. I don't know how he's connected to the Flag other than that. I'll keep looking." Jimmy slurps; keys tap. "But get this. You listening? I hear water pouring."

"Keep going."

"Oskar. Speer. Whatever. Twenty years ago, he sat on the board of an American company—they specialize in tungsten steel and make weapons and shit—with guess who. Milton Archer. Milton effing Archer. Your guy. The developer guy. It's him. Thing is, Carver, I can't find any other place where they come together. That board was a long time ago. Oskar Christensen only stayed on it a couple of years and Archer left not long after. I'm doing a deeper dive, but that's what I've got."

"Maybe Christensen brought Archer to the Flag."

"Or vice versa."

"Anything else from the Panamanian banks?"

"No. I ran Archer. He didn't come up. Unless there's another alias. You have any more?"

"Albert Speer's the only one so far."

"There were a shitload of Nazi dudes back then. Must be more aliases out there."

"I'll keep looking," I say.

"I'm getting tired, Carver. I'm fading. May have to take a few winks."

"Great work, Jimmy."

"You can get lost in all this shit," he says, his voice winding down. "It's like its own cosmos, you know? Fuck, it's bigger than the cosmos! It's what it's all coming to, you know. We're all going to vanish into the ether. Our brains uploaded. We won't need bodies anymore. Just the mind. The perfect computer. It's coming, Carver. You'll be gone before it happens. Me, too."

"Fascinating," I say, wanting to keep Jimmy on Christensen. "One other thing. How about real estate? Does Christensen own any land in LA? Any shell companies connecting him and Archer? That could be key. Might all be under fake names. Is Christensen married?"

"Three times. I'll check shell companies."

"Get some sleep, Jimmy."

"I'm sending you all the shit we just talked about," he says. "There's a few newspaper stories in there, too. I ran them through an app to translate them from Norwegian to English. Amazing place, the world. What time is it?"

"Little before seven."

"Can never tell in here."

I open my laptop and read what Jimmy sent. Christensen's net worth is $900 million. He owns mansions and villas. He skis. When he was twenty, he won a European championship in fencing and made Norway's Olympic team. He left the sport a few years later to work with the family money and, according to the *Aftenposten*, played in London nightclubs with the avant-garde artist daughter of a Belgian banker and a French actress who once worked with Goddard. By his mid-thirties, he had disappeared from the news, except for occasional profiles on his pharmaceutical and vaccine companies, and one story, during the Balkan wars, in which he vents his worries that refugees and immigrants will ruin Norway. "They are not us," he said in the translated version Jimmy sent. The only picture of him in the file was taken when he was fifty. He's walking alone on an Oslo street in a coat and fedora, a scarf wrapped around his neck. Light snow is falling. His eyes shine beneath the hat brim. They are bright green, the only color in the picture, and they lock on the lens with the intensity of a man not accustomed to sharing himself.

I close the laptop. The morning is gray, the streets wet. I walk down the hall to the bedroom—I haven't slept here since Lily died—and lie down. Her T-shirt is folded on the nightstand; a bandanna, gold chain, and pair of earrings lie nearby. I remember when she took the earrings off, sitting naked in the moonlight after we had come back from dinner and drinks. She put on a record, and we danced. "I should stay here more often, Carver," she said. "You're always flopping at my house." We danced down the hall. The music stopped. The needle crackled on vinyl. "Should I flip the record?" I said. "No," she said. "Pretend." It was the last night we spent together. A week before she died. Her towel is rumpled on the floor. White and new. A gift from her. "Carver," she said, "your towels are shit." I pick up the towel and lie back on the bed. I press the towel to my face and pull Lily's pillow close. I breathe her in, close my eyes. She is here. A scent, a faint trace, a pair of earrings. It is as if the room had kept her here, among the windows, dresser, rugs, and the painting we brought from Oaxaca, of two men playing cards at a wooden table. Candlelight against their faces, each thinks he holds the better hand. "We don't know who wins," says Lily. "I like that. A forever suspense."

I sleep.

CHAPTER 22

Alicia Bryant sits with two coffees in the lobby.

"I've been here an hour," she says. "I thought I'd come up, but I've never been up. So I thought I'd wait." She hands me a coffee. "It's cold."

I sit next to her.

"This was the old subway terminal, wasn't it?" she says.

"Yes."

"I love the columns and marble. They built better back then. More character."

"You've been drinking," I say.

She holds up a coffee.

"No," I say. "Something stronger."

"Long night."

"Case?"

"No. You still mad about Castillo?"

"I was never mad."

"You never believed it."

"It was your case, Alicia."

She sips her coffee. She wears no makeup or eyeliner; her nails are unpolished, the sheen of her left in another place.

"Trey split," she says.

"Split?"

"We broke up. He's keeping his studio downstairs. But he moved to the eastern building. How predictable is that? He's got money now. The big artist. The new Black sensation."

I reach out and touch her hand.

"Sorry," I say.

"It was coming. But it's still a surprise. Even when you know. He got tired of having a cop wife. Too intense. That's what he said. I got tired of all his slaves. All those faces looking at me, knowing they came from out of some ugly past. Living with paintings is not like seeing them in museums. There's no escape. They're on your walls, watching. Like family." She wipes her eyes. "I don't even know why I'm here, Carver. Not like we're close. I was just driving around and I saw your building. People do dumb shit. Sorry."

"You're out of sorts since Castillo."

"It was a good shoot. I was cleared."

"I know, but still . . ."

"Keep seeing him. Replaying it, you know. Thinking, did I pull too fast? I didn't. He was waving that damn gun."

"Any cop would have done the same thing."

"I didn't think it would be like that."

"What do you mean?"

"When the bullet hit, his body jerked. Really *jerked*. A shiver went over his face. Like a bee had stung him. He never made a sound, though. I kept thinking something would come out of him. A peep or gasp or something. But nothing, just a man falling to the floor. Even that didn't make a sound. Maybe I wasn't listening. Maybe there was all kinds of noise I didn't hear."

She sips her coffee; makes a face.

"Too cold," she says. "You ever kill anyone?"

"No. Shot at two guys, but never that."

"I might take some time off."

"They'll send you to a shrink."

"Already been arranged."

"They're quick about that."

"Don't want a woman on the verge of a nervous breakdown."

"That's a movie."

"I thought you'd get that. French, right?"

"Spanish."

The morning isn't new anymore; footsteps and open doors. A man in a ball cap hurries in with a small pile of newspapers. He lays them on the front desk and rushes out.

"I didn't think anyone got newspapers these days," says Alicia.

"Two are mine."

"Old school, Carver. A guy from another century."

"I like the feel."

The security guard returns from his rounds. I look at Alicia.

"You're spent," I say.

"This is me in morning light."

"I've seen worse," I say, smiling.

"Screw you, Carver. You couldn't hang with me on your best day, with your two newspapers and your rumpled, every-other-day-shaved cop thing going on. Who's that guy?"

"What guy?"

"That TV cop guy. The dude from all the novels. It's an Amazon thing. Ortiz likes it."

"Bosch?"

"Yeah, Bosch. Got a ton of bad shit in his life, but even that motherfucker shaves."

"I'm not so rumpled."

"You know what, though, Carver? You're balled-up. All reticent and shit. Like every word costs you a goddamn nickel. Tell me something I wouldn't guess about you."

"I dance the tango in silk shirts with women from Argentina."

"Get the fuck out."

"I do."

"You don't."

"Okay, but I'd like to. I'd like once to feel like I'm part of the air. Smooth like that."

"You in a silk tango shirt. I'd pay to see that shit."

She laughs.

"Like disappearing into someone else," she says.

"I've thought about it."

"A soul can't escape its place."

She cries, makes no sound, wipes her eyes.

"The Castillo thing didn't help with Trey," she says. "We were already in trouble. Then that shit."

"What happened?"

"He was done. It all sort of hit, you know? He got famous and it screwed him up, but it wasn't just him. It was me, too. Can't put it all on him. He didn't know what he was supposed to be anymore. The expectations. He can't keep painting slaves. Needs something new. But he can't find it. He keeps going back to them. He finds refuge in that pain. He pulled away from me. He's scared but won't admit it. He's a Black man. A lot of people want a Black man to fail. They don't want much better for Black women, either. Deep down. They don't say it. But deep down." She rubs a hand over her mouth. "I think I stopped loving him. I came from Compton. He came from some poor-ass neighborhood in Detroit. We both made it, you know. Why wouldn't it work? I think we carry too many of the same things inside, and sometimes you just want new things."

"I get that. I'd like some new things."

"Trey's working on another series. Like I said, same theme, different faces. He's bringing them present day. Ghosts from now. Trayvon Martin. Michael Brown. Eric Garner. Young Black men and boys killed by cops and racists. He's painting the faces as they'd look on a cell phone. That slightly blurred, viral look, you know, like it's hard for the one looking at it to understand. But you keep looking 'cause you can't believe it." She sips and puts the coffee cup aside. "What about you, Carver? You harder on a Black perp than a white one? You go for the gun quicker?"

"I try never to reach for the gun."

"You shot at two guys."

"They shot first. One was white."

"Okay, but when you come up on a Black guy, are you subconsciously reaching?"

"I don't think so."

"It's not thinking; it's instinct."

"I don't have that instinct."

"That's what all white people say."

"You an authority on all white people? Tough job."

"You know what I mean. That deep thing in the tissue. Your ancestors put it there. Put it in both of us. Black people learned to live with it. We had no choice. But white people never had to face it, not really, left it somewhere in a box. My father used to say white people don't know, 'cause they never looked for it. If you look, you find, and who would want to find that?"

I stare at her.

"Some of us have found it," I say. "Don't be so certain before you know. Mistake no matter what color you are."

"You're one of the enlightened, huh? A white liberal is a lot of righteous passion and not much action."

"Who are you pissed at? Me or Trey?"

"Right now, the world."

"You can be derisive."

"Experience."

"So, you know it all. See into every heart."

"I'm messing with you, Carver. Calm down. I like some white people. You might be one."

She laughs.

"Maybe I don't like you."

"I'm irresistible," she says. "Most days."

I almost smile.

"C'mon, Carver, I know you've got one in there," she says. "One day I'll see it."

We don't speak for a while.

"You think you and Trey will work it out?"

"No," she says. "I went to his studio the other day to give him something. All those faces on the wall looking at me. There was one clear white canvas hanging in the middle of them. Like a cloud between Trayvon Martin and Michael Brown. Trey stood beside me and said, 'There'll be another one coming soon.' Like he knew, you know, like he knew you could count on another dead Black man."

She wipes a tear away, takes a breath. She stills. I want to hold her, but I don't. She is accustomed to burden but not broken by it, which gives her a street kid's courage, although she would call it something else. The elevator opens. A woman pushes a stroller over the polished floor, humming a nursery rhyme, hurrying toward the front door, beyond which a man is talking on a phone and walking in tight circles near a black Escalade.

"You like being a cop?" I say.

"I do."

"Why?"

"The hours," she says.

"Don't be a wiseass."

"Putting a case down. Best feeling, right? Finding the asshole who did the deed. Who made the hurt, you know, who took something. You?"

"Watching the mystery burn away."

"Doesn't always," she says. "What's the perfect crime?"

"Disappearance."

"I know where you're going with this."

"I didn't say anything."

"You don't have to mention that name to say anything. You're one persistent man, Carver."

"You're a good cop, Alicia."

"It's too morning for this shit."

She stands. Hands me her empty cup.

"You keeping the car?" I say.

"The Merc? Damn right. Trey was good to me that way. Having nothing once makes you give easier."

She walks through the swinging doors onto the sidewalk. She pauses, looks at the sky, turns, and is lost in other faces. My phone rings.

"Facial recognition."

"What?"

"Get here."

I walk through Grand Central Market and up Spring to headquarters. Ortiz sits in Jimmy Knight's office. Jimmy's banging the keyboard.

"Guy's nuts," whispers Ortiz, nodding toward Jimmy. "All torqued up. Look at his eyes. He's a fucking bat."

"He doesn't sleep," I say.

Jimmy waves us closer.

"When we talked a couple hours ago, Carver, I didn't have much. Then I plugged Christensen's image into this cool facial recognition app. We're not supposed to use it—don't tell anybody, Captain Ortiz," says Jimmy, laughing. "I mean a whole lot of civil rights, privacy violation shit. The technology is beautiful. Beautiful. Designed by a little guy who looks like he sings in a boy band. Probably a billionaire now." Jimmy strikes two keys. "Look. Christensen's like where's fucking Waldo. He's everywhere."

Ortiz and I lean down toward the screens.

"Is that the guy?" says Ortiz.

"Yeah," says Jimmy. "Stick up his ass. Norwegian. Must be the cold."

A mosaic of Christensens looks back. A few pictures are blurry; most are clear. A man captured in moments. Some are posed, others candid, and I think we are strangers to ourselves when glimpsed unexpectedly. I'm sure Christensen would feel that way now, peering into himself, knowing it's him but wondering about the time, place, and date. The increments, the pixels and evolution, the evidence that we were here, we were there. Most of the pictures are Christensen with other men in restaurants, boardrooms, companies, a few in a hunting lodge, a couple in front of a castle, one at a zoo, another on a yacht, and three of him when he is much younger, dancing with a woman at a reception. He is in a tuxedo; she's in a gold gown. She is white-gloved and thin, hair falling past her shoulders. A sliver of a smile. It is night and they are dancing along windows. The glass reflects the room, faces, tables, waiters, but none are in focus—only Christensen and the woman, a wife or lover perhaps. I wonder who took the pictures and where the woman is now, what happened to her as the years went by.

"A lot of this shit," says Jimmy. "Most of these were posted by his friends on Facebook and Instagram, mostly Facebook. Guys his age don't 'gram. Nothing on TikTok. No surprise there. But look, a few from a street camera when he's out walking his dog. You put an image out there and it's everyone's. Nothing's your own anymore." Jimmy sips a Red Bull, bites a piece of pizza. "You guys want a slice?"

"It's nine a.m.," says Ortiz.

"Pizza knows no time," says Jimmy, laughing and pointing to an image, clicking on it.

"I want you to see the full screen, Carver. You're gonna love me. Look. There. Who is that?"

I lean closer and follow Jimmy's finger to the center of the screen. Two men sit at a linen-draped table in the middle of a crowded room. The soft glow from a chandelier. A bottle of red wine between them.

"That's Milton Archer," I say.

"Bingo," says Jimmy.

Ortiz bends in and looks.

"He and Christensen," says Jimmy. "Two guys on the town."

"Where?" I say.

"Budapest. Two thousand five," says Jimmy. "Some conference for right-wingers and neo-whatevers. See this guy over here." Jimmy's finger moves left. "That's Viktor Orban, president of Hungary. He wasn't president then, just some raving nationalist. Look here." Jimmy's finger traces right. "Sven Tomalsen. Know who he is? Of course you don't. He's the head of an alt-right Danish party. He's worth, like, five hundred million euros. It's like a party for Nazis. I face-checked a lot of these guys. Mostly all Europeans. No women. See this? Little swastika flags on sticks. On every table."

"They're not exactly swastikas," I say.

"Close enough," says Jimmy. "Redesigned for a new century."

"Where'd this come from?" says Ortiz.

"I told you," says Jimmy. "The ether. Someone posted it, sent it to a friend. It got reshared a few times, slipped beyond the firewalls."

Milton Archer has his hand around a glass. He and Christensen are looking at each other. A few men stand around them, smoking and drinking. A dinner has broken up and the room has relaxed in an end-of-the-evening feel—ties loosened, jackets off. Desserts half eaten. I scan the screen, looking at the faces. White men of means and hate. The kind of men who fund and inspire the lesser, desperate kind to do their work. Each carries a smug contentment, the smirks of money and secrets, of men untouchable. I wonder how Trey Bryant would paint them—the lines he would use, what he would pull from them and put on his canvas. What would look back into the world? I am drawn deeper into the screen, as if discovering an illicit scrapbook. Then I see him. A small face in the bottom corner, far from Archer and Christensen, gazing in from the edges.

"That's Bill Crenshaw," I say.

"Who?" says Ortiz.

"The head of the Flag."

"This guy?" says Jimmy, zooming in on Crenshaw's face.

"That's him," I say.

"Doesn't he have a brother?" says Ortiz.

"Charlie," I say. "I don't see him. Charlie's too rabid for this crowd."

"Bill looks lonely," says Jimmy. "All by himself at the table."

"Maybe he doesn't know many of them," says Ortiz. "First-timer. Looks a little uncomfortable. Out of his depth. Lost boy."

"They all know one another," I say. "This is the connection. Archer, Crenshaw, and Christensen."

"You mean Albert Speer," says Jimmy.

"Who's Albert Speer?" says Ortiz.

"Hitler's architect," I say. "Christensen's alias. He writes checks to the Flag."

"What the . . . ?" says Ortiz.

"Complicated shit, Captain," says Jimmy, reaching for another slice of pizza.

"So what are you saying, Carver?" says Ortiz. "What connection? I see a bunch of neo-Nazi types in a room. Probably a fundraiser, rally-the-troops kind of thing, who knows? A secret conglomerate of capitalists. A meeting for white men to keep ruling the planet. Nationalist, supremacist bullshit, okay, but you said connection and you're working on Skid Row murders."

"The Flag's flyers are all over Skid Row."

"The Crenshaws denied they have anything to do with those," says Ortiz. "Can you prove different? Can you prove they're involved in the homicides?"

"Not yet, but look," I say pointing to the screen. "Crenshaw told me he didn't know Archer. But he does."

"He's in the same room with him. It's a big room. Doesn't mean he knows him."

"C'mon," I say. "You must see it."

"I see three guys, okay? And I'll even buy your premise, three guys connected to the same ideology. Christensen sends checks to the Flag. So what? How's he connected to murders in LA? Archer's allowed to believe any hateful shit he wants. We know he's a right-winger. A closeted Nazi. Whatever. I've read a little about him. But how is he connected? Not hunches and circumstantial shit, Carver. But something I can take to the DA."

"Has Archer gotten to the mayor?"

"You mean after you ambushed him at the beach?" says Ortiz. "I don't know if he has or hasn't. I haven't heard about it. All I want to hear about is hard evidence."

"You sleep well last night?" I say. "'Cause you're being kind of a prick."

"No," says Ortiz, "I'm being a cop. I'm not saying it's not there." He nods toward the screen. "But we need more than this fifteen-year-old picture of guys at a dinner party."

Jimmy stands and stretches. Red Bull, glassy eyes.

"Let me run all faces again, see what's what," he says.

Ortiz taps me on the shoulder. We walk out of Jimmy's lair. We elevator down and head across the plaza toward Demitasse. We don't speak. Ortiz opens the door. I step in. We sit at the window. A gust of wind. Rain falls; cops and lawyers scurry. Ortiz smiles and orders espressos from Mariella. She smiles back. Ortiz likes seeing her face. It reminds him of things that aren't his but, perhaps in another time, could have been.

"You still got it for her," I say.

"I'm married," he says. "You know what it is. I just like knowing she's here."

We look out the window and back to one another.

"Keep working the Skid Row thing, Carver. It's not there yet."

"We know where it's going."

"Just get it done, okay? Lot of pressure from above."

"You must be on the mayor's good side," I say. "You looked official with him the other day at the press conference."

"I saw you in the back."

"I slipped out before the cameras turned."

"Best way to handle that crowd."

"I miss her."

"I know you do."

He stirs in a sugar. Mariella brings water, glides away.

"You haven't said much about the Castillo collar," he says.

"Bryant put it down. Case closed."

"You gonna let it stay that way?"

The rain falls harder. The café is quiet. Ortiz and I don't say anything for a long time.

CHAPTER 23

"Detective?"

"Who's this?"

"It's Manny, man. How come you don't know when I call?"

"You call from a different number each time."

"It's that bitch Wanda. She keeps changing phone cards."

"What's up, Manny?"

"Some motherfuckers stole my tent last night. Came by when I was playing guitar down the other corner, you know, the way I do."

"You need a new tent?"

"I can get my own fucking tent."

"Why are you calling, then?"

"You better get over to where Kiki stay."

"Why?"

"Just go, man."

I drive past San Pedro to the underpass where Kiki lives. Tweakers huddle around her mattress, faces aglow in candlelight. A few are stoned. Others are bent and weeping.

Two are going through crates of her belongings. Kiki lies in the arms of Marcus Robinson. He sits with her against the wall. She's frail and white, a bone child with bruised veins and needle marks. She wears underpants and a T-shirt, and her red hair is wild and tangled, as it was in life. I step closer. Marcus holds up a hand.

"Let it be a little longer," he says. "Ain't no need to take her right now."

"When?" I say.

"I came by last night and slept here. Woke and she was gone."

"OD?"

"What do you think, man? Look at this girl. Bad heroin and fentanyl shit been going around these streets."

Marcus wipes a tear, pulls Kiki closer. She seems a doll in his arms.

"I thought she might make it, you know?" he says. "Some of them do. But she was too much into this." He rubs a hand over her track marks. "Her baby died about a year ago. Stopped breathing before she could get it out. Slipped into the world dead. A junkie's baby boy. That was the end there. That's when Kiki gave up."

"She have family?"

"Crazy-ass coal miner dad in Kentucky. That's long broken. She was alone."

"She had you," I say.

"It wasn't like that. I roam. I told you before, I can't stay in one place. I'd see her from time to time. Stay with her on this rat-ass mattress. She kept a blanket for me, and sometimes we'd . . ."

He lets the words fall away. I sit next to him against the wall. I flash my badge and the tweakers scatter to the edge of the overpass, where the last of the day's light is dimming. Cars pass in the distance; nighttime boozers wander the sidewalk with fresh bottles. A tattered preacher stands on a box, waving a Bible and shouting about golden calves and Israelites. The boozers push him off. He runs west, shouting parables. The sidewalk quiets. I reach for Kiki's wrist. She is brittle and cold, her pulse long gone. Marcus, still holding her, fishes a cigarette out of his camo pants pocket. He lights it and blows smoke over her hair.

"In Nam," he says, "sat with a lot of guys like this. It's peaceful to let them pass through you. I never minded the dead."

"I saw my father dead."

"How?"

"Beaten."

"You a boy?"

"Yes."

The wind picks up; a few candles go dark. Marcus is not ready to let Kiki go.

"You been okay, I mean, before this?"

"Since them white motherfuckers jumped me, you mean?"

"Yes."

"They ain't been back," he says. "You know who's been burning tents?"

"I think so, but not enough yet."

"Don't let it go too long."

A tweaker walks over with a flower. He slides it into Kiki's hair. He puts a blanket over her. He turns and joins the others. Marcus watches him.

"Those boys got her hooked," he says. "Can't blame them. But still, they're the ones who did it. Used her sometimes, too." He kisses Kiki's forehead. "You, me, and these guys are the only ones who will know she's gone. Isn't that some bullshit?

Just the sorry-ass bunch of us. The girl should have had more, but that's bullshit, too. She's a junkie." He looks at me, looks at Kiki. "I'm going now. I guess you know who to call. They still bury them out at the place? I been there a few times, but I'm not going back. Sad little place. Even the ground don't want them."

"Where are you going?"

"On a long roam."

He lays Kiki on the mattress. He stands in his camo pants and boots. He pulls on a jacket and lifts his duffel. "Stay here till the men come," he tells me. He walks east out of the underpass and disappears into an alley. Night falls. I call the coroner. I sit next to Kiki. I pull the blanket up to her chin, touch her hair. I wonder what her trip to LA was like, years ago, leaving Kentucky, crossing state lines on a bus, seeing the country in window flashes, maybe believing it was waiting out there, beyond the driver's windshield—a place for her. She was a junkie. Needles and sidewalks. That was her place. She couldn't have known it then, or maybe there was a voice inside not listened to, a current to swim against. I lean my head against the wall. I am tired of bodies—the endless flow of them, the faces, the way they look into a sky they cannot see, lips holding words they will not speak. I pull one of Kiki's crates closer. Toilet paper, scarf, a shoe. The rest has been taken. A blue light shines; doors open. The bag is folded out; a zipper whines. The blanket is pulled off Kiki. Her skin is bright in the dark. She is small and thin, a run of bones. A scrap born and died. Hands in rubber gloves lift her. It is their work. The zipper, the crinkle. Footsteps, voices on a radio. The doors slam and the van drives away, its blue light seen for blocks and then gone.

I sit against the wall, pull my phone out. I play "Golden Slumbers," the song Kiki's dad sang to her when she was a girl and couldn't sleep. I keep the sound low, as if a man were beside me, telling me things. My father played Sinatra. He sang to himself, never to me, but sometimes I could hear him through the bedroom door, his voice trailing down the hall and into my mother's arms. I see him, too, in the mind's eye, holding her in those moments there were never enough of, when the house forgot its rage, and my father stepped out on the back stoop and looked into a sky clear and blue. A sky with no transgression.

I go to my car and sit. In the hour before dawn, I get on the 10 and drive toward Malibu.

CHAPTER 24

He is alone on the water. He sits on his board, tip pointing to low clouds, waiting for a wave. One rolls by. He lets it pass. Then another. He sits. Bobbing. Eyes on the horizon. He paddles farther out, getting smaller, but the sea has gone slack. The good waves will come with tomorrow's tides. He paddles toward shore, catching a short run, a spray of white. The splinters of a new sun on him. He picks up the board and walks to his towel.

"You may as well bring a board, Detective, if you're going to keep appearing like this," says Milton Archer. "Are you wearing last night's clothes? You don't look well, if I may say."

He drops his board, sits on the towel. Beads of water run off his wet suit.

"It'll be a good day," he says, looking at the sky. "But mornings often have deceptive promise." He wipes his face with his hand. "I thought I was clear last time we met. I have nothing to say. Is this the intimidation phase? Trying to get 'into my head'—is that the language? I am not who you want.

I am not your man. Why this fixation? I told my lawyer this. I'm sure he called the mayor. You may have heard. My lawyer's very good, but he's a fretful sort. Lawyers have to be these days, with so many men going down. White men of a certain kind. Yes, I think the age of men is coming to an end. Pity. It was a good run." He looks at me, then to the ocean, a thin wire of anger in his voice. "I wonder what the new ones will do. The Blacks, Asians, trans-whatevers, and the Latinos, who never tire of shouting out all the supposed injustices done to them. You'd think the immigrants had it worse than the Blacks. Name me one Latino country that works. No wonder they come here. Come here and bitch, crossing the border like they're owed. Imagine what they'll do to this country. The future will not be pretty. No, I'm sorry to say, we're on our way down. Jeff Bezos knows. He's building rocket ships to the stars."

"You weren't so talkative last time," I say.

"I've been thinking a lot. You do that out there," he says, pointing to the water, "when the waves don't come."

"How long have you known Oskar Christensen?"

"Intimidation and now the blunt approach," he says. "You know, Detective, you remind me of that Greek, the one who ran for miles to warn of war. What was his name? Pheidippides. That's it. Sitting here in the sand, rumpled, tired, you look like you've run a great distance. You look spent." He breathes out, shakes his head, but doesn't ask for his fretful lawyer. His face is shaven, a few lines around the eyes. Sharp in profile—aging, yes, but a face of vigor. "I've known Oskar more than thirty years. Corporate boards mostly. We'd see each other in Europe occasionally. He's made a few trips out here. We're not close friends, but we share the same ideas. He was an Olympian, you know."

I hand him the photograph Jimmy printed.

"That's Oskar and me," he says. "My, my. That's a while back. I think at a dinner in Budapest. Yes, it is. I'm sure of it. Where did it come from?"

"The ether," I say.

"A lot in the ether, I suppose. Maybe I should call my lawyer." He says nothing for a minute, watches the waves, turns to me. "This dinner was to raise money for political parties in Europe."

"Right-wing fanatic parties," I say.

"Call them what you like. I think in a democracy anybody can be represented. Even liberal fanatic parties, of which, in my mind, we have too many."

"Do you know Christensen's pen name?"

"Pen name?"

"Alias."

"No."

"Albert Speer."

Archer laughs.

"How wonderful," he says. "A little over the top. That's so Oskar, though. He's quite a character. A prankster, but you wouldn't know to look at him. 'Albert Speer' is a bit further than I would go. I wonder if most people even know who Speer was. It's a clever allusion. A kind of wink, I think."

"Do you know who he writes checks to?"

"Many people, I would guess."

"This man," I say, pointing to the corner of the frame. "Bill Crenshaw. The founder of the Flag."

"The Flag?"

I hand him a flyer.

"Oh, this thing. You showed me this last time. Skid Row fires, right?"

"Yes. You said you didn't know the Flag."

"I don't."

"But there you and Crenshaw are in the same room with Albert Speer."

"That was many years ago. Am I supposed to remember all the faces in a room? You'll have to do better."

"There's another alias, too. PureLand."

"That's quite Aryan," he says. "Is that Oskar's, too?"

"We don't know whose it is. Is it you?"

"No, Detective, it's not me. But I like the ring of it. PureLand. That sums it up perfectly."

"Whoever it is posts on the Flag's website about getting rid of the homeless in LA so Skid Row can be developed. And, I quote, 'so this great city can thrive again.'"

"I share that sentiment," says Archer, standing and unzipping the top of his wet suit as if shedding a skin. "But I don't know this PureLand. I do know Oskar, as you can see. I know he's further to the right than I am. I don't know how far, but he has his views. Very European-centric. Europe is the heart of nationalism. Two World Wars were fought over it. It has been trying to become something else, to go against what it is. It can't. Not in the end. Europe is quite right-wing at the core. As for this Crenshaw," he says, looking closer at the photograph, "he may have been in the same room, but I do not remember meeting him, and I certainly know nothing of the Flag."

"Christensen does."

"That's his business. I don't know why I'm still sitting here talking to you. I am not part of this. I don't know about your tent burnings. Do I want the homeless cleared out of Los Angeles? Of course. Do I want a border wall? Most definitely. Am I a supremacist? There are many iterations of that, but if I look at myself through your eyes, then yes, I am. Too many immigrants, too many on welfare. Too many who don't want to aspire to what they can be, because they have found easier ways. This destroys. Inclusion destroys the very thing that allows it in. Like an infection. Little by little, it destroys. Civilizations die. You can see it now. I fund right-wing causes. I helped swiftboat Kerry. I despise Obama. That smugness. Hillary's a psychotic in a pantsuit. And Trump is all the things he appears to be. Despite all his bumbling, lying, and conniving—the man himself cares only about money—he's made this country face the existential question: Who are we?"

"We're not that."

"We are more that than you think. Don't be condescending, Detective. That's what gets the left into trouble."

"Who said I was on the left?"

"I don't know or care what you are. But condescension is the fatal flaw of liberals. Trump has played them all so well. They thought he was a circus act. But look. The circus is in the White House. Maybe not for much longer. But he got there. He's got this singular belief in his own lies and bullshit. His gap between perception and reality is extraordinary. That got him elected. How do you defeat a man whom truth will not bring down?"

He glances at the photograph once more and hands it to me.

"You still don't believe me, do you, Detective?"

"I see three men in a room."

"But you don't see the picture."

"We're not done," I say. "I'm looking into everything."

"I'm sure you are. You are Pheidippides."

He picks up his board, throws the towel over his shoulder.

"Goodbye, Detective."

He turns.

"Who matters in this world you want to create?" I say.

"That's a question for another day," he says, not looking back.

I watch him walk away briskly over the sand. He gets to the highway, arrows his board into the back of his Thunderbird convertible. He drives into a new day, far from Kiki and Marcus Robinson, far from the Latinas on their bus rides into Santa Monica, far from all the things he hates. Pheidippides. What an asshole. But I do feel as if I've run a hundred miles. Sandpipers race along the surf line, following its curves like whispers. The beach is empty. The surf boys are other places. It's cold. I pull my jacket tight. I lie back and look into a sky of promise. Is that what Archer said? I listen to the waves. They rise and fall out of tune. I close my eyes. I could sleep. I could sleep for as long as Pheidippides ran. I get up and walk to the car. Jimmy has called. Ortiz, too. Two calls from Mariana Sanchez. Bryant has texted me a picture of one of Trey's slaves.

> You see what I mean, I had to escape. lol. #history.

An email from Dylan—nothing but a subject line: "I'm soooooooooooooooooooo bored. Let's play."

The phone rings.

"Detective Carver?"

"Yes."

"Sergeant Tremble here. We've been running the plate number you gave us. It's only a partial. Best we can do is a couple of possibles given the variables we had to factor. What's still registered. What's not. All kinds of shit. Even then I'm not sure. Neither of them matches the kind of vehicle your witness described. Something old, seventies, maybe—isn't that what he said?"

"The witness is a homeless pill popper, not entirely reliable."

"Most people can't keep seven numbers and letters in their head more than five seconds. I'm amazed when we do get an accurate match. A rare thing."

"He said three guys in an old car drove into Skid Row and threw Molotovs at tents. There's video, too, but it doesn't show the make of that car."

"Okay, well, good luck, then. Here's the two possibles. One registered to a Sam Li. A 1994 BMW. San Marino address. The other is to a Jimena Guerrero, 1983 Ford pickup. Saco address. Up near Bakersfield. Almond country. I know your guy didn't mention a pickup, but it's a close plate match. I don't think that truck's been on the road for years, though. Nothing active with DMV. That's as good as we could do. Sorry it took a while. Short-staffed here. I'll text you the street addresses and put them in a report."

"Thanks, Sergeant."

I drive south on the coast highway, stop for a coffee at a pier, and after thumbing through the *Los Angeles Times*, which has been running editorials on the mayor's "homeless problem," I hop on the 10 to the 110 and head north to San Marino, a patch of green and comfortable wealth tucked south of Pasadena. I check the address Tremble texted: a brick Tudor with stained-glass windows and an ancient door. A magnolia tree stands out front. The BMW parked in the driveway is slate blue and well kept. A man on his knees is gardening in a beekeeper's hat, long-sleeve shirt, and gloves. He turns dirt with a small shovel.

"Mr. Li?"

He looks up through the mesh of his hat.

"We don't want any," he says.

"Any what?"

"Whatever you have."

"I'm a detective."

"No crime here," he says, lifting his hat off and smiling. "Too much rain to garden. The soil is drenched. I've never seen this much rain in one season, even in winter. More is coming."

I show him my shield, hand him my card. A black Lab runs out of the house, circles him, jumps on me, and takes off down the sidewalk.

"Very complicated day," says Li. "We have a wedding. How can I help you?"

I nod to the BMW. "Is that your car?"

"Yes," he says, glancing to the curb at my Porsche. "I see you like vintage, too, Detective, but you should take more care. Rust in the back."

I ask him where he was on the night of the tent burnings. He slips off his gloves and pulls a phone from his pocket. He scrolls.

"I was in Los Robles," he says.

"Overnight?"

"Visiting my cousin."

"This car with you the whole time?"

"Where else would it go? What has happened, Detective?"

"I'm looking into a case. Your plates came up as a possible match. But I see they're not."

"What kind of case?"

"Just something we're checking into."

"That could be many things," he says, slipping his gloves back on. "I hope you find it."

"Who's getting married?"

"My sister's kid. Third time. It's like shopping for him."

"Maybe this time it'll take."

"No. He's a tragic case, but what can you do? Family."

He kneels and reaches for his shovel.

"Hope you find what you're checking into, Detective."

I walk toward my car and call Ortiz.

"I'm going to Bakersfield to check on a plate."

"Skid Row case?" he says.

"Got a partial match."

"Never cared for Bakersfield."

"You don't farm."

"I don't like country music, either," he says. "I do like Taylor Swift, though."

"I wouldn't have thought. She's not really country. She's her own thing."

"Whatever. Seems country to me."

"I saw Archer again," I say.

"I wish you wouldn't keep doing that. You don't have anything, Carver."

"I'm getting there."

"You on the Five?"

"Yes."

"How's traffic?"

"Light all the way to the valley."

"It's good when that happens."

He hangs up.

I get off the 5 and head north on 99 at Wheeler Ridge, passing Panama, Gosford, Bakersfield, and north to Saco, a sliver of a town along the old Southern Pacific Railroad line. A land of almond farmers and oil drillers. I turn onto a dirt road, then another, dust trailing me in the dry air. The sun is out. I roll down the window and let it warm me. The sky is clear, weeks of rain forgotten. I cross an intersection. Jimena Guerrero's house—two stories, faded yellow with a slanting roof—rises on the left. I turn through a broken gate and into the driveway. The porch is shaded by trees. A barn of dark wood planks stands at the edge of a field, the sun bright on its tin roof. A woman steps out from the screen door. She's small, print dress, ankle boots, white hair in bobby pins, a purse hanging from her arm.

"You here to take me?" she says.

"Take you where?"

"The store. I called the Uber."

"I'm not from Uber. I'm Detective Sam Carver."

"You're not the Uber?"

"No."

She sighs.

"The Uber never finds me. Must not be from around here."

She sits on the porch steps.

"I'm from Los Angeles," I say. "I'm looking into a case."

"I hate it when the Uber doesn't come. I'm all dressed."

She opens her purse and pulls out a flask.

"Kombucha," she says. "My granddaughter taught me how to make it."

She stares at me, then at the road.

"Do you have a 1983 Ford pickup?" I say.

"I don't know what kind it is, but there's one in the barn. It's old. Doesn't run. My cousin took away the engine a long time ago. It's just sitting in there. It was my husband's. He's been dead a while. I drove it after, but then I stopped driving. Bad eyes."

"Are the license plates still on it?"

"I wouldn't know. This is strange."

"What?"

"A cop instead of an Uber. Something about my old truck. Is there trouble? I'm not good with trouble anymore."

"No trouble. May I look?"

She stands, leaves her purse on the porch, and walks toward the barn with her flask.

"What do you grow?" I ask her.

"That's not my land. Only this house. We tried pistachios and mandarins. Ended up with a small carrot farm. I gave it up when my husband died. I don't like carrots anymore."

Cool air from the cracks in the barn threads over us.

"Lift that latch," she says. "Give it a push. It sticks."

The door swings open. Needles of light shoot through holes in the roof. A small tractor is parked on the side, beneath beams of cobwebs and wasp nests.

"It's been a while since we used it," she says. "I liked coming out here when I was young. It was quiet. Like a church. I went to church, too, but this was better. More your own place. Smell it. Earth and time, my husband said that about this land. *Earth and time.* He loved that expression. After we put the kids down, he and I would sit right over there and share a cigarette. Sometimes we'd walk to the fields. They were wide and dark as the sky." She sips from the flask, points to the pickup against the back wall. "There's the truck. Not much of anything now."

Tires flat, headlights missing. Scavenged over time. I bend down. Two screw holes shine. I rub a finger over them. The back plate was recently removed. I feel the ground for screws but find nothing.

"Anyone been in here in the last few weeks?" I say.

"No."

"You said your cousin removed the engine."

"That was long ago. He's dead now."

"Any children, grandchildren, or friends who could have come and taken parts?"

"My children died. One in an accident, one in the fields. My two grandchildren moved away. I'm alone here."

She caps her flask, slips it into the pocket of her dress.

"Is something wrong?" she says.

"The license plate is missing."

She steps around back and looks.

"They sent you all the way up from Los Angeles for that?"

"The plate matches the plate of a car we're looking for."

"This is a truck. It's gone nowhere."

"I think your plate was stolen."

"I wouldn't know. Only wasps and dust in here."

"Where do your grandchildren live?"

"Seattle and Chicago."

"Can I get their names and numbers?"

"They haven't been here. Who would take a license plate from an old truck?"

"I just want to check. To make sure."

"You think I don't know things. That I'm confused."

"That's not it."

"People do that when you get a certain age," she says. "They think you don't know things."

We walk out of the barn. I close the door.

"Slam the latch tight," she says.

We get to the porch. She pulls her phone from her purse.

"The Uber didn't call. No text, either."

"What do you need?"

"A few things at the market."

"How far is it?"

"Up the road. Ginny's Market."

"I'll take you."

"Will you bring me back?"

"Yes."

"How much?"

"Nothing."

"Let's go, then."

We get in the car.

"Back way," she says, pointing out the window.

We drive over dirt roads, passing shorn fields and rows of almond trees.

"They take a lot of water," she says. "One little almond needs gallons of water. Most people don't know that. Almond farmers steal a lot of water, too. That's a rich man's game. No poor man can sink a well that deep."

I park at Ginny's.

"I won't be long. You're gonna be here, right?"

"Yes."

Jimena walks in. I stand in the sun. I call Jimena's grandchildren: Martin, a teacher in Seattle, and Camila, a set designer in Chicago. They visited Jimena last summer but haven't been back. They can't think of anyone who might have gone into the barn. "Who would have known the truck was there?" says Camila. "Jimena's been alone since our parents died. No one comes around. My husband and I invited her to move to Chicago with us. But she wants to stay. She came to the valley as a girl from Mexico. She worked the fields until my grandfather died."

I drive Jimena and her bag of groceries back to her house.

"You want a sandwich?" she says. "I bought ham."

"Thank you, but I have to get back to LA."

"I was there once. We brought carrots down to the market. We thought we'd open a little stall. We saw other people do it. Sell our carrots in the city. My husband liked the idea. But it was too far. It must be all different now. I see it on the news sometimes."

I lift her groceries and carry them to the front porch. Jimena passes me and opens the screen door. The house is small: a couch, a few chairs, two bedrooms off the living room. Photographs of Martin in a Little League uniform, ball cap tilted sideways, the green field spread behind him, and of Camila, missing teeth in a First Communion dress, and later as a young woman looking over the Chicago skyline from a balcony in a high-rise. Her hair is long and black, her face half-lit in the dusk reflecting off windows. Jimena stops in front of Camila. "Like an angel," she says. "So many boys. But a good girl." Jimena leads me to the back of the house, to a tiled kitchen floor of white and cerulean-blue, which I imagine must have been an extravagance for a family of carrot farmers. I set the bags on the table. Jimena taps my arm. She points to a corner of the floor. Her name and her husband's—Izan—are written in paint beneath a crucifix on the wall. She stares at them, Izan's in blunt letters, hers in calligraphy. She opens the curtains over the sink. Light pours in. She stands in it for a moment, her hands, small and nicked, aglow on the porcelain. "There once was a tree out there," she says. "Lightning hit it one night and it burned down." She turns and unpacks her groceries.

"Look, I have ham," she says. "You want a sandwich?"

"No, thank you. I have to go."

I head south on the 5. Clouds appear over Santa Clarita. I drive into the rain.

CHAPTER 25

The phone rings.

"Barry Wilkins. Oregon State Police."

"You're better than an alarm clock," I say.

"Hell, it's already six a.m." He laughs.

I sit up on the couch. Throw the blanket off.

"Went to the Crenshaws last night," he says. "I showed Bill the picture you sent from that Nazi thing in Budapest. Bill takes it, sits down, and studies it, you know, like some ghost from the past just reappeared. Brother Charlie gets in my face. Says I'm harassing them. Says, I 'got no legal right.' Pain in the ass. Amazing how brothers can be so different in temperament. I tell Charlie to back off or I'll cuff him. He goes off and sulks in the corner. Like a scolded dog or a little kid."

"What did Bill say?"

"Nothing for a long time," says Wilkins.

"You in the car again? I hear car noises."

"Heading downstate to serve a warrant. I don't know what

you hear, though, just tires and road and a whole lot of quiet
woods. No one else out."

"That's what it is. Silent but not. The sound of moving."

"You need coffee, Carver."

"Water's on. So Bill's got nothing to say?"

"Contrary. Bill opens up. Says he remembers that night
in Budapest. Changed his life. That's when he—and I'm
using his words—'committed myself to the cause. I felt a
brotherhood.' I'm thinking, where's he going with this? He
says Oskar Christensen gave a speech about immigrants and
refugees spoiling the 'white stock of Europe.' How God had
ordained the white man to rule over all his creations: animals,
Blacks, browns, yellows—you name it. It got to Bill. Made
him a believer."

"Did he meet Christensen?"

"Says he only 'shook the great man's hand.' He sent
Christensen a letter after he got home. The Flag was nothing
much then, not fully formed. Bill was still searching.
Christensen wrote him back and encouraged him. Couple
years later, Bill sent Christensen a link to the Flag's website.
They swapped emails but never saw each other again. I asked
if he thought Christensen was the Albert Speer sending the
Flag money. Bill said he would have no idea of knowing about
Albert Speer. A man can support whatever cause he wants,
under whatever name. Bill's words. I think he's maybe right."

Wilkins takes a breath. I imagine him lifting a cup to his lips
to spit his snuff. "My gut, Bill doesn't know, or decided he
didn't want to know, who Albert Speer is. I went over his tax
forms and other paperwork. He declares all donations. Meets
disclosure requirements."

"You sound like an accountant," I say.

"Income forensics—part of the job."

"What about Milton Archer?"

"Bill zeros in on Archer's face. Real close. Says he didn't meet him in Budapest. Saw him from a distance in the room. It was a big room. Bill's words. Bill said he was new to the cause. It was his first meeting of the Nazi sort other than small rallies in Oregon. Bill didn't know a lot of people. Claims he still doesn't know Archer except by reputation—you know, billionaire right-winger. My gut, he's telling the truth."

"Your gut tells you a lot."

"Guiding principle."

"There's got to be a connection. It's too coincidental."

"Send me more when you get it. Always happy to help."

"You've got doubts."

"A little skeptical."

"The Flag flyers on Skid Row."

"Anyone could have done that. If you were going to start burning people up, would you advertise it?"

"These guys are all about brand."

"ISIS is about brand. I don't know about these guys."

"They're all the same. They want notoriety. To be paid attention to."

"Maybe, I don't know."

"You think Charlie could have gone rogue?"

"Charlie's mean. Probably has it in him. But he wouldn't take a shit without Bill's blessing."

"Where are you now?"

"With this case? Metaphorically?"

"In the car."

"Coming through the Tillamook woods on the way to Neskowin along the coast. You know it?"

"No."

"Green until you hit the ocean."

"Bill could be good at playing dumb."

"Wouldn't be the first. He's a believer. I could see it in him. A real soldier for the cause."

"Thanks for your help on this," I say.

"You'll get there."

I hang up, pour coffee. I sit in the chair by the window and lift Lily's ashes. So small a box. I'll take her soon and scatter her over the place she belongs. I pull the gold ribbon and open the box, touch her gently with a finger, feel the slight cool, the almost insubstantial softness of what body and bone become, and the sacred loss of what was, here, ash-gray and silent in my hands. I close the box and slide it under the chair.

I make more coffee and call Ortiz, tell him about Jimena Guerrero and her old truck.

"Could be our plate, huh?" he says. "I love what you can find in barns."

"Crenshaw denies that Archer or Christensen has anything to do with the Flag."

"Surprise."

"Where are you?"

"Heading in. That crazy fuck come up with anything else?"

"Who? Jimmy?"

"The bat in the room with all the computers."

"He's still looking."

"All changed, hasn't it, Carver? Catching a guy."

"Modern world. Technology is your friend."

I hang up. Sit back. The phone rings again.

"Is this Detective Carver?"

"Yes."

"Jonathan Morrow. I represent Milton Archer. You must stop harassing my client."

"I like the beach in the morning."

"You're harassing him, Detective. If you keep this up, I must inform you, action will be taken. We will file suit."

"He was willing to talk. He's a big boy."

"You'll not speak to him again without my being present. Is that clear?"

"He said you were a fretful man. Are you fretful?"

"You've been warned, Detective. Goodbye."

I reach for a notebook. Write. Names, lines, connections, all expanding, folding out. It helps me see. My story of a case. I have hundreds of notebooks. Diaries of crimes. I mix myself in with perps and vics. A mostly reliable narrator. That's what Lily called me, but she meant in our relationship, and she would tease me that one day she'd find the notebook with her in it. I told her she was in a few, and she said, "No, not the ones with the cases, the one with just us, or don't you have that kind? Maybe, Carver, you only write down things about others. Write down your own crimes." She laughed. I didn't answer. My own crimes. Where to begin? Nothing big, but still, infractions committed along the way, known and unknown marks left on others. The things we inflict, the things inflicted on us. I told Lily that. And she said in barely a whisper, "Carver, seriously, lighten up." I did. We laughed. We laughed so long that night. We went to the Grand Central Market and ate pizza, and I took Lily's picture next to the neon on the wall, and we walked into the Second Street tunnel and watched skateboarders fly out of the darkness and glide toward the Bradbury Building.

It's night when I close the notebook. Archer. Christensen. Crenshaw. Burning tents. Nazis. Marcus. Kiki. Pages with the word "rain." I shower and make ramen. Music comes from the street. I go to the window. "Summer Wind" plays from a boom box. A woman is dancing on the slick sidewalk beneath the fire escape in front of the Hotel Clark. A few people stand around her. She wears heels, a short black dress, and a fedora pulled low. She sways and spins. A man shadows her in dance and drifts away, but she stays with the song. Words and music from my childhood, when my mother, in the days after my father was gone, would dance in the moonlight of our kitchen. The woman is tall, every movement a long, slow ripple running through her. Like a black scarf in a breeze; a flickering piece of night. She lifts the brim of the fedora. A magician with a trick. A reveal. But I know, and she knows I know. Her eyes look up and find me in the window.

She smiles.

Dylan Cross spins once more and bows.

I run out of my apartment, bolt down four flights of stairs, to the street. She has vanished. The boom box plays "Summer Wind" on repeat. I stand wrinkled, in my socks, with a gun in my hand. A couple looks at me and hurries past. A man in rags picks up the boom box, puts it in his shopping cart, and heads down the sidewalk. The music mixes with traffic noise and disappears. I breathe in, thinking there might be a scent of her, a faint trace in the air. I hadn't seen her in so long—often felt her presence, yes, but to see her again so close, so brazen and dangerous, and if you didn't know the history she comes with, you would think, watching her dance beneath pink-and-orange neon, that she is lovely. But she is not. She is the assassin of my small dream. Yet she is here, invisible in the night, an unfinished file. I tuck the gun into my pocket and return to my apartment. The phone on the counter glows with a message.

All for you, Sam. Love, D.

CHAPTER 26

It's an hour until last call at the Little Easy.

Lenny has the sports pages open on the bar.

"A sin, really, when you think about it, Sam," he says, sliding me a whiskey.

"Who did what to who this time?"

"Astros."

"That's history."

"They're writing about it again."

"Flat-out cheating."

"Robbed the World Series from the Dodgers. Sign stealing. They knew what pitches we were throwing."

"I didn't know you were a Dodgers fan," I say.

"It's the principle."

Lenny folds the newspaper, pushes it down the bar.

"Place looks good," I say.

"I've been straightening up. Polished the piano."

He looks at me.

"You want to play?"

"Not tonight," I say.

Lenny's white shirt is open at the collar; his bow tie dangles. His face is long and red in profile. He has one foot up on the ice bin, his thin body leaning forward, his glasses, pens, and papers scattered over the bar. He could be the captain of a ship in rough seas. His hair is gray, swept back, a slight sheen to it, and his New York accent—just a trace of what it was when I met him years ago—edges his syllables. He pours himself soda water, slides me another scotch.

"On the house," he says.

"You get laid? You're happy."

"Horse came in."

"Yeah?"

"Made a few bucks. Thinking about Cabo. You ever been?"

"Acapulco once."

"No one goes there anymore."

A heavyset guy tosses a twenty on the bar, waves, and walks out.

"So, Sam, you know that guy Michael, the one who runs the homeless clinic or whatever?"

"Michael Ruiz."

"In here the other night. He was in a bad way. Drinking too much, slurring. Kept talking about the homeless. How no one cares. The world is fucked up, that kind of shit. Sounded like St. Francis on a bender—you know, morose, I'd say."

"He's been running that clinic a long time. He could have had a house in Brentwood and a tee time, but he came down here."

"You know him pretty good, right?"

"I know him okay."

"You should talk to him. He seems alone, you know?"

"Aren't we all?"

"No joke, Sam. Guy's in a different way. It's been gradual, you know. You see it with people. Little by little, the world gets at 'em."

"All right," I say. "I've got to see him about a case, anyway."

"The tent burning shit. I think that's what it is. The good doctor can't save 'em."

Lenny reaches for a rag.

"Who does that, anyway—burn people up?"

I cut him a glance.

"I know, I know, open case," he says. "How about the Astros?"

"Cold case."

"Hey, did you hear about this virus in China? This Corona thing. The radio had a big report on it."

"I saw a headline."

"It could be bad if it comes this way. They don't know yet, but it seems pretty nasty."

"Epidemic?"

"Maybe worse. Comes from bats. Like Ebola or something. Remember that? It makes you wonder, you know? All this rain. Can hardly breathe the air most places. It's not good no matter where you look. I worry about this virus."

"It's always the things you can't see."

"The Chinese locked down a city called Wuhan. Won't let anybody in or out. Like millions of people or something."

"No vaccine?"

"Nothing."

"Whales are dying, too."

"Yeah."

"No one knows why."

Lenny tucks the twenty from the bar into the cash register.

"C'mon, Sam, play something."

"You ever notice there's never any women in here?"

"You come too late. Anybody respectable is home."

"You've got it figured out, huh, Lenny?"

"Mostly. You gonna play?"

I take my drink to the piano. I drift through a few things, but nothing takes shape; notes hang shallow, elusive. I return to the bar.

"Not feeling it tonight, huh, Sam?"

"A little off, maybe."

"Gotta play every day to keep it."

"Like anything."

"The discipline of a thing. Lose that and you're fucked."

"I might stop coming here."

Lenny laughs.

"How you holding up, seriously?" he says.

"I don't know anymore."

He polishes a glass, rags the bar, stays close.

"Lily was a good kid," he says. "Quick, you know, always had a wiseass comment, but the good kind, like she liked to keep things moving. Knew herself. Don't get many of those."

He lowers his voice.

"I went to her funeral," he says.

I look at him.

"I did, Sam. I stood at the end of rows of cops. Impressive. All that dark, shining blue standing outside the chapel, spreading over the grass. The flag. Lily's picture in her uniform out of the academy. She had that smile, you know? Smile of a believer. I guess you have to. Looked like a teenager. I stayed for a long time after it was over. Wanted to pay my respects. No grave. I guess she was cremated. Was she, Sam?

I don't answer.

"Remember that first night you brought her in here? 'So,

Carver, this is your dive.' Remember she said that. You played the piano and you two danced. We stayed until breakfast. She went back and made eggs and coffee and we sat right over there and watched the light come up."

Lenny slides me a clean rag. I lift it to my eyes.

"There was something about it," he says. "Three right people in the right place at the right time. Rare thing." Lenny slants the bottle to pour me another. I wave him away. "How about all this rain? You think it's ever gonna stop? It's the world, Sam. Things are going badly."

"Going that way for a while, or haven't you noticed?"

"More dire now. My thinking, anyway. This virus thing."

"You mentioned."

"It bears repeating."

I look at myself in the mirror behind Lenny. I could be almost anyone.

"They still doing that shoot over on Spring?" I say.

"Location manager and a few extras were in yesterday. Financial thriller or something. They were vague about the whole thing. Extras were in suits, dressed like guys in the eighties. That was a big-hair time. Hedge fund guys and big hair. That's what the eighties were. And Reagan, of course. The pope, too, let's not forget JP the Second."

"You should be in a movie, Lenny."

"Surprised I haven't been asked. I've got the face for it."

"Lily loved old black-and-white movies. She'd watch them through the night, one after the other. 'Hey, Carver,' she'd say, 'wake up and check this out.' Loved all the Bogart films. Had a thing for Ray Milland, too. *Lost Weekend.*"

"Classic," says Lenny. "That's going back. Simpler then. Even the bad tragic shit was simpler then."

"That's bullshit."

"Nostalgia, maybe, huh? Makes things seem less bad. My guess. But I like the black-and-white ones."

I listen to the quiet.

"I loved her, Lenny."

"I'm pretty sure of it."

"I keep driving by her place."

"What do you see?"

"Empty windows. Rain on the grass."

"You ever think about all the stuff inside us? Where it all goes? I think about that a lot. Where's all the shit go?"

"It goes when you go."

"I read somewhere that it doesn't go until your name is spoken for the last time. The last time your name is heard in the world, that's when you no longer exist. It's not death."

"It's the last syllable."

"It's centuries for some. Mozart. Shakespeare. Much shorter for most."

"It's what you leave."

"Exactly that."

I look into my glass, then up to Lenny.

"I have her ashes," I say.

"What are you going to do with them?"

"I know a place. A place we had."

"Wonder how it will feel."

"What?"

"Giving her back to the world," he says. "Keep saying her name."

"How about half a shot, Lenny."

"That's a new one. Never poured one of those."

He slides it to me. I sip, a slow taste, letting the warmth spread through me.

"You think anyone really knows us?" says Lenny.

"No."

"Lily didn't know you?"

"A lot, not every speck."

"I guess. Of course, you're not the revealing type."

Lenny smiles.

"Somebody out there knows me."

"Who?"

I don't answer. I slow-sip again. The warmth goes deeper. Lenny puts the bottle on the shelf. He opens the cash register, takes out the day's cash and receipts. Opens his ledger. Writes.

"There are computers and spreadsheets, Lenny."

"This way suits me."

I walk to the window.

"Is it . . ."

"Yes," I say. "Still coming down."

I button my coat. Finish the last sip of my shot. I head into the dark. Down Fifth, up Hill, fog streaking streets, rain falling hard, but I don't mind. I point my face to the night. Feeling lost, as if I should call someone or go back to Lenny. No. It is all mine. I walk into my building, dripping over the floor, past the sleeping guard, into the elevator, down the hall to my apartment, where I keep the lights off and let the cold stay in my bones a little longer.

CHAPTER 27

A tent burns along a chain-link fence at the edge of the Flower District. The flames spread to a dumpster and race into an abandoned building. Homeless faces are lit, as if drawn from outer reaches toward a light in the night. They stand squinty-eyed, wrapped in blankets, talking strange words and madness. A million whispers. The fire crews have it nearly under control; the flames fight and fade; gray plumes roll and press against the sky. I walk over to a barefoot man standing with two uniforms on the corner.

"It's his," says one of the uniforms, nodding to the tent.

I step closer to the man. He's Black, ancient, curled fingers at his lips. Liquor on his breath.

"All burned up," he says. "I need a new place."

"What's your name?"

"Ezekiel."

"From the Bible," I say.

"I don't know about that."

"What happened, Ezekiel? You high? Drunk?"

"A little sip earlier. I don't do that no more. Not in a big way."

"You smoke?"

"No."

"Didn't start it by accident?" I say.

"Hell, no. Who burns up their own place?"

A paramedic hands him a coat, checks his pulse, looks into his yellowed eyes.

"You're okay," she says.

"Okay? Shit, my tent's burned up. Shoes too."

The guy's shivering.

"What happened?" I say.

"I was sleeping. A car come by. Low sound like a animal. It stopped. Went on again and stopped. Then a pop and like a *fsch, fsch* noise." His head jitters. He pulls at the air with his fingers as if trying to find threads of sound in the air. "Fire came fast across the sidewalk. Into my tent. I had the zipper open. Crawled out fast. Thought I might die, but then didn't think so. I have cancer. Gonna die of that. Can't die of two things."

"You want to go to the hospital?" I say. "Get checked out."

"What I got, they can't fix. Already told me."

"We'll get you a tent."

"And shoes."

I tell the uniforms to drive him to a shelter. The tent is charred and wet. I can see Ezekiel's shoes, sodden in black and ash. Bits of cardboard, burned clothes, a pocketknife, its handle melted. Specks of a shattered bottle, probably from the Molotov cocktail, glint on the sidewalk in police lights. It seems like a movie on replay—a loop of fire guys, white-suit guys, confused homeless, yellow tape, reporters, Ortiz in a blue flash, me calling Jimmy Knight to say watch for anything new from PureLand on 8chan.

"Same MO," says Ortiz. "Car, fire, tent."

"This one went a little further," I say.

"That building used to be a piñata factory. Run by a family from Juarez, bunch of kids. Shut down a long time ago."

"It's getting to be a habit," I say.

"Let's stop it, then."

"Where's the mayor?"

"His people are afraid if he shows up at another tent fire, he'll look more like a failure than a protector. Project the wrong image, or some shit."

"Valid point."

"We're going to start double patrols in Skid Row," says Ortiz. "Heavy presence."

"That's a good image."

"Just find who's doing this. It's gotta stop, Carver."

Ortiz walks toward the fire chief. I call Jimmy Knight.

"Nothing yet," he says. "They might not post a video right away."

"They?"

"PureLand, whoever."

"Any more facial recognition hits on Archer, Christensen, or Crenshaw?"

"Not much. Christensen running a red light in Oslo. Traffic camera caught him."

"You can get traffic cams from anywhere, too?"

"I told you, Carver, once an image is in the ether, doesn't matter the source; it's out there for anyone to find."

"How about ours?"

"Been through most of it. But, you know, we don't have complete coverage, not like London or Beijing. I mean, in those places, you can't hide from the lens. Everybody's on TV. Big Brother to the hyper max."

"Let me know if another tent-burning video pops up."

"Anyone dead there?"

"No."

I drive toward Malibu and Escondido Canyon. Three a.m. A cop with questionable motives and nothing solid. I leave the Pacific Coast Highway and wind north. Headlights cut through fog, but then, higher up, the night clears to crystal black. Stars far off. Thicket and scrub. The road narrows; the ocean fans below to my left. This is the edge of the continent, the last prayer before the horizon. I stop in front of Milton Archer's house. Turn off the engine. Bougainvillea on a courtyard wall. I'm parked in front of the security camera at the gate, not in the driveway but just off to the side. At 3:45 a.m., a text from the fire investigator: "Looks like a Molotov. Similar to the others." I lean back in the seat, put on Chet Baker low, that lonely, brilliant horn like a silk thread being pulled through the night. Maybe the same sound the old homeless guy was looking for, the one he couldn't quite find as he stood over his ruined tent. It'll be a few hours. I pull my jacket tight, feel the coldness in my feet. I stare up at the security camera, another face in Jimmy Knight's ether. I find a cigarette deep in the glove box. I crack the window, blow smoke. Fog passes over the windshield, but only for a moment. The sky clears. I drift in and out of sleep.

Dawn. The click and hum of a gate. I wake, lean forward, rub my eyes. My windshield is fogged and blurry. I wipe it with my sleeve. Archer's Thunderbird, a surfboard poking like a wing out of a back window, eases down the driveway through the drizzle. He stops in front of my car and walks toward me in a ball cap and a windbreaker. I roll down my window.

"Early," I say.

"Best time."

"Another tent fire last night."

"Why are you here, then, Detective? Shouldn't you be out investigating?"

"I thought I'd stop by and let you know," I say. "Keep you apprised."

"You enjoy this, don't you?" he says, eyes hard, words barely slipping through his teeth. "This act."

"I'm following leads."

"You're harassing. You have nothing. So you come here in your beat-up car to sit and hope. It's quite sad. You're missing it."

"Missing what?"

"Whatever will lead you to the right place."

"I'm getting there."

"No," he says, "you're not. You're going after the idea of me. Fine, hate me. Hate all I am. But don't confuse that with whoever's setting your fires."

"Did you see me on that?" I say, pointing to the camera on the courtyard wall.

"I called the security company."

"Suspicious car."

"They're on their way. My lawyer called your department. This is going to end. Now. You can sit here until they come. It's a beautiful view on most days, but not today. The clouds are low."

He steps back, turns toward his car. A flash streaks my rearview. Alicia Bryant gets out of her Merc and walks toward Archer and me.

"Detective Bryant," she says, looking at Archer.

"Your colleague has been harassing me," he says. "I want it to stop."

"Why don't you go, Mr. Archer. I'll take care of things with Detective Carver."

She looks at his Thunderbird.

"Is that a James Perse?" says Bryant.

"Yes," says Archer.

"You seem surprised."

"Well, I just . . ."

"Just thought a Black woman wouldn't know dick about surfboards."

"Most people don't," he says. "It's a classic."

"Probably cost three grand or so."

"Do you surf?"

"When I was a girl."

"Amazing," says Archer.

Bryant looks at me, looks at Archer, rolls her eyes. I start to open my door. Bryant leans into it.

"Stay there, Carver," she says.

"You'll take care of this?" says Archer.

"I got a call. Came to see if Detective Carver needed backup."

"Backup?" says Archer. "He's the *problem*."

"Call came in said Detective Carver at this address might need backup. Homicide investigation."

"Homicide?" says Archer.

He points a finger, bites his lips. His face goes red. Bryant doesn't flinch.

"You'll be sued, both of you," he said.

He walks to his Thunderbird and drives away.

"No kidding! Bryant, you surfed?"

"Don't be an asshole," she says. "You're harassing this guy. Ortiz filled me in on the way over. Don't know why he called me to keep your sorry ass from getting into more trouble. If you've got evidence against this guy, bring it. Otherwise, don't fuck it up."

"I'm building a case," I say.

She leans against the driver's side.

"You look like hell," she says.

"Drove out here last night after the fire."

"Just to get into his head."

"Looks like it worked."

"Didn't seem that way to me," she says. "I saw a pissed-off man of privilege. Come at a guy like that too early, you lose him. Bush-league move. What do you have, Carver, seriously?"

"Archer's all over this. I can feel it."

"You didn't answer my question."

I say nothing. The drizzle has stopped. The sky is morning tin with blades of sun. Bryant walks around the car and gets in the passenger side. We look to the ocean: gray-green, whitecaps.

"I surfed one summer," she says. "I knew this boy. He grew up in Hawaii. Navy kid. He was staying a few months with his aunt in Compton. He had an extra board. He took me every morning at five." She shakes her head, laughs. "You really want to know you're Black, go surfing in Manhattan Beach. We didn't even have wet suits. He was good, though, best one out there. He taught me. After a few weeks, I was good, too—not as good as him, but man, I could drop down on a wave and let it sing under me. You know, that's what he'd say: 'Let it sing under you,' and you moving, fast, and for those seconds it's just you, wind, and water." She opens the glove box, closes it. "That's how white people feel every day. That's what he told me."

"He left?"

"Back to Hawaii. Never saw him again."

"What was his name?"

"Michael Lee."

"You remember."

"I remember a lot of shit."

"Let's go surfing," I say.

"I'm not pulling your ass out of the ocean."

"I've surfed."

"You need sleep."

"Tell me a good story, Bryant."

"That was a good story."

"No, a story where you're not the Black girl."

"I'm always the Black girl."

"I know, but you know what I mean."

Bryant cracks her window.

"When I was a kid," she says, "my father brought home an aquarium and twenty fish all in bags. It was amazing. My mother said it was too extravagant, but my father could be like that. Surprise you in that way. We opened all those bags and slipped the fish into the water, and we sat back and watched it like it was TV. All those fish and colors darting around. My dad was happy, and even my mom came out, and we just stayed in front of the aquarium until way past midnight, naming fish and making up stories about them."

She rolls her window all the way down, breathes in.

"All those little fish," she says.

"A metaphor."

"No, Carver, I was too young for metaphors. It was real."

"Are they hard to clean?"

"What?"

"Aquariums."

"Hell, yeah."

"Thanks for coming," I say.

"Two misfits."

"We're not so bad."

"I don't know you that well, Carver, but I see a man in slide."

"Slide?"

"Not good."

"Going down?"

"Yea, but not in free fall. In a slower way. Worst kind of way."

"Odd way to look at things."

"It's what I see," she says. "Lily . . ."

"Let's not talk about her."

"She needs to be talked about."

"She needs to be missed."

I start to say more. The words won't come, but I almost tell her about Dylan Cross dancing on the sidewalk to "Summer Wind." Bryant would think it a delusion. That's what Dylan is: not there yet ever present. *A man in slide.* It sounds frictionless, quiet, tempting. A slow descent. Into what? We sit a little longer. We don't talk. Bryant knows the edges of how far to push. She can be in a place without words, too. Not many can. I like that about her. The clouds break. The sun is on the water, but only for a moment. The clouds close and the water is shadowed again. The rain comes and the ocean disappears from the windshield. Bryant opens her door. "See you, Carver." She runs to her Merc and drives away.

I turn the key, click the wipers. A new day. I drive away from Archer's gate and wind down the hill. The phone rings.

"Carver."

"Jimmy?"

"Yeah, it's me. Who'd you think it was? My number's in your phone. 'Jimmy' pops up, right? That's me."

"Where are you?"

"In my forever place, where else? My laptops and software are working overtime for you, Carver. LAPD doesn't pay me enough. You gotta bring that up with that captain guy who was in here with you the other day. Ortiz, right? Bring it up with him." Jimmy takes a breath. "I've been running down all the shit Archer owns. It's a lot, man. Stuff all over. He's got enough land to make his own map. Downtown—Skid Row, like we thought. Basically, if you think about it, he's kinda like a homeless landlord."

"Too much Red Bull, Jimmy."

"I'm on coffee now. Easing into things. Anyway, here's the greatest hits: Archer owns land and buildings in Santa Monica, Beverly Hills, La Cañada, Pasadena, et cetera, et cetera. That's just in California. The list goes on, man. Worth billions. He's one of those guys, you know, those guys you don't see flying under the radar but have their hands in all the shit that matters. Like invisible power. It's cool, really, to see the world that way. I'm going to buy some property."

"I thought you needed a raise."

"After that," he says.

"Anything connecting him to Christensen or the Flag?"

"Nothing obvious. Maybe shell companies inside shell companies. That'll take time."

"Anything more on photos, facial recognition?"

"No. I've been on land stuff." I hear clicking. Jimmy's scrolling. I can see his face pressed close to a screen. "You know Archer even owns an almond farm?" he says.

I pull the car over.

"What?"

"An almond farm. I like almonds."

"Where?"

"Outside of Bakersfield. Bought the land a long time ago. Do you know almonds need, like, oceans of water to grow? I read that in the *Times*. You wouldn't think, right? It's their density. Almonds are small but dense like bricks."

"What's the name of the farm?"

"Paradise Almonds. His wife's actually on the deed. Must have been a gift. 'Here, honey, here's three thousand acres of almonds.' What the fuck, right?"

Jimmy laughs.

"I was up near Bakersfield the other day," I say. "Running down license plates we got on those partial numbers. Plates had been stolen off a broken-down pickup in a barn near Saco."

"Pretty close to Bakersfield."

"Could be . . ."

"I don't know, Carver. I get it's a pretty cool coincidence, but Archer doesn't strike me as the stealing-license-plates-off-old-trucks kind of guy."

"Text me the farm's address."

"Already did," says Jimmy. "You going up?"

"On my way."

"What's it like out?"

"The rain's stopped. I'm coming down from Malibu. Sky's clear."

"It won't last. I'm looking at weather imagery from this cool app. Looks like more clouds from the west."

"Why don't you go outside and look."

"Virtual world's more reliable," he says. "Get me some overtime, Carver. And pick me up some almonds."

Jimmy hangs up. I head north.

CHAPTER 28

Paradise Almonds lies southeast of Bakersfield, about fifteen miles from Jimena Guerrero's house in Saco. The oven summers and just-above-freezing winters of the San Joaquin Valley are ideal for almonds, like Tuscany and Napa for wine—lands that grow perfection and allow men like Archer to believe they are conspiring with God. I pass Arvin and head toward Fig Orchard. I pick up Route 58, then take a dirt road, passing a few Paradise Almonds billboards. The windshield fills with bloomless orchards. No one is in the rows. The gate is locked. I pull off to the side of the road and park. I take notes. I should have called ahead, but the best leads often happen when you don't. A few cars pass. A helicopter skims low over the orchards and disappears to the northwest. I like this quiet, this space, the earth in browns and greens, and the almond trees a dark army beneath the sky. A knock on the window.

"You lost?"

"No."

I roll down the window.

"Drunk?"

"No."

"A lot of guys drunk this time of year."

"The place looks closed," I say.

"They're done for the day."

"You work here?"

"Used to," says a man about midfifties with a cowboy hat pulled low. "Helped manage Paradise for a while. Started my own business a few years ago. Little north of here. You a buyer? Don't look like one."

"I'm a detective."

"Something happen?"

"I'm from Los Angeles. I came up hoping I'd find Mrs. Archer."

The man laughs.

"You won't find her here," he says.

"I thought she owned the place."

"That may be true, but I don't think she likes almonds."

I get out of the car and stand near the man. A sheathed Ka-Bar as old as he is rides on his hip; his hands are thick and chapped. We look over the land.

"You gotta be careful with almonds," he says. "They're sensitive. Soil. Weather. Can't be too hot, can't be too cold. A frost can wipe you out. Don't want a frost, not here."

"I can barely keep a houseplant."

"It takes a certain type, I guess."

"Mrs. Archer wasn't that type?"

"No. What'd she do?"

"Nothing."

"Drove all the way up here for nothing?"

Small birds scatter past and land in the branches. The air settles.

"Did you know Milton Archer?"

"Met him once or twice," says the man. "Walked him through the orchard years ago. He do something?"

"I'm looking into a case. He might have a connection. How many people work here?"

"A couple hundred at harvests."

"They live here?"

"Some do. Some come and go. Follow the seasons and the fruit."

"I read in the paper that the land is sinking."

"Lot of the valley that way. You gotta suck tons of water from underground to feed an orchard. Take all that water from below, the land sinks. A little bit of hollow beneath, here and there, dips and indentations. You can feel it beneath your feet. Squishy-like."

He takes his hat off, runs a hand over a gray crew cut.

"I didn't like Archer," he says. "Mr. or Mrs. They wanted to own an orchard, you know, just to have it. You can't have something if you don't work it. Not in their blood. Don't know why they called it Paradise Almonds. This land is mostly not paradise."

"So, they don't come here much."

"Not that I recall. Never looked for 'em much, either. That type of people. I think they have a house in Malibu."

"They have a lot of houses."

"I would imagine."

He scans the orchard, looks back at me. He puts his hat on.

"Peaceful this time of year," he says. "You get much peace in LA?"

"Rarely."

"Figured."

The birds lift from the trees.

"I used to date a girl in LA. Way back. She wanted to be something she wasn't."

"City's full of those."

"I liked that she was trying, though, you know, like she wanted it so bad. I admired it until it drove me crazy. If you're going to drive that far every weekend, you want a smooth landing. She was anything but."

"She make it?"

"No. I called her a few years ago, just to say hi. She had moved back to where she came from. Her voice was different. I felt sad about that."

A car slows and passes.

"I gotta go," he says. "Hope you solve whatever you came for."

He drives away in his pickup; a phone rises to his ear. I head for Jimena's.

It's dusk when I arrive and roll through the broken gate. The porch light is on. I can see Jimena sitting in the living room in the dim flare of a TV. I knock. She opens the door; her white hair hangs combed and long over a print dress—a different color but the same pattern as the one she was wearing when we met a few days ago. She pushes open the screen door, looks up, squints, slides on silver-rimmed glasses.

"You the Uber man?"

"No."

"I didn't want the Uber."

"I'm Detective Carver. We met the other day."

She leans into the porch light, looks at me, waves me in.

"I remember. You were the one in the barn," she says. "About that old truck."

"Yes. But I wanted to ask you something else."

She turns off the TV and nods for me to sit. A pair of scissors and two shoeboxes of pictures rest on the end table.

"I was going through stuff," she says. "Pictures make you feel good about things not here anymore. They make you feel old, too. I feel old today." She holds up a photograph. "Look how young I was. I don't even remember the year, it's so long ago." She puts the photograph back into the box. "You're not so old," she says. "But it comes. Let's have tea. I have honey."

"I really—"

"We should have tea."

We go to the kitchen and walk across her cerulean-blue floor. I sit at the small table; she places a box of pictures before me. A boy on a tractor, a man in a field, the virgin mother carried on the shoulders of field hands through a candlelit alley. A flame rises on the stove. She pulls down cups and honey from the cupboard, two spoons from a drawer. She doesn't speak. The kettle whistles. She pours two cups, turns to me, and sits down. She laughs.

"I thought you were the Uber. Sometimes I butt-dial. My grandson told me that. 'Butt-dial.' It's a strange expression. The Uber hardly ever comes when I call, but then when I don't, you come. But you're not the Uber."

"I didn't know you could butt-dial an Uber."

"Apparently, you can. I thought that was odd, too."

"I'm Detective Carver."

"You said."

"Do you know anyone who ever worked at Paradise Almonds?"

"Is that around here?"

"About fifteen miles away. On the other side of Bakersfield."

"A lot of almond places around here. We grew carrots mostly. Let me think, Paradise Almonds. Drink your tea. You want more honey?"

I shake my head.

"I like a lot of honey," she says. "My husband and I worked in almonds when we were young, before we went to carrots. But I don't think I've ever heard of Paradise Almonds." She sips her tea. "Let me call Roberto. He might know. I owe him a call, anyway." She lifts her phone. She speaks Spanish for five minutes, her voice younger, alive. She laughs—reminiscing, I suppose, or catching up on the things that can slip past without notice. She sets the phone on the table. "Roberto doesn't know about Paradise Almonds, but he said a cousin worked there two summers ago and then went to mandarins, then back to Mexico."

"Do you know a man named Milton Archer?"

"Doesn't sound like a name that works the fields."

"You said when I was here the other day that no one had been in your barn."

"Not that I know of. You're the only one who's been in the barn. I never go back there anymore. You said someone stole license plates off that old truck. I don't know who could have done that. Maybe kids. You know how they get into things. Drink your tea."

She pulls the shoebox closer, lifts out pictures. A boy running in a rainstorm, mud spattering around him. Men building a house. Jimena in a blue dress, young, her hair tied back, at a dance. A coffin coming down church steps. A lone woman, distant in rows of gravestones. She sips her tea, adds a spoonful of honey. She holds up a larger black-and-white photograph of three people sitting at a table in a restaurant. They are young, early twenties, maybe, their faces bright in the flash, the rest dark around them. Her grandchildren Martin and Camila, and a third person, smiling, his black hair swooped back. He looks familiar. I know him. I take the picture from Jimena and stand with it in the light over the sink. I hold it close, the face expectant, the beam of a smile, blue eyes with no burden. I hand it back to Jimena.

"Who is this?"

"That's Camila and Martin. My grandchildren. I told you about them."

"This man?"

"Oh, that's Michael."

"What's his last name?"

"Ruiz. Michael Ruiz. He's a doctor now. They were best friends."

"For how long?"

"Michael grew up in Los Angeles. The Eastside, I think. We visited his family once or twice. His father was a mechanic and a deacon. His mother—I don't know, a seamstress, maybe. From Mexico, like us. Michael came to Saco every summer to live with his aunt. She worked in pistachios. His parents wanted him to live in the country." She laughs. "Michael always thought that was funny. He came to Saco after every school year. They became friends."

"When did you last see him?"

"It's been a long time. I don't even know when. I think it was when Camila came for a visit from Chicago. That was years ago." The kitchen clock ticks. She looks at me. "You're very interested in Michael."

"He hasn't been here recently?"

"I would know if Michael came. He brought me flowers every summer."

"Do Camila and Martin stay in touch with him?"

"Maybe. They were good friends."

She stares at the picture. Sips her tea.

"It's cold. I'll put the kettle back on."

"It's late. I have to go."

She gets up and steps to the window over the sink.

"Michael's a doctor now," she says. "I think, in Los Angeles. But people move around so much, you never know."

"What was he like?"

She smiles and stares at Michael Ruiz.

"He walked around with a Coke can full of change. Always collecting for some charity. My husband gave him handfuls of quarters over the years. A small fortune." She shakes her head, wipes away a tear. She lays the photograph on the table. She turns to the stove, puts on the kettle. I snap a picture of the photograph with my phone. We say nothing for a while. I stand. Jimena shuts off the stove and walks me over her cerulean-blue floor, through the living room, and to the front door.

"I think something has happened," she says. "Will Michael be okay?"

I look at her but don't answer. She closes the door.

I race south on the 5. A picture. An unexpected face, a young man looking out from years past. I invert the math. It could be. It seems impossible, but it could be. The things I didn't see the first time—Michael handing me the Flag flyer in his office; the way he stood distraught in the rain in the alley near the second tent burning; how he spoke of Marcus Robinson; how no one listened anymore to the clinic doctor's pleas to help the homeless. An unheard prophet. The quiet rage inside him. "A powerless man is a dangerous thing, son." My father had told me that as a boy. Michael knew that the pickup was in the barn. He must have taken the license plates. But what connection could he have to Milton Archer or the Flag? To the drive-by men who set tents on fire? It doesn't fit.

I call Lenny at the Little Easy.

"Is the doctor there?"

"Yes," says Lenny. "Getting to be a habit. Remember? I told you."

"Keep him there."

"He's three in. What's up, Sam?"

"Just keep him there, Lenny."

The rain sheets hard. The highway is a blur. The skyline rises, half lost in the mist, as if part of the city had been erased. I step into the Little Easy a few minutes after midnight. The place is empty except for Lenny, newspaper spread before him, and Michael Ruiz, sitting at the corner of the bar, looking into his glass, his phone beside him. I nod to Lenny and sit next to Michael. He turns as if waking from a slumber. He downs his scotch, waves to Lenny for another. "And one for the good detective," says Michael. "On me." Lenny pours and returns to his paper.

"You okay, Michael?" I say. "You seem like you've had too many."

"Building up a tolerance. Haven't seen you in a while."

"Saw you a few days ago."

"Oh, yeah. Sorry. I'm a little woo-oozy. Did that come out right?"

He takes a swallow, turns toward the piano.

"Play us something," he says. "Something smooth and . . . you know . . . soft."

"Not tonight, Michael. It's cold. My fingers are tight."

He cuts me a glance.

"It is cold up in the valley this time of year, Sam."

"Who called you?"

"Camila," he says. "Jimena called her after you left."

"So, you know."

"What do I know, Sam?"

"The license plates."

"We used to play in that old truck as kids. I kissed Camila there. My first kiss, Sam. You remember your first kiss?"

"Sandra. On a beach road."

"You don't hear much about Sandras anymore. Pooor Sandras."

"You and Camila?"

"Young love. I should have married her, Sam. I should have done a lot of things."

"What's going on, Michael?"

He looks at me in the soft light. His hair uncombed, his face red, tears rimming his eyes. He takes a short sip. Rain rattles the front window, calms. Lenny turns a page.

"No one listens, you know, Sam. Go open the door and look toward Main. You know what I mean. It's acceptable. Homelessness is like overdoses and car accidents. Tragedies that aren't tragedies anymore. Statistics we live with. When did we become like this? I think we always were, Sam. That's the thing. We just told ourselves we were different." He finishes his drink, nods for another. I wave Lenny away. "A guy came in the clinic today. Pneumonia. Schizoooo, schizophrenic. Diabetes. A madman shouting at himself. Soaking wet. Shivering. I gave him a handful of pills and a blanket. That's it, Sam. Not even a prayer. He'll be dead in two days. I tell people this. Commissions. Mayors. But the madmen keep coming. Keep dying, like they all live on this i-i-island no one can see."

"I see them."

"Maybe, a little." He leans away, points at me, winks. "You just might, Sam." He edges closer, steadies himself on the bar. "I should have been a plastic surgeon."

"You wouldn't have been happy."

"I'm not happy now. But at least I would have been loaded. I never married. Not Camila, not anybody. I should have

married, you know. A few kiiids. I would have taken them to
Europe. I've never been. Imagine that, Sam, never being to
Euuurope. My words feel stretchy."

"I need to ask you something, Michael."

"Always business with you, Sam. Let's have another. I think
we might need another."

Lenny heads our way with the bottle. My eyes tell him no.

"Did you take the license plates off the truck?" I ask. "Have
someone else do it?"

He rubs a hand over his mouth.

"There's always a flaaaw, isn't there? In your line of work,
I mean."

"Why don't you tell me, Michael?"

"You sure you don't want to play something, Sam? Soft,
maybe, like jazz. Really slooow."

"No."

I look at the two of us in the mirror, half hidden amid rows
of bottles.

"I can't figure it out, Michael."

"What?"

"How you might be connected to the Flag and those hate
groups."

He shakes his head. Combs a hand through his hair.

"Noooo. You don't get it, do you?"

"Tell me what I don't get, Michael."

He takes a deep breath.

"I am PureLand. Pure . . . Land."

He stands, opens his arms, spins. For all he has drunk, he
stays on his feet.

"PureLand, that's me," he says. "Pretty clever, huh?"

He sits. I stare at him. I can't believe what he is saying. He
reminds me of one of those men you sometimes come upon in

a bar, a man near ruin, rumpled, not himself, talking in liquor tongue, playing out the consequences of something lived with and left unspoken for too long.

"You posted all that hate about the homeless?" I ask him. "Race wars. Nazi slogans."

"Don't forget white supremacy. Ironic, huh? I mean, *Ruiz* won't get you into the Klan."

"I don't get it, Michael."

"You do look confused, Sam. Play something."

"Michael—"

"I created PureLand. I read all the alt-right literature. Studied their webs-s-s . . ." He pauses. "Websites. The creeds of racism and Aryan superiority, right-wing economics, that whole agenda, and you know, Sam, those guys on Fox News and talk radio." He pauses again, looks up as if searching for words. "They're the polished version—if you can call them polished—for a lot of bad shit the rich want to do to the country. The rich guys you don't see—they're behind it all. The guys who go to church on Sunday."

"You read the Flag?"

"My favorite. The Crenshaws and their adolescent, predictable ideology. That's the thing with all of them. There's no wit, just predictability. A bit vague, too, some of them. They're all so easy to mimic because they're caricatoons—ah, sorry *caricatures*. But dangerous, veeeryyyy dangerous."

I glance into my empty glass and back to Michael.

"You still look confused," he says.

He starts to stand. I put my hand on his shoulder.

"Sit, Michael."

He looks down the bar at Lenny, back to me.

"It came to me one morning, walking on San Pedro," he says. "I kept passing tents. Faces looking up. Piss stink everywhere. Junkies, rags. The whole wreck of it. It wasn't going to stop, you know. I couldn't keep testifying to committees. Couldn't keep talking to the media." He pushes back a tear. "No one was listening, Sam. I needed a new approach." He waves for Lenny again. I nod, okay. Lenny pours. "PureLand. It's a wonderful word," says Michael. "A trick of a word. Seems innocent but it's evil. I started posting about the homeless. How despicable they were, invading cities. I put it out there. I sent letters to the Flag. They loved PureLand. I was a great impostor. I was fooling them. I fooooled them allll."

"The letters to the Flag were mailed from different places."

"Martin and Camila mailed them from Chicago and Seattle and other cities for me." He looks at me. "They didn't know, Sam. Had no idea. I sent them envelopes already stamped and sealed. They thought they were doing favors for me. I told them they were angry letters to the Flag that I didn't want to be traced. They didn't ask much. They thought I was a little crazy but said okay."

"Tell me."

"I know the next question."

"Did you set the tent fires, Michael?"

He finishes his drink. He pats my arm, stares down the length of the bar to the neon in the window. He begins. Planning to kill someone was easier than he thought. He decided to make martyrs. People paid attention to martyrs. And in Michael's mind, it offered a degree of absolution that what he was doing was sanctioned by a higher cause. A calling. He picked his martyrs from clinic files, looking for names of those already dying. James Fincher had inoperable cancer. Warren Simpson's liver was failing. But Michael could not end a life. The doctor in him, the long-ago boy with the change in a Coke can, would not allow it. He tried, walking nights through Skid Row, holding matches and lighters in his hands. But he couldn't. He hired two drifters—the same men who attacked me—who had come into the clinic one day. Ex-cons and pill addicts, trying to cop a high. Michael gave them oxy and Xanax; he tweaked their cravings. He paid them three hundred dollars each. The father of one of them had a 1973 Dodge Challenger parked under a tarp across the Santa Clara River in Fillmore. It had no plates. Michael knew where to get them. The men made Molotov cocktails, put on ski masks, and hired a third doper to video the fires, which Michael later uploaded to 4chan and 8chan. PureLand became a hero in the chatrooms of the alt-right.

"How, Michael? It's not you."

He looked at me, didn't answer, fixed his eyes on the neon.

The plan worked. Michael's martyrs turned Los Angeles into a national story about homelessness. The country felt ashamed. The mayor scrambled. Congress promised bills; musicians wrote songs; graffiti blazed from underpasses and billboards. The woke took to the Twitter-sphere. Michael watched it all on TV. The alt-right and neo-Nazis were vilified for what they were, but they also had what they wanted, a cause célèbre: PureLand, a patriot, a man of resolve who took a righteous stand to win back America from the freeloaders, Muslims, Jews, Blacks, browns, and anyone else who did not look like Richard Spencer, David Duke, Milton Archer, or the desperate souls dressed in camo and carrying a picket sign outside of a shut-down steel plant.

"You didn't do this on your own," I say.

"Strange thing is, Sam, I did. I'm sorry about the men that night. I hope they didn't huuurt you. Just wanted to make it seem om-m-minous."

"But . . ."

"I became what I hated most."

"A lie."

"An invention. But people finally paid attention. That's what I wanted. People looked."

"Only as long as the fires burned."

This stings him. He shakes his head.

"That's not true, Sam."

"It is."

"No."

"You killed two men."

He balls his fists as if trying to hold something in. He relaxes, lets out a deep breath; he puts his face into his hands and weeps. Lenny pulls a clean rag out of a drawer and slides it to him. Michael wipes his eyes, bows his head. He shakes, then calms, but the thing keeps welling up in him, a great shudder. I rub his back. It's how it is, that moment, not of absolution but of feeling the insides of a sin that will never lift. I have seen it in too many others—that instant when all the calculations fall away. Michael looks up.

"They were dead already, Sam."

"You don't believe that."

"I do. People paid attention because of them. They're sain . . . saints."

"Don't make yourself feel better, Michael. They're victims."

"You don't understand."

"Do you know Milton Archer?" I ask.

"No." His voice is flat. "I know he owns a lot of property on Skid Row."

"You never met him?"

"I don't think Milton Archer and I have the same friends."

"I'm having a hard time, Michael, believing that this is only you."

"You get to a point," he says. "You think you're doing right, and the thing is, it starts becoming right."

"It's never right. Not that. What about guys like Marcus Robinson? What do you tell them?"

"He's dying, too. He came to the clinic the other day. Not himself. He looked small and shattered. So big a man. Not anymore. He didn't have his duffel bag or his saxophone. He said he had been on a long roam and lost them."

"What does he have?"

"You don't know with a lot of them. They just fall away."

"You burned his tent."

"I knew he wouldn't be in it." He stops, mumbles something I can't make out. "I kneeew he had let James Fincher use it. He often did. I would never hurt Marcus."

"Kiki died."

"That crushed him. That sad little redheaded junkie beneath the underpass. She came to the clinic a few times. He cared for that girl but could do nothing for her. Just like I could do nothing for him. I just got tired of not being able to do anything."

I stand.

"I have to bring you in, Michael."

"I've got to go back to the clinic. They'll be there. They come at dawn. I have to be there."

"Not tonight, Michael."

"Nooo, Sam, I have to be there."

I lean closer to him. I tell him it will be all right. He jumps up and steps back. He pulls a .22 pistol from his jacket, lifts it with a shaking hand.

"Put it down, Michael."

He fires. The bullet hits me in the shoulder, spins me a quarter-turn. He fires into the mirror over the bar. Glass and bottles shatter. Lenny dives to the floor. Michael holds the gun on me. "I'm sorry, Sam." His eyes will allow no convincing. He backs away three steps. He turns and runs out the door into the darkness. I follow, bracing my right arm over my chest. A night of drinking has not slowed him; he runs across Spring toward Main, a silhouette in the blowing rain. I'm half a block behind. The blood down my arm is warm; the rest of me is cold. Michael takes a left on Main, running past fences, tents, and razor wire. He looks back at me and crosses the street. The last few hours finally catch up with him. He wobbles. He doesn't see the truck. It hits him square, knocks him twenty feet, as if a sudden wind had lifted a shirt on a clothesline. I get to him. I lean down, listen for a breath, but feel only brokenness beneath his clothes. His eyes are open, still, shining in the rain. "I didn't see him," says the driver, standing over me. "I'm making a delivery to the flower market. I didn't see him." I sit beside Michael in the street. I reach for his hand. I squeeze it. Nothing back. So much I had wrong. I look at the tents and the lean-tos. No faces. No one is moving tonight. The ragged army sleeps. I hear sirens, see red flashes in the dark. Like the ones at Lily's house. I lie back and feel the rain on my face.

CHAPTER 29

They cut off my wet clothes. My skin is incandescent in the ER light. Voices, needles, blood on gauze, gloved hands, quick as wings. Silver gleams. The bullet is shallow. I feel a tug, hear a *ping* in the stainless-steel bowl. Voices calm. A nurse hurries past. I fade.

"Carver. Carver."

I open one eye.

"You'll live," says Ortiz, standing over me.

"Bullet hit nothing important," says Alicia Bryant, leaning in from the other side of the bed. "Small caliber. Didn't even have to take you into the OR."

"What time is it?"

"Seven a.m.," says Ortiz. "A little after."

"It's still raining," I say.

"Goddamn biblical," says Bryant.

I look at them both.

"We doing this now?" I ask.

"Might as well get it done," says Ortiz.

I tell them about Michael Ruiz. It's hard to fit words to the story, but I unwind it slow, still trying to believe it myself.

"Savior complex," says Ortiz.

"Ends justify the means," says Bryant. "Never underestimate the ability to rationalize."

"He was a good man," I say.

"They crack, too," says Bryant. "I feel for the guy, though. Crying out from the wilderness all those years and no one listening. I get that."

I hear Bryant's pen move across a notebook. Her face is unmade, shadowed by a ball cap; her eyes are bright and clear, tuned to the task.

"The Flag. Archer," says Ortiz. "Oskar Christensen. Albert Speer. The grand conspiracy of yours. None of it, huh?"

"All Ruiz," I say. "He was drinking and he just spilled."

"You believe it?" says Bryant.

"All fits."

"You read him his rights?" says Ortiz.

"I let him talk. He wanted it out. The burden got to be too much. He would have confessed. He *did* confess. I was bringing him to the station when he pulled on me."

"What was that about?"

"He thought he could go back to who he was. Pretend it would all go away."

"Delusional," says Bryant. "People make all kinds of plans in the shit."

"He wanted to go open the clinic," I say. "I pressed him, and he reached for the gun."

"Couldn't live with it," says Bryant. "Couldn't get away from it." She scribbles a bit more and closes her notebook. "And all that time you're dogging Archer."

"The wrong man," says Ortiz.

"I thought it was bigger," I say. "I missed things. But Archer looked good for it. At least connected."

Ortiz steps to the window. Looks over the city, back to me.

"You saw what you thought was the big picture too early," he says. "You fixated. That'll mess up a case."

"Guilty on all three," I say.

"It happens," says Ortiz. "But it should only happen once."

"I like it when you're like this," I say. "Playing the boss."

"I am the boss. You screwed up."

Ortiz looks at me hard but lets it pass.

"Ruiz was clever," says Bryant. "I mean, who would have thought?"

"I wonder if someone will open his clinic this morning," I say.

"There'll be a line," says Ortiz. "Always a line outside that place."

"I bet the mayor's happy," says Bryant. "Story turns another way. No neo-Nazis. No rich-developer donors. Just a fucked-up Good Samaritan."

"That's not a good story."

"There are no good stories," says Ortiz. "Just the stories we have."

"That's way too philosophical for the hour," says Bryant. "You guys, you know, are like Frick and fucking Frack. We've got a case down. Be a little happy."

"I got shot," I say.

"Glorified flesh wound. Man up, Carver," she says.

Ortiz and Bryant leave. I drift, sleep. I wake at midafternoon. I lift the bandage. A few stitches; horizontal, a yellow stain around them. I put on the clothes Ortiz had brought from my apartment. I stand and look out the window. I reach for my phone and call Mariana Sanchez. I tell her I have a story for her.

"I didn't think I'd hear from you," she says.

"Meet me at that Portuguese place over off Fifth. You know it?"

"I'll be there," she says. "I'm bringing my cameraman."

"Just you and me. There'll be plenty left for your cameraman after."

"I heard about a shooting," she says.

"Be there."

CHAPTER 30

Sanchez's story airs. It's solid. Interviews with homeless and social workers and people who knew Michael over the years. Jimena made a cameo, sitting on her porch, shaking her head, calling him a good boy. Looking back at a life gone, she and others had no premonition, no inklings of what lay deep in Michael. It's like that all the time, as if we are separate from ourselves in the eyes of others. But the deed, even the unexplainable kind, invariably fits the man. Sanchez captured him in full. The intricacies that gather and set a course. I liked that she said: "Many will say Michael Ruiz fell from grace, but, in the end, that may not be true. Desperation pushed him beyond the small hope he carried." She looked at the camera, the way she can, pulling you through the lens toward her, and turned and gazed over San Pedro and Skid Row, letting tents, junkies, shopping carts, soaked cardboard, a man in rags, and the crooked, sad line outside Michael's clinic have the last unspoken word.

I pack a bag, reach for Lily's box of ashes. I head west on

the 10. I know where to go. The sky is gray, but no rain. Cracks of light in the distance open and close. I hit the Pacific Coast Highway, the beach empty, the Palisades quiet. I speed north, listening to Robert Williams sing about Baton Rouge and the floods the past brings. That fades to the Pretenders and Tom Waits and slides into a hymn sung by Icelandic monks and then Fado ballads from Portugal. I round a curve, look into the cove, and see a lone surfer. I park and walk over the sand to the shoreline. I sit and watch. He seems at one with it, smooth, a black figure rising, accelerating, disappearing for a moment, and then back into the sight line, an arrow through a spray of white, the horizon behind him. He would do it all day, forget about the rest, but he cannot rule the tides. He paddles out once more, catches the last good ride, steps off his board in the shallows, and meets my eye.

Milton Archer walks toward me.

"This has become our spot, hasn't it, Detective?"

"You're consistent."

"Perhaps you, too."

He lifts a towel from the sand, rubs it over his silver hair. He sits next to me.

"Cold," he says.

"Winter's gone on too long."

"I saw you got your man. The right one, thankfully."

"I wish it had been someone else," I say, glancing toward him.

"Poor Michael Ruiz. Imagine the torment. How's your shoulder? I read you got shot."

"Healing."

"What does it feel like?"

"What?"

"To be shot."

"Nothing at first."

"I had always supposed a numbness. A kind of limbo before the pain. Is it like that?"

"A bit, maybe."

A gull skims close and lands.

"I know you wanted it to be me," says Archer. "You had it all figured out. The right-wing hate, the rich developer. The homeless scourge. My word, not yours, *scourge*. A plausible scenario but one woefully short of the mark." He wipes water dripping from his face. "That's not the way it will be. Not some violent act by a misguided disciple. I know, Ruiz wasn't a disciple for the cause, but he was certainly misguided. What a conflicted soul. You appear conflicted yourself, Detective. But let's not get into that. The change I want in this country will come right before your eyes. It's happening now. Like a low-grade recycling virus. It will build."

"Virus?"

"Nothing purges the weak like a virus. Cruel, perhaps, but an occasional necessity for the species."

"What will it look like when it's done?"

He stares at me.

"What was always intended."

"I don't like you."

"I've gathered," he says. "But we've come to an under-standing. That is rare in itself."

"I despise what I understand."

"Yes, yes, I know."

We sit with no words; the waves roll in, slower, smaller. He stands. He picks up his board.

"I come here every day," he says. "It's the same but always different."

"Like Skid Row."

He laughs, shakes his head.

"Yes, I suppose so. For now."

"It's dangerous, what you're doing."

"To me it doesn't seem so. Just the opposite."

"You won't live long enough to see it."

"That is a consideration. But I have hope, and, if not, maybe you'll see it and know I was right. An architect knows his building will stand long after he is gone."

He turns.

"I have to go," he says. "I don't imagine I'll see you much anymore."

"I know where to find you."

"Goodbye, Detective."

He walks over the sand. Wind catches his board; he leans, finds his balance, and heads toward his Thunderbird. I turn toward the ocean. I sit a little longer. I think of Archer's world and how he's right about one thing. It is happening before us. The gull takes flight, veering beyond the surf break over calmer water. Bright against the gray sky. The rains came in autumn, but they have stayed, and although they are not falling now, I can smell them, feel their brisk advance. I used to welcome them—an inviting change, but not anymore. They have settled in with an air of permanence, and I wonder if this is how life will be for a while. I stand and brush the sand off. I have delayed too long what I must do—the task at hand, as my mother would say.

I continue north, past Oxnard, Santa Barbara, Morro Bay, the road curving, rising, vistas shining, waves breaking along cliffs and coast. I stop at an overlook, sip scotch, feel the warm net spread through me. Onward, like a pilgrim, or a lost frontiersman suddenly come upon a view beyond his powers to imagine. Past San Simeon, toward Big Sur. The markings on the road come back to me. I hear her. "Hey, Carver, it's right up here, around this bend; don't pass it," said Lily, holding her map. A year ago. "This is my favorite place along the whole damn coast," she said. "Stop. Here. Park. This is it." She is not here; only this box of what's left. I take it from the seat and walk down the steps Lily showed me on that day we joked about leaving all the cop work behind. Disappearing. "It's good, you know, to think what you might do even though you know you won't." The stairs are slippery. I descend to a small cove. I take off my shoes and roll up my pants. I walk through the shallow surf and climb up a rock just as Lily and I did when she kissed me and held me and said: "Carver, how about this goddamn view!" I open the box. She is more than this, but this is all I have. So much of what we collect through life is forgotten, but if we're lucky, the best things stay with us as if we'd had them all along. I hold up the box. The wind takes her, little by little until she is no more. The only prayer I have is unspoken, moving through my blood, an offering, maybe, but I think something more. I give it to Lily.

I walk through the shallows to the beach. I turn back toward the ocean. I stand for a long time. I will not come back here. The wind lifts hard and calms. I wait for it to come again, raising whitecaps, whistling through rocks. I put on my shoes and climb the wooden stairs. The rain follows. I sit in the car, close my eyes and listen, and then drive to a small hotel and restaurant south of Big Sur. It's an old place with a row of cabins along the cliff. The parking lot is empty except for another car. I check in, shower, lie on the bed, and watch the night come.

CHAPTER 31

The restaurant is small. White linen, candles, tables by big windows, threads of waves beyond in the dark. I order a scotch and scroll my phone. Ortiz checking in. Alicia Bryant, too. I don't answer. I slide the phone aside and read a book I keep coming back to but never finish—a long-ago story about a flier in a silver jet streaking above foreign terrain, finding home in the sky, high above the things that ruined him. The rain is steady on the roof. The waitress, a woman with cropped blond hair, dressed in a paisley vest and white shirt, brings two glasses and a bottle of wine I didn't order. She holds the bottle before me: a merlot from Los Robles. I know it well. She uncorks it and leaves. I close the book and look at the glasses. I pour. I wait. The door opens. A woman sails through, slips out of a raincoat. She is tall. Her hair shines with mist. Sleeveless black dress, black heels. I know them, too. She walks toward me, holding a small clutch. She sits, pulls the wine bottle close, knowing I remember it's the same label and vintage she brought the night we first met. She is pleased with herself. Like a child. She smiles and reaches for my hand. I pull away. I feel for my gun. I want to shoot, to end it, but I let it be, as she knew I would.

"Sam, darling. It's just us."

She looks around, waves a hand in the air.

"I knew you were coming," I say.

"But to be here, huh? You and me. Mmm. I've been watching you. I've been quite a shadow, haven't I? An angel floating around you. How about my little dance? Did you like my notes and letters? Not too intimate, I hope. Don't publish them until after my death—isn't that what all the writers say?" She laughs, leans toward me. "Let's be quiet for a minute, Sam. Let me look at you. So close again. As it should be. You feel it, too. I know you do."

"I'm going to arrest you."

"No, darling, you're not."

Dylan Cross sips her wine.

We stare at each other. For so long, I have wanted her this close. But it is not the way I imagined. It has never been that way with Dylan. I granted her something long ago—absolution, perhaps. But no, she is a killer, avenger to the men who broke her, murderer of Lily. But she is other things, too, as am I. We are both more than we appear to be in our accumulated wreckage, and no, that is not enough, but it is what we bring to each other. I don't know what to do, but I am calm, as if I have been through this moment many times. That is the thing with Dylan: the line to the truth itself is suspect. She sips her wine. Her lipstick is red and glossy, her black hair long and brushed back over her shoulders, her face a sharp and lovely mask. Small pearls encircle her neck, and her movements embody the ease of the tennis player she once was, and the precision of the architect she willed herself to be. I wonder what the waitress thinks. A quiet couple on a rainy night? An affair? An anniversary, or maybe a chance meeting earlier in the day, strangers in separate cars traveling opposite directions and finding a hotel out of season when all the others are closed. There is an air of nostalgia about this evening. Perhaps our lives have resumed from some distant time, and the things that have brought us together are not as I know them, but something far different. The pearls around Dylan's neck suggest at least the possibility that what I know to be real may be only one of many passing shadows. I think my mother felt the same with my father. She invented a parallel life to the one she knew, and over time she crossed between them until there was no border.

A tear runs down Dylan's cheek, drops on the linen like a tiny star. I try to reach for my gun, but my hand will not obey.

"You're crying," I say.

"The good kind. One tear for you, Sam." She lifts her napkin to her face. "I haven't felt a tear in so long." She pulls a compact from her clutch, checks her eyes, snaps it shut. "You still go to the desert, don't you?"

"Why do you ask? You watch me."

"My addiction." She laughs—the nervous kind. A sound I don't remember from the night we first met. "Is that too much? I think I tell you too much. I should be more discreet, but why, really? Why? Some women are quite discreet, aren't they? Schemers. But, you know, I find discretion a kind of deceit. I've never been good at it. The games. People play too many games. But yes, I've been watching. You love it, don't you, my church in the desert?"

"Yes."

"The best thing I've ever done. I say that with humility." She rolls her eyes; humility is not one of Dylan's traits. "Just saw it in my mind. Like an epiphany, hah, get it? Lines clear and simple. Out of the earth, you know, my stained-glass gift to God. When you visit it, do you pray, Sam? I've wondered. Do you pray? I've read your diaries, except they're not really diaries—just writings at the end of the day. Not much self-reflection. You still haven't changed your password. I think you like that I've hacked you. You pretend you don't, but, Sam, then why no firewall? Why am I so easily let in?" She pours more wine. "But they're not prayers."

"You don't know as much as you think."

"Oh, darling, tell me a prayer. Sing me a hymn."

She lifts the stem of her glass, sips.

"Why did you—"

"Let's not talk about *her* now," she says. "This is my night. *Our* night."

"Only one of us will survive it."

"Oh, Sam, don't be so melodramatic. It's not your nature."

"I loved her."

Dylan's eyes flash hard, a fingernail scratches into the linen.

"No, Sam. You didn't. You know that's not true. An infatuation at best. But I'm not talking about *her*, Sam. Is that clear?" She takes a breath, closes her eyes, opens them. "Let's start again. As I imagined, as I have imagined since that first night."

"The night you broke into my apartment and tied me up."

"I taped you up. Be precise."

She winks.

"I felt bad about hitting you on the head. But what's a girl to do? I wanted you to love me," she says. "But you didn't. You weren't ready to come away with me. You just weren't ready. I should have anticipated that. But things were hectic then."

"You killed two men."

"You're a man of annoying details, my darling."

"Truths."

"You're good at truths, aren't you, Sam, even though you avoid your own. But, okay, I'll play. Truths. I killed the ones who raped me. You saw the video; you knew. You didn't love me, but you understood. It was all in the writings in your laptop. That's when I knew, Sam. You were different. You had to learn, though. You didn't see it right away. Something of a disappointment, I must say. But I was hoping for too much, too early. A girl must be patient. That's why I taped you up. I had to be sure. But you were still wavering. My wavering, darling Sam. You would have arrested me that night. Admit it."

"I would have, and I'm going to arrest you tonight."

"Yet here we sit. Tell me, Sam, why do we sit? You keep feeling for your gun, but where is it? You can't anymore. You're not wavering. You know now, after all this time. The things we have."

"You're crazy."

"Let's order."

"Did you set up Angel Castillo?"

"He is on the menu?" she says, laughing. "You mean the one who killed *her*."

"He didn't kill her. You did."

"The cops said he did. Alicia Bryant arrested him. Gun, evidence, motive. All your little police-stuff thingies to make a case. I saw it on TV. With the mayor and everything. Poor little mayor, always seems engulfed by some misfortune."

"You set it all up."

"Alicia Bryant's pretty smart. You better watch out for that one, Sam."

"You're smarter."

"You're sweet, darling. Thank you. But, seriously, let's order. I'm starved."

Dylan orders steak. I take fish. The waitress brings

another bottle of wine. She walks away, past empty tables and candlelight, mirrored in windows streaked with rain.

"Will it ever stop?" says Dylan.

"It's the most ever."

"It's a sign." Her eyes widen. "Doom."

She laughs.

"You like yourself," I say.

"I don't know if *like* is the word. I enjoy myself. I'm quite amusing, Sam."

"You need help. Let me help you."

Her jaw tightens. She cuts her steak, doesn't look up.

"I helped your mother, didn't I, Sam? Where were you? Out here while she was losing her mind in Boston with Maggie. Poor Aunt Maggie. I liked her. I liked your mother, too, but day by day we were losing her. Maggie could see it. She cried in the kitchen at night. I bet she never told you that. It's hard on the ones who care. How is Maggie?"

"You tricked her. She doesn't know the truth."

"The truth?"

"That you showed up at her house pretending to be a nurse sent from the hospital."

"To know you better, Sam. Maggie told me all about you. I saw all your little-boy pictures. So cute. Little pirate Sam in his Halloween costume. Opening Christmas toys. Did you like the picture I left you of the three of us? I thought you might fantasize about me in my nurse's whites. I did feel like a nurse. Florence what's-her-name. I brushed your mother's hair, rubbed cream on her hands. Took her pulse."

I rush around the table. Fury burns through me. I lower my face to hers.

"Can you do it, Sam?" she says.

My gun inches out of its holster.

"Can you do it, darling?"

I smell her wine and perfume. Her blue eyes narrow, unfrightened, inviting. The waitress takes a few steps toward us. Stops. She can't see the gun, hidden by my blazer. I slip it back into the holster. Dylan looks toward it. She kisses me on the forehead, whispers in my ear.

"I know you're mad, Sam."

"You don't know a goddamned thing."

"But you're making a scene. Like a little boy. Sit. Please, sit. There's so much to talk about. You don't want to spoil things, do you? Sit, darling."

I take my seat. The waitress retreats.

"How's this supposed to end?" I say. "You're so good with plans."

"It will never end, Sam." She reaches across the table, pats my hand. "Now, eat. My steak is just right. How's your fish?"

I pour the wine. I look at her, a storybook queen, a menace in a castle.

"Let me tell you about my travels," she says. "When I left you that morning—I hope it wasn't *too* embarrassing, taped up like that. Did your cop friends tease you? It was still dark, remember? Of course you do. I had a fake passport. I have a number of them. So many men out there doing illicit things for money. You can get anything if you call the right number. I flew to Argentina. I love the architecture of Buenos Aires. I stayed a few weeks, walking the streets, sketching. So many designs in my head." She pushes her plate aside, leans on the table. "Then I went to Europe. Greece. Italy. I found a house in a hill town in Umbria, the fields below me scattered with ruins. You would have loved it. I'd lean against those ruins, Sam, and feel the ancient men, architects like me. But I felt very sad for the longest while, sad about what had been done to me, sad at not having you. But I kept drawing. My salvation. I drew whole cities, buildings like you never saw. You said I would never have that. You told me that night. But I did have it, Sam. One day I will show you all that I designed, the world I drew to live in."

"What kind of world is that?"

She looks to the window, pretends not to hear.

"Are you sad now?" I ask.

"Sad? Me? I'm delighted."

"I don't think so. You were hurt bad, Dylan."

"Oh, well. There's that. What they did to me. I hated for a long time. But then I thought, what's to hate? The men who made me hate are gone."

"You killed them."

"What else to do? That's how we met, Sam."

"I still can't figure it. How—"

"I'm not done telling you about my trip. I left Italy and ended up in Croatia."

"Your father was from there."

"Yes, a village outside Split. I stayed along the Dalmatian Coast. I went out on fishing boats and played tennis on red clay. I hadn't played in so long. But it came back and for a while, Sam, I was the girl in the tennis picture I left you the night we met. The girl before. The naive girl who didn't know the things she should. I kept wanting her to come back, but she's gone. The men who made me hate scared her away. But she wants to come back."

"How did you do it?"

"You know how I did it. You saw them."

"No, in your mind."

"You sound like a shrink. Really, Sam, don't analyze. Why this fixation?"

"You block it out. You become someone else."

"No. You're very much yourself. The purest self."

"Vengeance is not pure."

"It's delicious," she says, her eyes on me, then away. "For a while."

"I don't believe that, either. That's not you."

"What *is* me, Sam? I want to hear."

I don't answer. The waitress takes our plates. I watch her quick hands and pursed lips. The soft clatter of forks and knives. She is efficient at her task, leaning in and out, not disturbing, stacking plates until the table is only napkins and linen, wineglasses, and a silver sugar bowl. She brushes crumbs and is gone. *Lily, your killer sits before me.* The words drift through me, but still, I sit with my useless gun, as if waiting for other words to make sense of it all. But those words don't arrive, and Dylan, content for a moment in her silence, rims a finger around her wineglass, making a kind of music.

"It's a hard one, isn't it?" she says. "What I am. Who you are."

"The riddle eternal."

"Ooh, who said that? Is that you, Sam? It's a bit over the top."

"A monk I knew."

"Monks don't believe in riddles. They have it all figured out."

"Their riddle is believing that."

"Are you being clever? Smart little Sam."

"No."

"I think you are. It's so good we're finally together."

The music from her wineglass stops.

"Do you suppose we ever know, Sam?"

"Know what?"

"The riddle."

"No."

"I don't think so, either. It's a mystery, isn't it? The trick is to play along. But you know about my mother? I told you that night."

"Not much. She burned your house down."

"Her finest hour. Her church. She was the crazy one. Hah. But I loved her. Children can love anything because they so much want it to be. She was in and out of institutions. When she was home, I thought she was magical. Isn't that strange? All her moods. Her flying rage and slow tears. She was a storm in our hallways. My father told me that. He didn't know what to do. But he loved her. He gave her metaphors. It was his way of coping, I suppose. I gave her love until one day she was gone. Lying on the floor. I remember thinking how the pills scattered around her head looked like stars."

"That's pretty."

"Don't patronize me, Sam."

"I mean it."

"Fuck you."

She sips her wine, cuts me a sideways glance.

"Forgive me, Sam. I shouldn't be so vulgar."

"You have that, don't you?" I say. "A little of your mother."

"I saw a shrink for a while. Took meds. I stopped it all a long time ago."

"After."

"Yes, after. I needed to see, think clearly."

"To kill two men."

"You love saying that, don't you, Sam? Whatever you like. You saw."

"Michael Gallagher's slit throat. Up from behind on Main Street."

"It was empty that night. I remember how cool it was. Just a few homeless, wandering."

"Paul Jamieson, though. That was theatrical."

"Performance art. I slipped a little drug into his wine."

She looks at me, my wineglass. She winks.

"Don't worry, Sam. You would have felt it by now."

"Knife in the heart."

"Slow, too, you know. I knelt before him. He couldn't move. Just sat there. His eyes twitching. He was so frightened. Imagine. All he could do was count the seconds and watch. Then he knew. The final thing he saw was the face of the girl he raped."

"Why the makeup?"

"I wanted to take away who he was. I made him something else. It took a while. Mascara is never easy, but there he was, drugged, naked, and made-up. Sitting like a puppet. A little ashamed puppet."

"They were architects like you."

"Let's stop the interrogation, darling. We know how it ended. But they were nothing like me at all." Her hands drum the linen. "Sam, Sam, Sam, I'm bored with this. Let's dance."

"I don't dance."

"*I don't dance.* You sound like a man who bowls."

"There's no music."

"We'll pretend."

She stands and twirls. She waves for me, but I do not come. She frowns, a play pout, and closes her eyes and slowly spins around the empty restaurant. A shadow in candlelight. The waitress watches from the bar; the chef peeks from the kitchen. Dylan dances. No music. Only the rustle of her dress, the slide of high heels over the carpet. She dances closer, spins behind me, wraps her arms around me, coaxes me to rise. "Come, Sam, don't be shy. It's only us. Dance." I pull her arms away. "Chicken," she says. "You're no fun." She laughs. She twirls along the windows. Her black dress becomes one with the

night, her face and arms bright white in the glass, as if floating
without the rest of her. I remember when I saw the video of
what Gallagher and Jamieson had done to her, and how I felt
pity and desire, the way a vic can draw up the things that are
sacrilege to all you ever thought was good in you. But here
she is, splendid in her delusions and pearls, a woman who, if I
didn't know her past, I might have asked to dance.

Dylan stops. She stares out to the rain and the ocean. She
turns toward me, lost, her eyes not quite sure, as if she were
a refugee just landed from a distant country. It is only for a
moment. She finds herself again and glances around the room,
back to me. Her eyes tell me she knows me, she has read all
my words. Yes, she says, not like the others, not even like Lily,
but only she knows. She twirls back to me. A dark feather in
the air. She sits.

"Let's eat cake," she says.

"I'm not hungry."

"Everyone's hungry for cake, Sam. You can have a bite of
mine. We'll get two forks, like lovers do."

She waves for the waitress and orders.

"Have you read about this virus thing in China?" she says.

"A little."

"Scary. It's spreading fast. The world is dangerously
connected, Sam, don't you think? All the invisible killers out
there. I wonder if it will come here. I think it will. No one's
immune anymore."

"Were we ever?"

"We thought so."

The waitress brings cake and two forks. Dylan takes a bite,
closes her eyes, and smiles.

"Chocolate is heaven. Try some, Sam." She leans over,
sails her fork toward me. I open my mouth. She thinks she

has won. Content with herself, as if the night were leading toward my discovery that I belong in her strange pageant. Her presupposing smile makes me wonder if she's sensed surrender in me. I don't think so, but this is Dylan's world, and like the flier in the book I have yet to finish, the terrain is foreign, but also—even in my grief for Lily and my hate for the hand that killed her—tempting. Transgression too deep for penance. I am here in the night at the tip of her fork, knowing that the betrayals we allow ourselves are, in the end, what define us. The waitress brings brandy. Dylan takes another bite of cake.

"Delicious, right?" she says. She wipes the corners of her mouth.

"Your father, Sam," she says. "He is your mystery. Like my mother. The ones we love but cannot have. You write most about him. Do you know that? Not your mother, who raised, loved, and never left you, but your father. The bruised boxer. I can see him."

"You know nothing about it."

"Oh, but, darling, I do. Tell me one father story and then we'll leave him to the past. Just one."

"Don't call me darling."

"Just one story, Sam."

She reaches over, touches my hand.

"He taught me to box. He was murdered in an alley by men who got away."

"You were only a boy," she says. "Tell me more, Sam. I want to know."

"This won't work, Dylan. This night you've imagined."

"A few more hours, Sam. Until dawn. How can it hurt? I know you better than anyone, yet I am a stranger. What does that say? I'm *not* a stranger, though. It's hard for you to understand that. It goes against all that you think you are.

That's unfair to me. Unfair to all we have. We're not like other couples, Sam. Tell me one story about your father."

She pours more wine, runs a fingernail through frosting, licks.

"He'd get up in the morning and tape his hands. He'd make fists so the white tape fit like new skin. He'd put on his sweats and disappear into the street before first light. Running and punching the air. That's what I remember most about him. He seemed at war with the air." I stop. What's this for? This recounting of ghosts. But Dylan wants more. She leans closer. "I followed him one morning. It was winter. I knew his route. He'd go way out beyond the city and circle back to the beach. I cut across the city, so I'd get to the beach before him. I stood on the cliff above and waited. He came. Small, out of the distance, his taped hands blurring in front of him. It was snowing. He stopped. He opened his arms and looked to the sky. He let the snow fall around him. All the anger and confusion in him was gone. I could see it even from where I was. He was just a man in the snow on a winter's morning. That man never came back to the house. He kept that man outside."

Dylan is crying. She gets up, puts my face in her hands, and kisses my forehead. I let her.

She sits back down.

"We can't have the things we want," she says. "You wanted him. I can see you standing there. A little boy on a cliff."

"No, Dylan, you can't."

"Your mother," she says.

"Sometimes, he would bring that man to her. She told me after he was gone."

"It's why you're a cop."

"No, it's not."

"We won't talk about it anymore. Past is past. My mother

would say that when she wanted me to forget one of her episodes. As if she could will her broken mind away." She laughs. "What odd, sad places we come from, Sam."

"Why me, Dylan? Why am I here?"

Her face is still; her eyes not as clever as they were a minute ago.

"You know," she says.

"I don't."

"It was the newspaper. A story about you, remember? You solved that famous case. The one with the movie producer, bodies in dumpsters and drug money in the Caymans. There you were, Mr. Reticent Cop standing in front of the Bradbury Building. You both looked so beautiful. I knew then, Sam, that you'd understand me. Know me. Why I had to do what I did. I could see it in that picture. You know how you just know? I knew. I knew you'd be my detective. I killed them where you would be the first one called. It took a lot of planning. But I was patient."

She laughs.

"Not always," she says. "That's when I hacked you. Entered your laptop and all your little writings. You let me in, darling, with your predictable passwords and pathetic firewall. I lived in your laptop. I absorbed all of you. Then I watched. Followed. You were my game. Did you ever sense me? I've often wondered. I saw you at the Last Bookstore one night. You were browsing Hemingway and that crew. I brushed right past you on my way to Chaucer. You never looked up, and I thought I must get whatever he's reading. Ha. And at the Phil one night. Dudamel conducting Mahler, or was it Brahms? I sat a few rows behind you. I passed you in the lobby. I breathed in your witch hazel and scotch."

"Is that true?"

"All is true, Sam."

She stands and goes to the window.

"The rain has stopped," she says. "Let's walk on the beach."

Dylan lays four hundred dollars on the table. We walk to the door. The waitress holds her coat. Dylan slips into it. We step into the night.

"I have a story about her," she says.

"Who?"

"The waitress. Stanford dropout. Drifted down here, partly desperate, partly searching, fell in with the cook."

"He could be her father."

"Yes, but it works. They open the restaurant every night and close up late. They go home and wash it all off and watch TV and make love until dawn. They drink—he more than her, but she is catching up. Don't you love to make up stories about people, Sam? To play God. I think they're quite happy in their little lives, and when he dies, she'll drift somewhere else and find another man. You can tell."

"It's cold," I say.

Dylan takes my arm, pulls me close. We walk along the cliff, through a row of pine, and down the stairs to the beach. Moonlight appears and disappears through broken clouds. The air is damp. Rain will come again, but the earlier winds have died, and I feel a stillness as if, for a moment, we have stepped into a photograph. Dylan takes off her high heels and tosses them by the stairs. We walk along the white rim of the waves. I wonder if it will snow inland, but I don't think it's cold enough, and I imagine Lily as part of all this, beyond the breakwater in the quiet at the horizon.

"Why?" I ask.

"Why what, Sam?"

"Did you kill her."

Dylan stops. She turns toward me. She hugs me. My face is lost in her hair.

"Oh, Sam. I didn't mean to. I really didn't."

"I don't believe that."

She presses me close. I feel the length of her. We are suspended, but only for an instant. She releases me. "I went to scare her," she says. "I wanted to frighten her away from you. You were falling for her, darling, and that couldn't be. You were forgetting about *us*. Past is not past, Sam. But I had been away too long. I blame myself for that. I had been watching the two of you together. This infatuation of yours. I thought it might be harmless. I tolerated it for a while. I got jealous. The consuming kind." She steps closer to the water, a silhouette with her back to me. "I went to her house that night. That crummy little neighborhood below Saint Mary's. It was raining. She left the downstairs door open. She was waiting for you. I went in and up the stairs. She was in the shower. I sat. I waited. I heard the water go off. I stood. She came out in a kimono, and I thought, just for a second, oh, yes, now I know why my Sam has this infatuation. She had something, darling. I saw that up close. In her eyes."

"She was . . ."

"Yes, she was. I was terrified. This wasn't supposed to happen. I knew then I could lose you. That could not be allowed. We both stood, looking at one another. Her hair was dripping, and I thought how tall I was next to her, and I remembered how as a girl I never liked being tall, all the looks you got for being the tall one, the strange, lanky kid at the back of the class. My father taught me to love my height, to find beauty in it. I did. Eventually. But standing there with *her*, I felt the odd one again. Oh, dear, I thought. What is happening? It's that simple, Sam—no more complicated than a sudden feeling. An impulse. And suddenly, well, you know, that sound and that smell and the way she fell."

She turns toward me. A wave breaks; water swirls at her feet, recedes.

"I did it," she says. "But, Sam, you must know, I didn't set out to. It wasn't like the others. I only wanted to chase her away. You're mad, I know. We'll get past this. All couples have challenges. But here we are, darling, the beach, the water, and the night. All ours. As it should be."

I rush toward her. I grab her neck and squeeze. She gasps, claws me with her nails, one striking my face. But her eyes are not frantic, not desperate. They flash in moonlight, looking into me, knowing my weakness and the things I cannot do. I release her. She folds to the sand, facing the sky, her black hair in the night, her face white as a star. She coughs, gasps, closes her eyes, touches her neck. She reaches up, takes my hand, and draws me down. I sit beside her. I feel blood on my cheek, the sting of a cut. Her breaths mix with the sound of the waves, and I can see the shadow of a tanker on the horizon. The clouds close and the rain comes—not hard, but steady around us. Dylan takes my arm and pulls herself up. We sit side by side. I listen to the rain, feel it cold on my scalp, seeping through my clothes, chilling my bones. I can feel it in Dylan, too. She shivers and cries, but then she stops. She stares out across the water. The rain dances on our clothes. She turns toward me, runs a hand through my wet hair, kisses me on the forehead. She stands, reaches down. I take her hand and rise. We say nothing. We walk to the stairs; she leaves her shoes on the sand. We head up to the cliff and back through the pines and toward the cabin at the end of the row, where Dylan slides the key into the door. We step in. She brings us towels from the bathroom, so warm and white in the dark. My clothes heavy, I dry my face and hair. Dylan unzips her dress. Let's it fall to the floor.

CHAPTER 32

She stands tall, slender, stepping toward me. She pushes back my jacket. She unbuttons my shirt, peels it off. She holds me, her skin cold, her hair wet on my shoulder. Clouds and moonlight play tricks in the window. Her breaths are slow. She kisses my cut face. I taste my blood on her lips. She says my name. The room is cold. Dylan is cold. I undress. We lie on the bed, slip under the covers. She slides under my arm. She lies still. We stay for a long while like this. I feel her tears on my chest, the slow rise and fall of her. I hold her and close my eyes. I want nothing remembered. But no, this is not so; I want her and all that must come from it. She has led me to this bed in a rented cabin, a lonely place by the sea, my gun on the nightstand.

"I'm scared," she says.

"Why?"

"Let's stay like this."

"I thought you wanted more."

"That will come, but let's just hold each other. Can we do that?"

"Yes."

"See, Sam, you know me."

"What do I know?"

She doesn't answer. The rain stops. The wind quiets. I think of the time I went to her house and stood on her lawn. She had killed two men and was hiding—this is what she told me tonight—behind a lace curtain on the third floor, watching me. I circled the house, an old Victorian she had restored, and stood on the porch. I peeked through the stained glass of the front door. Staircase, Persian carpet, vase of flowers. I went to the backyard and looked over the city. She almost ran down the stairs and out the door to stand beside me; she wanted to tell me how skylines were born, and of all she wanted to build. "Wouldn't that have been something, Sam? You would have understood so much." I remember her backyard. The grass, the garden, the hillslope into the thicket. I thought a man could come home to this every evening and see the last of the day succumb to night. I had never wanted that until that moment. It was a passing thought, but it struck me. I pretended a radio played in the kitchen, and the house's lights were just coming on, and a woman—an image of one—moved over the carpets, her presence filling the rooms. I left Dylan's house that night, not knowing she was watching me from her turret and smiling at the prospect that I was close to finding her.

"Maybe one day," she says, her body now warm beside me, "we can drive to my church in the desert. You know, Sam, we could live out there. I have money. We could disappear into the desert. People get lost all the time out near Joshua Tree. I stayed lost for a while." She laughs; she is coming back to herself. "It's really not that hard. If we got tired of the desert, we could disappear somewhere new."

"Your voice is different."

"You choked me, Sam. You didn't mean to. I knew you wouldn't hurt me too bad. I confessed, didn't I? I never meant to do any of it to *her*. You forgive me, don't you, darling?" She kisses me. "I sound raspy, don't I? Like an actress in one of those old movies your father liked. I know how you'd sit with him way past midnight watching old movies."

"Lizabeth Scott."

"Who?"

"She was his favorite."

"I wonder what it was like back then. When it was all in black and white."

She turns away and slides open the nightstand drawer.

"I have something for you," she says.

She pulls out a bottle of scotch, two glasses.

"You took it for granted," I say.

"I knew I'd get you back here. It's all gone as I planned, mostly. Here."

She pours one for each of us. She slides back under my arm, rests her glass on my chest.

"You drink too much," she says.

"I hadn't thought about it."

She touches my bullet scar.

"It's small," she says. "Does it hurt?"

"No."

"It'll be morning in a few hours," she says. "I wish it wouldn't come. It'll all be different."

"What will?"

"Everything. It always is."

She sips. Kisses me.

"You kissed back," she says. "In the day will you kiss back?"

She slips away from me and walks to the window. Her hair falls around her shoulders. Her body is like one of her designs:

all in place, lines and angles smoothed by night. I think about what it has survived, how it has, in its defiance, kept its beauty. As her father wanted. She tells me it's snowing in Joshua Tree. White rocks and frozen canyons. She wonders who had this cabin before us. An older couple, maybe, still in love, or perhaps a woman like her mother, escaping with a borrowed suitcase and stolen credit cards. She says she wishes she could paint the window black and put stars in it so it would always be night for us. She laughs. She traces herself on the glass. Her reflection is strange and white, as if pressing in from the darkness. It disappears when a cloud passes. She turns toward me, wearing nothing. She looks back out the window. I rise and go to her. Only the ocean sees us. I slide my arms around her.

"I've only been with one other man since that night," she says. "It was a mistake. He wasn't the right man—he wasn't you, Sam—but I had to know if I could. It wasn't good. I wasn't ready. I ran to the bathroom and cried." She reaches back, touches my face. "Can we try? It may be no good, but I think it might be. Will you understand?"

She kisses me, leads me to the bed. I can feel her shaking. We hold each other; she is crying. Her manic confidence, all her cleverness, gone. She is without armor. She kisses me. I can feel her tears. It is what she has thought she wanted for so long, and now it is here, her pretend world becoming real in the cold night. She presses her lips harder to mine, and then her body relaxes and I feel her warmth. She slides on top of me, looking down in the dark, crying, moving slowly, finding me, drawing a long breath, releasing it, but still crying, a sliver of pain and memory. This is what I see looking up at her, knowing how she wanted it to be so perfect, and maybe it is, in its own way, all that she had imagined. But it is not. She closes her eyes tighter to try to find it, but she is moving beyond what her body will allow. It will not relent. It will not accept what she most desires, but she keeps trying. And what I see, even in her desperation, is the grace that she taught herself long ago as a tall girl finding her way through the air. I hate the men who took that away. They are with us, as is Lily, in this cabin of voices and ghosts. Dylan stops, goes still. She slides off me and sits on the edge of the bed.

"I'm sorry, Sam."

"It's all right."

"No."

She is bent, sobbing softly, hair wild.

I sit up and reach for her. Her skin is cool and damp.

"You think it will go away, you know," she says. "That it will disappear inside you. It doesn't. Even with you, my darling Sam, it doesn't. It's here. My little tragedy. Do you suppose that's what it is? A little stain deep inside. They put it there." She turns back to me, takes my hand. "It was good almost. Did you feel it? Those few seconds. Is that what it's like, Sam? Is that what it was like with *her*? I feel like a child who knows nothing. But how could I know? I know the bad things. Why are the bad things so real and the good ones so pretend? I have wanted you for so long, but it was no good, and I'm sorry because I thought it would be. I fooled myself. I'm such a good fooler. But I'm a disappointment. I have disappointed you, darling."

"What happened to you was—"

"Let's not. We know all that. No need for words. It is part of us."

"It always was."

"Yes, but I thought maybe it didn't have to be."

"What were you expecting tonight?"

"Peace."

"You really thought . . ."

"Yes."

She goes to the nightstand, pours two scotches. She hands me one and sits naked in a chair by the window. We sip. We say nothing for a while. I feel the warmth spread through me the way it does, but even more so. A soft fire in the bones, eyes heavy, a pleasantness. I hear the rain on the window. A million whispers. I used to think that as a child alone in my room, watching rain blow like invisible bees down the street.

"You'll have to arrest me now," she says. Her words stretch and drift in the air. "I'm curious, Sam. Would you have arrested me if we could have, you know, made love the way we both wanted? I don't know. We'll never know. But I like to think you wouldn't have, that you would have crossed to my side. I so much wanted you on my side. I wanted you to love me. You do love me. I know you do. But Sam is Sam with all his moral equations. You'll do the right thing. Why is that?"

"I haven't done much that is right."

"Bless me, Father, for I have sinned. Spare me the confession, darling. I'm the bad one."

I try to lift my glass. It will not move.

"It won't last long," she says. "A few hours. Until morning."

"Wha . . . ?"

"A sedative, my darling. Something to help you sleep. You haven't been sleeping. I know. I read your little writings." She sips; her glass catches the moonlight. I can barely hear her, yet her voice has returned to what it was, sly and sharp with mischief. "Can you see me?" she says. "I'm here before you. Look." She stands and spins. "All for you, Sam. I like to think that. Wouldn't it be something if this was a night we looked back on, sitting in lawn chairs and watching the skyline at the end of the day? Talking about things. Oh, yes, Sam. I know. I have read. How in that moment at my house you loved the twilight, imagined something different for yourself. Isn't it lovely to think so?"

I feel her lips at my ear.

"Imagined things never happen, do they, darling?" She is a blur, a pale brushstroke. She walks to the nightstand. She pours more scotch. She takes the glass from my hand. I feel it slip away. She sits beside me, lifts my hand to her breast. I can feel her heart. She bends down and kisses me. She leans back, strokes my hair. She unholsters my gun. "They're so much heavier than you think," she says. She takes aim at the window but doesn't fire. She lowers the gun, traces the barrel over my lips. "You've never killed anyone," she says. "Not in all your years as a cop. I smell only steel. Did you ever think you'd shoot me, Sam? Back then when I was a killer on the prowl?" She laughs. "I'm still a killer, but I don't prowl anymore." She presses down, looks into my eyes. "Maybe I gave you too much, darling. I'm out of practice. Sleep, my pretty. Who said that? I know who. The pointy-nosed witch. But Dorothy got away in her ruby slippers." She turns toward the window. "Look, Sam, it's getting lighter. Our night's almost over. You love me. You do."

Silence. My eyes are almost shut. I see a shape in the window. White. It moves toward me.

"It's time for goodbye, Sam. All the boys and girls must go home. Mothers and fathers are calling. Can you hear them? Put on your ruby slippers. If you could have seen me once, darling, the way I was before, you would have been so pleased." She is crying. "That girl is gone. But she was pretty, Sam, not the pretty when you think of *pretty*—a different kind, but still. So tall and pretty and alone, the way girls are before the bad things. Take her with you, Sam. Wherever you go." A kiss. "I'm sorry, darling." Another kiss. "Bye, Sam."

CHAPTER 33

My eyes open. My head aches. Scotch glasses, unholstered gun, Dylan's black hair on the pillow. Clothes on the floor. Rain falls through the pines and over the sea. Low clouds roll toward the horizon. Two gulls skim past. They dive beneath the cliffs to the beach. The room is different in early light. A scuff on the wall, a cracked picture frame. The moments of strangers come and gone invisible in the air. Dylan sleeps. I pick up her dress, still wet, and drape it over the chair. I check my phone. Ortiz and Bryant have texted and called. No one else. They can wait. Bits of last night are coming together, but not all. I remember dinner, the walk, rain, this room, dark, and Dylan kissing me, and the two of us holding each other—not what I expected. But what was I to expect? I sit and look at her, lying on her side, face hidden in hair. Killer, lost girl, my torment and desire. How can she be so much, sleeping beneath the sheet, a fugitive? I am a fugitive, too, I suppose. I wonder if it fits me. Can I disappear down roads and erase all I know?

I reach for my badge, feel its weight and the halo of rays

embossed above city hall. I slide it away. I should have danced with her, just for an instant, so I could have seen us together in the window. She said something about the trick of us in the glass, the way our reflections give us two selves. We drank too much. We talked and I felt a tug toward the shadows. An inviting darkness. I remember hearing faint, vanishing words. Then nothing.

I go back to the window and pretend a little longer that the day hasn't started, even as the gulls take flight from the beach, lift over the cliffs, and wing toward the horizon. I turn and look at her. She is still. Too still. I know. How else could it be? This final offering beneath white linen. I walk from the window and sit beside Dylan on the bed. I brush the hair from her face, kiss her forehead. She is cold. Pills on the nightstand. I lift back the sheet. She is curled, like a child sleeping. I kneel beside her. Her eyes are closed, her lips parted—a sliver of space, hanging on to an unknown word. A streak of lipstick on the pillow, an empty bottle, two glasses. The pills. Blue and white. So subtle for her. What a quiet way to leave.

The drug she had given me lingers, but the warmth of it and the scotch are gone. I reach for my phone but then let it be. I slip beneath the sheet. I hold her and think of only hours ago, when she walked into the restaurant, and how I wanted to kill her and knew I couldn't, and how, in her way, she had won. How must that have been to her? To have come so close to the strange dream she constructed, an architecture that must have been tempting and beautiful. So close. But the lines and angles would not obey. Her body would not comply, not forget the cruelty done to it. It all fell to nothing in the bed we shared. It had never been like that before—the touch of her, the way she wanted to consume, to make us part of her fable. She saw us as unmended yet deserving. Of what? She

never said, only that we could escape, and that she knew me
best. She was my confessor, dancing beneath my window in a
fedora. I loved her, but not in a way that should be, although
I'm not sure anymore what those ways are. They cannot be
measured. Would I have brought her in? I don't know. I like
to think I would have, that my oath as a cop went deeper than
my need for her damage—my damage—but I don't know. She
took the choice from me.

I kiss her shoulder. I pull her tight. She is cold and gone.
Like the others. I have only people who are no more. Lily,
father, mother without memory. Dylan. I wipe away a tear and
close my eyes. I listen to the wind. It rattles the window and
the roof, and I hear the rain and imagine it falling through the
pines and over the cove and across the distant fishing boats
that sail the rough waters off the coast.

I rise and dress, my clothes still damp, and read the note
Dylan has left.

"It could never have been. Why, darling, couldn't it have?
Take me to my church, Sam."

I fold it into my pocket. I walk to the bathroom, splash
my face with water. I collect her things: lipstick, perfume,
toothbrush, not much else. I slip them into the small suitcase
she had left in the corner. Shirt, pants, sneakers, scarf, a
notebook of self-portraits, pages of drawings and changing
faces—the way she must have seen herself from day to day,
a constellation never the same. I fold her dress—it smells of
the ocean—and put it into the suitcase with the pills from the
nightstand, along with the glasses and empty scotch bottle.

I check the drawers, under the bed, behind the picture.
No trace. She does not exist. I wipe down the table, chairs,
headboard, nightstand. The window is bright with rain and
shades of gray. I close the curtains. I lay Dylan on her back. I

gaze at the long flow of her, breathe her in. I wrap her in the sheet and sit, listening to footsteps and far-off cars and long spools of silence. I close my eyes, calm myself. I rise, put the "Do Not Disturb" sign on the door, and go to my cabin. I rustle the bed, take my bag, and go to the front desk to settle the bill. The old woman tells me the rooms have been paid for—in cash—by "the woman you had dinner with last night." She looks at me as if we share a conspiracy. "She left a few hours ago. Before the light." I turn and look out the window. Dylan's car is gone. My Porsche is alone in the lot. "Seems she was in a hurry," says the woman. Dylan must have taken her car, probably one she stole, dumped it someplace, and made her way back in the dark. I tell the woman I want to rent the cabin—Dylan's—for another night. "That'll be no problem. Slow time of year." She looks through a ledger. "Not a single reservation." I pay her in cash. "Do you want housekeeping?" I tell her no and return to the cabin. I undress, take a shower, dry, and sit in the chair, staring at the white sheet, remembering the dead man on the sidewalk who brought me to her, and how, for the longest time, she left no clues.

I sleep, wake in midafternoon. Looking at my bag, a few clothes, a book. Nothing for a journey. I glance at the sheet and Dylan's suitcase. I want to bring her to where she wants to go, and then escape, myself, to a point unfixed. Take a new name and start over. I have chased other men who have tried, but there is a part that never lets go. There is not enough magic in the world for a soul to dissolve from its burden. One of the men I chased years ago told me that. He was right. I walk to her, fold back the sheet. The blue-pale of death is settling in. Her lips are ashen, her face serene, calm. Dylan was neither, but there she lies, disappearing by increments on a winter's dusk. I can still hear her first whisper, a mischievous hymn in the pitch of night. So in control—at least, that's what she believed—but then she was out my door and gone, vagabond, architect, woman of fleeting disguises, speaking to stones, wandering ancient lands. I run a finger through her hair and cover her once more. The dead need only a final tenderness, a marking, without judgment, between what is and what is no more. I peek through the curtain. The rain has stopped. My car waits.

CHAPTER 34

"Where the hell are you, Carver?"

"You need to come."

"Where?" says Ortiz.

I give him the address and cabin number.

"Stay put," he says.

I sit with Dylan and wait. She was right. "Sam is Sam with all his moral equations." I couldn't run. But I almost did. I had her in my arms. I reached for the door but couldn't turn the knob or slip her into my car or lay her in the ground in the shadow of her church. She knew my bounds and her own.

I look out the window. No moon. No rain. A cold black to the ocean. It is after midnight when I hear footsteps. The door opens. Ortiz steps in, sees the wrapped linen on the bed. He turns on the nightstand light and reaches for the sheet. Her face glimmers, a flash of white. He looks at me and back to Dylan. He covers her. He shuts off the light. We pull chairs to the window and sit for a long time in silence. I tell him all in the hour before dawn.

"I knew as soon as you called," he says.

"She thought I'd go away with her."

"You should have cuffed her right away."

"You know better."

"Yeah, but you should have. She really killed Lily?"

"I told you."

"I guess I knew but didn't want to. Castillo looked good for it. Bryant had it solid."

"Dylan made it look that way. Set up the whole thing."

"Too clever for her own good. The whole time she's sending you notes, following you around."

"She kept getting closer. I sensed her sometimes, but I'd turn and she wasn't there. Her notes got longer. Love letters, rambling thoughts. She never admitted to Lily until last night. She said she only wanted to scare her."

"Lily was taking you from her."

"That's what she thought."

"How do you reconcile that, Carver? Sleeping with the woman who killed the woman you loved."

"You haven't been listening."

"I'm a goddamned good listener. I know you had this weird thing with Dylan Cross. Hell, I don't know what it was, but she got in too deep, you know, messed around in your head. And you let it happen. I can almost understand it. I saw the video of what they did to her. I get it. The whole vengeance thing. But you let all her mad shit run wild. She put you in her world. I don't know what that says about you. I'm trying to figure that out."

"I almost killed her when she told me about Lily."

"You should have."

He grabs my arm, yanks me toward him.

"You goddamn should have," he says.

He lets go, walks to Dylan, folds the sheet back in the first thread of morning light.

"I thought she'd stay gone for good," he says. "I was hoping. Strange when they're dead, isn't it? The broken ones, I mean. There's a kind of still beauty to them, you know, like they got free. Not like the normal ones. They look different."

He covers her.

"What was it like?" he says. "To be—"

"I wanted to go away with her. I thought I could. She made it seem possible."

He walks to the window.

"We've got a problem, Carver."

"What do you want to do?"

"Fix it."

He hands me my bag and tells me to go sit in his car. I wait in the passenger seat, watching the world slowly come back to itself in the splintered gray of a new morning.

He knocks on the window twenty minutes later and leads me back to the cabin. Dylan is no longer wrapped in the sheet. She lies beneath it as if in slumber, black hair streaked across the pillow. The way I saw her hours ago. The pills are back on the nightstand next to the notebook of her drawings, a pencil slid between the pages. Her suitcase is open, clothes scattered. Her dress hangs on the curtain rod in the bathroom. Her toothbrush slants from a glass on the sink. A troubled woman, a fugitive, on her own in a roadside cabin for the night. That is true, but Ortiz has altered it. It is another story now, not Dylan's, not mine—an invention, a lie that will fit into a police report.

Ortiz hands me the scotch bottle and the glasses. I run them to the cliff and throw them into the ocean. I stand for a moment at the edge. Watch the waves. I turn toward the cabin.

Two local detectives arrive. Ortiz knows one of them and does all the talking: Dylan Cross killed two men, escaped to Europe, disappeared for a while, returned to California. We got a tip and tracked her here, but it was too late—crazy and a pill addict. She OD'd next to this book of drawings. Look at those faces—is that a screwed-up woman, or what? Ortiz is smooth, lets it flow. "I guess," he says, "she sensed we were close. Who the fuck knows?" The detectives take notes; a photographer clicks away; crime scene guys snap on gloves, open kits. Dylan is another vic. A nude woman in a bed among vials, evidence bags, and voices of men who know nothing of who she was. It is like that with all vics. We need only what lies before us. Ortiz doesn't tell them Dylan killed Lily. Why complicate a solved case?

"You guys can take off," says the detective who knows Ortiz. "We pretty much got this."

"Let me know if you need anything," says Ortiz.

"I'll give you a call after the autopsy," says the detective.

"Right," says Ortiz. "A lot of pills is what it looks like."

"Second time this year I found one like this. Kinda peaceful, huh?"

"Maybe."

"You float toward it, right? Drift away slow, sleeping-like."

"You think that's how it feels?"

"Got to be."

"Could be there's something at the end. Something that shakes, you know?"

"I don't think so."

"Who the fuck knows, right?"

"Can't ask her."

Ortiz and I step out the door. He opens an umbrella. I huddle beneath and we walk to the parking lot.

"Won't work," I say.

"It'll work."

"Hotel staff saw us. We ate dinner together. I rented the cabin again from the old lady at the front desk."

We stop at my car.

"The detective asking all the questions. His name is Lorenz. Great guy," says Ortiz. "We fished together years ago right up here off the coast. We meet every now and then and do the same— charter an overpriced boat and go for an afternoon. Lucky thing, too. For your sake. I called Lorenz into the bathroom when he and his buddy got there. You remember? Of course you don't. You were in a haze. I gave Lorenz a quick version of the real story. I mean, I couldn't give him the whole thing—not enough time—but I'll fill him in, in a few hours. He knows you and Dylan met here, but he's gonna take care of things."

"Why?"

"'Cause he's a cop and a friend, and as screwed up as you are, I know you didn't kill her. You did worse, though."

"What?"

"You fell for her. That's a goddamn sin."

"It'll come back on us."

"No, it won't. Lorenz will handle it. Don't ever talk about it again."

"And it just goes away."

"Don't pull the self-righteous shit on me, Carver. I'm saving your career."

Rain blows sideways. The ocean is lost in fog. Ortiz's face presses closer in the mist. I can see him as he was when we met long ago—younger, putting down a case, reaching for another file, the glare of a new crime staring up at him, and his dark eyes, relentless, knowing that you never count vics and the work is never done.

"Drive home, Sam. I'll stick around and make sure it's fixed. We'll talk about it all later. A lot's come down on you, but you're jeopardizing things. Too many mistakes piling up. We've got to stop that, bring you back from the bad place you've landed. Go home and sleep for, like, a million years. You look like a ghost walking."

I stare at Ortiz and back to the cabin. It feels unnatural to grieve for a killer, but what do you do with a woman who willed herself on you? Ortiz knows. He'll let me have it, even as he holds it as my crime against Lily, and a violation of all he believes. Dylan died unredeemed. But God alone knows what's in a sinner's heart—that's what the nuns told us in catechism class—when the last breath is drawn. It comes to that, and the few sacred things we may have done, the quiet faith we held in the time before the last bit of grace left us. Dylan designed a church in the desert, a perfect church of saints, stained glass, and stone, and that must count for something even for Ortiz and his Sundays of communions and confessions.

"You still go to Saint Joe's?" I ask.

"Me and Consuela. Not today, though."

"You have a cigarette?"

"We quit. It's raining, Carver. Get out of here."

"You still sneak one."

He winks.

"You holding out on me?"

"I'd rather have a drink," he says.

"You should have stayed in Costa Rica."

"Who'd have saved your ass if I had?"

Rain rattles the umbrella.

"This thing doesn't work," he says. "I'm soaked."

"Don't tell Bryant."

"I'm not telling anybody."

"I keep thinking about her."

"Bryant?"

"No, Dylan. The way it all . . ."

"Drive away, Carver. Hey."

I turn.

"Lily is the tragedy in all this," he says. "You know that, right?"

CHAPTER 35

I pass a week in my apartment. Reading, roaming rooms, watching night fall on slick streets, sneaking out once to the Little Easy and playing piano for Lenny, who was half-stoned and sang a song about a girl he knew long ago in Brooklyn. He poured me one on the house and sent me away after last call. I walked to the underpass where Kiki stayed, but there were only tweakers and mad prophets. The fires had stopped.

"It's done," says Ortiz, standing in the hallway outside my door before dawn.

I wave him in.

"Can't stay," he says. "Lorenz called. Autopsy showed enough drugs for a cartel. It's going down as an overdose-slash-suicide." He stares into my eyes. "You look better. Rested. Take another week off, Carver. Stay in here; go someplace. Meditate. Do whatever. Just get clear of it. She's gone."

I start to say something, but he holds a hand up and walks down the hall. I shower, shave, run through a Miles playlist, sitting at the window, watching a hawk perched on a fire escape at the Hotel Clark. It drops for a moment as if suspended, and takes flight, gliding out of sight over the city. I make more coffee, switch to Coleman Hawkins. I feel as if I'm coming back—from where, I don't know, but the music, newspapers, magazines, Afghan carpets bought in a past life, and the sliver of light in the sink offer a familiar though long-missed peace. My fortress. I sweep the floor, shake out the rugs, dust the books except the one about the lost flier in skies over foreign lands, which sits open on the counter, eighty pages still left. The phone rings.

"Sam Carver?"

"Yes."

"My name is Father Roland. You don't know me, but I was asked to tell you something."

"How did you get this number?"

"A woman gave it to me."

"What woman?"

"Let me just tell you what I must tell you."

"What is it, Father?"

"Dylan Cross will be buried tomorrow."

"I'm hanging up."

"Please don't. I can explain. Dylan and I met years ago, when she arrived in Joshua Tree with blueprints and a deed for a piece of land no one wanted."

"For her church?"

"Yes."

"I know about that."

"Maybe not everything," he says. "The materials and the builders came. Dylan used to say she wanted it to be part of the land, the way God made Adam from clay. She loved metaphor. Always little things like that."

"What's this about, Father?"

"Dylan and I became friends. I suppose that's what we were. She never came to Mass. I didn't know her crimes. She would sometimes appear unannounced on a Saturday afternoon and we'd sit in a pew and have a glass of wine and then walk into the desert. We'd turn back and look. She'd watch the shadow off the steeple, and how the stained glass glowed in purples, blues, and scarlet. She reached down once and held my hand. For an instant. She said, 'It is as it should be. My little box of secrets.' I looked at her and she was crying. She walked back to the church, lit a candle, and left."

"Had you been in touch with her?"

"She stopped coming a while ago," he says. "She called one day and told me she was traveling to Europe and would be gone a long time. I received a text from her a few days later, saying she wanted to be buried in the plot beyond the altar door, where two trees stand alone in the desert. That was the last I heard from her until . . ."

"Until when?"

"She mailed me a letter the night she died. She said she was near Big Sur and that it would be over soon. I read about it a couple of days later in the papers. I arranged for a funeral home to bring her to her church. Burial will be in the spot she wanted."

He pauses. I hear a breath.

"Will you come, Detective? Dylan wrote that only you should be there."

"What else did the letter say?"

"Nothing. It was short. Just a few details."

"She asked for no one else?"

"No. Her mother and father are gone."

"You read the papers," I say. "You know what she had done. She was a killer."

"I cannot judge."

"Can you forgive?" I ask.

I look out the window to the blurred neon of the Jewelry District.

"It's still raining," I say.

"Here, too."

I hear falling water.

"I'm outside under the eaves," he says. "You were the one who used to come to the church and sit for hours."

"Yes."

"I thought that might have been you. I don't know why—an inkling, I suppose. I sit in the church often. In the silence. Something about it. The design, where it is. I can't explain, but you know what I mean. Dylan wasn't religious, or so she told me, but the church for her was something permanent. She often talked of mortality, wanting somehow to beat it." His voice has a trace of the South, the way the syllables curl and hang, in no particular hurry. "I imagine we all hope that. To be the one to outlast it all. She had studied all the cathedrals, you know, but her church is nothing like them. It is simple and beautiful, like an act of faith."

"Faith in what?"

"I can't say."

"I had hoped that she'd show up one day and sit in a pew beside me."

"To arrest her?"

I don't answer.

"Did she ever confess?" I ask.

"Not to me. One could see she was hurting. I thought she might tell me in time."

"It ran out."

He draws a long breath.

"This is odd, isn't it?" he says. "Two strangers bound by the same person."

"What time?"

"The first light of the sun."

"Goodbye, Father."

I awake and put on the best suit I own. I drive east in the dark. A little rain in Chino, but stars over the desert. No music. I listen to the wind. The land, its slopes and patterns, its rock and brush and deep rippled layers made before time, all out there in the cold, enduring beyond comprehension as my car races past in a moment that, unlike the tremor of a fault line, will go ungraphed and die with me. There is refuge in that. There must be. I turn north. I feel the dawn but don't yet see it. Trailers, shops, and homes are emerging from the darkness. I turn onto a dirt road with no name. The church rises in the distance. Stained-glass windows, like eyes of many colors, watch me. I park and stand alone. The vestibule door opens. Father Roland, dressed in a white tunic, walks toward me, older and taller than I expected, like some missionary released from a forgotten village in equatorial Africa.

"I'm glad you came," he says. "She's inside."

He touches my arm and points the way. I follow like a child.

"She wanted a wooden coffin," he says. "Wood and nails. I made it with two men from the parish."

We enter the church.

"She asked for all these candles," he says. "I'll let you sit with her."

"I . . ."

"Just for a short time. She hoped for that. She wanted to be alone with you here. The coffin is closed. She wanted that, too. I like when people do that. The final image should not be the last thing left of us."

He leaves. I sit in a middle pew. Dylan and I are alone, but I don't want to be. I walk to the box, run my hand over the sanded pine, breathe in its scent, look at the silver-framed photograph. She is standing amid ruins, sun in her hair, alone in a linen dress, the sea behind her. Greece or perhaps Sardinia. I wonder who took the photograph—a stranger, man or woman, walking along the columns and fallen statues of a distant empire. They came upon her, a statue herself, but no, that isn't right. She is a lost, beautiful girl in the light, a sly smile on her lips, her eyes knowing she would come my way again. She took Lily. An innocent. She stole the life I might have had, Lily and me in that Boyle Heights house, sitting on the porch, listening to the radio, watching rain fall over the cross at Saint Mary's. Pointing out faces, telling cop stories in the twilight. Growing old. It could have happened.

I walk to the door and step outside. The sun is edging over the rocks. Father Roland and three other men carry the coffin from the church toward two tamarisk trees. They wave me over. We slide ropes beneath the box and lower it into the earth. We stand around it. "Go in peace, Dylan," says the priest. It is the only prayer. The men take their shovels and do their work, the sound of the dirt fading softer as the first light comes through the trees, striking the ground around her. It is done. The men smooth the soil and leave in a truck. Father Roland lays a single white rose on the gravestone. *Dylan Cross. Architect.*

I nod to the nameless stone beside Dylan's.

"Who's that for?" I ask.

He turns.

"You, Detective."

He steps closer.

"Should you decide, of course," he says. "It's all written out."

He walks toward the church. I stare across the desert. I am alone. The sun rises higher, the night cool gone. I think it might not rain, but I see far-off clouds that will darken with the hours, as they have all winter. I walk to my car, look back to the two trees and the church. All that she had imagined on a plot of land no one wanted. I stand for a moment longer. I close my eyes and listen. I want to crawl into the stillness, away from it all, but a man is seldom granted refuge. A breeze kicks up and dies. I drive away, down the dirt road to the highway. I head east. It is still early. I can make good time to wherever it is I'm going.

ACKNOWLEDGMENTS

I am grateful to have worked on this trilogy with my editor, Michael Carr. His discerning eye and gift for story were wise and vital. Thanks to my agent, Jill Marr, and everyone at Blackstone, including Shira Schindel, and Alenka Linaschke, who designed the art for the series. I am indebted to Mace Neufeld and Diane M. Conn for many nights of wonderful meals and endless stories about times and places both present and gone. And, as always, I am amazed at the steadfast and true: Clare, Aaron, and Hannah.